Hannah's Call

By Paul Hart

Printed in the United States of America

First Printing

ISBN: 978-0-578-68409-3

Email: twopdhart@yahoo.com

Who You Say I Am
By Reuben Morgan and Ben Fielding
© Hillsong Music Publishing

Cover
Max Guillory

Contents

For Emily

For Amy

*"Train up a child in the way he should go:
and when he is old, he will not depart from it."*
—Proverbs 22:6

Chapter 1
Upon This Rock

"Here they are!"

Hannah ran her fingers lightly over the weathered initials. Dust, rain, sleet, ice, snow and floods had abused them for seven decades. Lichen nested in them.

But they remained.

The girl's dear grandfather carved these letters she now delicately touched when younger than her as he sat on the spot where she knelt, one little moment in a big and still-unfolding story about two amazing people.

What a lucky young lady.

The thought made her sigh, sweet Grandpa Tom, and his very special wife.

For years, this big, flat rock, the size of a basketball court, had been the go-to place for passionate Randall High guys to declare true and eternal love for their gals. The senior class picnic every spring filled Randall, Missouri's, beautiful Hoot Owl Hollow Park, and maybe a dozen boys would be up here with knives, chisels or old screwdrivers, clinking away.

Hundreds, thousands, of letters, plus-signs, Cupid's arrows, hearts and numbers—here's one: DS+EW73—scarred the flat, gray stone.

Plus, more summer sunsets, moonlit nights and other romantic moments occurred across the decades around this rock than anyone knew. Couples leaned against each other, listening to the creek murmur below:

"Let me get my pocketknife...."

"Oh, honey...."

Tradition.

History.

Permanence.

And yes, mystery. Very special things happened out here.

Want to find a particular set? Think needle in a haystack.

Charley loped back to her across the limestone slab that had fallen from the bluff above in some geologic cataclysm eons ago. He had looked too; no luck.

But after an hour of searching in the hot sun, the granddaughter found them: TB+CD.

Hands on his knees, Charley stared down at the letters, just above his sneakers, as Hannah touched them again.

"This is just so awesome," he said as a drop of sweat fell off his forehead on the "C."

"Wait, hand me your phone, I'll get a photo. Keep your fingers there," Charley said as the phone clicked. "Your initials out here?"

"No way!" Hannah answered, laughing. "Me? Too busy being popular in high school to have a boyfriend."

"Good," Charley said.

Hannah snickered.

"Here, help me up. The rock hurts my knees," the girl said to her companion as he gave her a lift. She wiped dirt off her legs and cutoffs, and sweat off her face.

"Boy, it's hot!" she added with a glance up at the cloudless, end-of-May sky. "I have drinks in the cooler, let's go."

He took the girl's arm and helped her jump down from the big rock, her hair flew up for an instant as she bounded easily to the ground. Long-legged Charley came down beside her in one, long step, but he slipped and fell as he landed. No problem, just some wet gravel on his jeans, brush it off. They trudged up the creek bank together.

They made a pair.

Her: Petite, pleasant, pretty, and perhaps just a mite plump, a young woman everyone called "cute"—always smiling, liquid brown eyes, chipper, with a frequent and cheerful laugh.

She squinted when she grinned—her eyes smiled.

You couldn't help but like her. She had a quick wit, "feisty" comes to mind. This afternoon found her in typical attire, a sleeveless top and cutoffs. She spoke in alto, high school cheerleading left her with a raspy, Peppermint Patty note to her bouncy voice.

Perky.

Him: Tall, thin, taciturn, a thoughtful young man most rated plain, maybe boring, clumsy. But he proved always helpful, a hard worker, cordial and polite, quiet and rather aloof. Spare time found him with a book or music.

As usual, he wore an older, worn polo and jeans. He spoke, and sang, in a thin tenor.

Nerdy.

Both had brown hair.

They headed to the parking lot where Hannah's dark green Jeep sat, the one with the spare tire cover reading *Silly Boys, Jeeps Are For Girls* below MIZZOU and ΨΣΗ stickers on the hatch window.

"Gosh, pretty out here," Charley said, looking at the towering trees that lined the gurgling creek, shading the park's picnic tables. "You've been here before?"

"Ha! I nearly grew up in this park," she replied brightly. "My family came out here all the time, we're all really outdoorsy. That's why we have the Jeep. My softball teams played over there on that diamond, or over at Bentley Fields by the high school."

Charley cocked his head.

"*Bentley* Fields, as in Hannah *Bentley*, like, your family?"

"Sure, my great-grandfather gave money to the parks department to build them."

Charley's jaw dropped.

"Well, um, uh, what position did you play?"

"Catcher, mostly, or first, Grandpa Tom's a big baseball fan, he came to all my games. I'd get a hit and he'd be up there in the stands yelling: 'RUN! RUN!' It felt great."

"Your famous grandfather… at ho-hum softball games?"

"Well, he wasn't famous back then! Plus mom and dad came, always there for me, sometimes my brother came. I went to his games; pitcher.

"We do everything together."

Charley shook his head in wonder.

"You don't walk like a softball player, they strut or something," Charley added.

Hannah laughed. "I'll take that as a compliment!"

"Sure."

"Maybe that's why my softball career ended in high school," she added with an ironic smirk.

The boy smiled.

"So, did you ever see your grandfather's initials before?"

"Heavens no! I didn't even know about them until he mentioned it on his radio show."

Hannah opened the Wrangler's passenger door and reached back to the cooler.

"You want water or Gatorade? I think I have a Dr Pepper too," she asked.

"Same as you."

"Okay."

She grabbed a couple waters, closed the cooler and Jeep door, and the pair walked to a picnic table and sat down. They enjoyed long drinks as they rested in the cool shade of huge oaks. Charley put his arm behind her on the table—not too close, too hot on this sticky afternoon.

"TB-plus-CD, that would be Tom Bentley… and Claire's maiden name?" Charley asked.

"Dearborn," Hannah answered, "Claire Dearborn."

"Your grandmother?"

"No, my step-grandmother, is there such a thing? My grandmother was Grandpa Tom's first wife, Linda, Brown was her maiden name," Hannah explained between swigs. "She died of cancer as my dad finished his sophomore year in high school. Of course, I never knew her, but grandpa's old buddies around town say I'm her double.

"We'd run into some little old lady out shopping who grandpa knows, she'd stare at me and say something like, 'My, oh my, she's so cute: She looks just like Linda!' Then Grandpa Tom would smile and give me a hug.

"She must've been an amazing woman, Grandpa Tom talked about her a lot, he really doted on her—well, *before* he married Claire!

"Grandpa and my dad would tell stories: 'You remember when she...' this or that? Then they both laugh, clap their hands and, well, then they get quiet, change the subject."

"So then, Tom and Claire dated in high school, went their separate ways and met decades later at a nursing home?" the boy asked. "Thought maybe they divorced, remarried."

"No, you have it. They met in high school back in the '40s," Hannah answered. "It's all so wild. I'd never heard the story until after he proposed a year ago this spring. It shocked everyone. We all felt sad about having to put our dear grandpa in a nursing home and then—Surprise!—here he finds, and marries, his old high school flame.

"I remember when he called my dad and said, 'I want you to buy an engagement ring.' My folks just walked around like zombies," she said with a laugh.

"Can you imagine? Both of them past eighty! And then they start that national radio show, and now a book's coming out, and they're talking movie deal. I don't know how they do it, Grandpa Tom has these bad fainting spells and Claire had a stroke and has to have a wheelchair. But they meet with writers, producers, agents—oh my—it's amazing!

"Claire, something special," Charley said quietly.

"Yes, and we've become close," Hannah replied fondly with a faraway look, "They are two remarkable people, different, but they complement each other."

"Remarkable," Charley repeated.

"Oh, yes!" Hannah continued.

"Anyway, daddy took us all out to this great Mexican place here, Rio Bravo. Maybe we can go eat there while we're in town this weekend, love their taco salads. Grandpa explained it all that night, how he went to the Korean War and nearly lost his leg, he still walks with a cane. Meanwhile, Claire went away to law school, became a federal judge in Dayton and Cincinnati, then ended up on the shortlist for a Supreme Court nomination. What an amazing woman!

"Grandpa didn't talk about old girlfriends, or girlfriend, as you might expect. But wow, what a life she's had. She met presidents, ruled on these big cases, all kinds of things."

The boy smiled.

"Tomorrow's their first anniversary?" he asked. "I remember the wedding on TV. My gosh, that's all you heard for days on the news—that old couple in Missouri! You would've thought they were British royalty."

Hannah chuckled.

"I know, crazy!" she added. "I had just finished spring finals. My roomie recorded it on her DVR, and there I am on national TV in this springy-pink dress with a corsage, sitting in the crowd next to my long-lost Aunt Brenda. Oh, she's another story! The governor and our congressman are in the row behind us.

"You, in a dress?" Charley asked.

"Yes! It does happen!" Hannah replied, laughing.

"I still can't imagine, my own sweet Grandpa Tom—a celebrity! Oh, I remember that day!"

"I'll get to meet them?" he asked.

"Sure, that's why you came, right? Well, besides to meet the rest of my family."

Charley hung his head and sighed.

"Yes, that too."

"Don't worry, they'll like you!" Hannah said with a wave. "Just be yourself. If you like Grandpa Tom and Claire, you'll like them. That's why I thought you should meet them."

"Hope so," the lanky boy replied, nervously rubbing his face.

"We're family, all of us. I'm one of what grandpa calls 'my kids,' and we are, well, close."

Charley sighed and looked at the ground.

She sensed maybe she'd said too much.

"Look, I hope you aren't disappointed," she continued. "They're just regular people. Grandpa Tom's funny, Claire's thoughtful and deep. But she has a tender side once you get to know her."

"But, but, they're famous! They do that radio show, the podcast, millions listen," Charley said in awe.

Both drained their water bottles and chunked them in a trash can, then headed back to the Jeep and climbed in. Hannah started it up and hit the steering wheel's phone button as she turned on the air.

"Bluetooth, ready," the car's feminine voice responded.

"Call daddy," the driver commanded as she shifted into first.

"Calling daddy," the Jeep answered.

The phone rang and the familiar voice of Tom Junior came through: "Hey, Ladybug, where you at?"

"Hi, Daddy, we're at Hoot Owl! Charley asked to see those initials grandpa talked about on the radio a few weeks ago. We're headed to the house now."

"So, you found them? Wow!"

"Yep, kind of up in one corner, weathered but still there. We'll have to tell grandpa, we got a picture."

"Great, put it on Insta' and Facebook, see you in a few. Your mom ordered a pizza for dinner from that new, coal-fired oven place out on the bypass. Love you!"

"You too, 'bye," Hannah responded brightly and the Jeep responded with "call ended" as it slowed at the park's guard station.

"Let me turn in the off-road trail pass, we can do that Sunday afternoon, ran out of time," she explained to Charley.

The guard shack door opened and a tall, muscular young man with shaggy blond hair swaggered out in an ill-fitting ranger uniform. He held his hand up for them to stop. He was in charge here—and he wanted you to know it.

The ranger had an Elvis Presley sneer. Think "macho."

Rough.

Hannah gasped, then moaned.

"Oh, no! Oh, no! WHY?"

Facepalm.

The Jeep stopped and she painfully lowered her window.

"Well, well, well, look who's here: Hannah Bentley!" the ranger said as he leered at her with a wicked smirk, hands on hips.

"My, oh my, if it is not just the hottest cheerleader to ever yell for the Randall Rams. Those pom-poms always made you look even bigger where it counts, babe."

She grimaced.

"Hello, Randy," Hannah responded icily. "You're home for the summer?"

"Let me put it this way, lover: Missouri State has certain expectations of its students that, like, you know, do not meet my expectations. I'm workin' for the city now."

"Okay, whatever, we didn't get to the Jeep trail, I need to turn in the pass," she explained flatly as she took the hanger off her rearview mirror.

The guard stared at her chest, not her face. She knew it, she did not like it.

Randy reached for the pass, making sure his fingers slid over her hand slowly as he took it.

Hannah winced.

"Sure, sweetheart, I get off at nine, you free? We can visit some really pretty spots up there in the woods—only we park rangers know about 'em. There's a moon tonight, we can be alone and have a good time."

"NO!" Hannah responded sharply.

Randy just then noticed Charley in the passenger seat and scowled.

"Tell me he's a long-lost cousin," the ranger snarled, pointing at her passenger. "I don't like competitors."

"This is Charley. We are friends. He is nice," she explained curtly.

"Well, remember I'm watching you," the ranger said with a sneer.

She did not like that reply.

"And *you* remember I do not want to deal with you! Understand that?" Hannah shouted, shaking her finger. "My dad and my brother are expecting us, and if I am not there for some reason, they're both pretty good with a gun, Randy. *You* remember *that*!

"Gotta' go," a testy Hannah said as she popped the clutch and the Jeep rolled past the guard shack.

Hannah let out a loud "UHHH!"

But she also looked back in the rearview mirror, sighed, and shook her head as they drove away.

"Who's that? You both got kind of rude," a puzzled Charley asked.

"Let's just say I'd rather not deal with Randy."

Chapter 2
Something Solid

A couple miles rolled by in silence and the Jeep pulled to the stoplight at Ninth Street and the turn signal came on. Across the way, a construction crew worked on a small building behind a COMING SOON STARBUCKS sign. Rebar in place, a crew would soon pour a driveway.

"Randall, a Starbucks?" Charley asked.

"I guess," Hannah answered. "I know they talked to daddy about Grandpa Tom's house, good location, but they couldn't agree on a price. I'm glad, they would've torn the place down."

The light stayed red for a while as traffic crawled by. Charley leaned over and awkwardly planted a quick peck on her cheek as they waited. It shocked her, he had never been affectionate.

"Are you having fun yet?" she asked, surprised, as she touched her cheek.

"If I'm with you, I have fun," Charley answered.

"You're so sweet!" she replied, dazed.

The light turned green and Hannah turned right onto Ninth from behind a truck as traffic moved again. An assortment of doctors' and professional offices, a C-store, an event center and mini storage passed them.

Charley laid his hand on the console and she laid her hand on his.

"You're clammy, what's wrong?" she asked.

Charley sighed.

"Nerves."

"Look, silly, you don't have a thing to worry about. Like I told you when we left campus, just be your sweet, courteous, loveable self. Grandpa Tom and Claire, and my family, will think you're wonderful!" she replied.

Charley shrugged.

In a few blocks, very commercial Ninth ended at residential Poplar and the familiar Victorian masterpiece the girl had known all her life—the Bentley homestead where she had played Barbies on the porch and fell off her tricycle in the yard—still towered above the intersection.

"That's Grandpa Tom's house, he talks about it on the show," she explained, pointing out Charley's window. She saw something different, trucks and builders' supplies, out the corner of her eye as they drove past. Hey girl, watch the road.

The familiar red mailbox that read "902 BENTLEY" stood at the curb. How many times had Grandpa Tom asked his granddaughter to go get the mail?

"A beauty, yes, he mentioned it," Charley replied, admiring the mustard yellow-and-green mansion with its turrets and gingerbread. "Your family's owned it, like, a hundred years?"

"Oh, longer than that, my great-great grandparents built it in the late 1800s."

"And your family has lived here in Randall, Missouri, all that time?"

"Yep, came to the Ozarks in the Civil War, so the story goes. They supported the Union, left Tennessee when the war started, not safe. The Ozarks remained a Union stronghold."

"Amazing," Charley said. "It must be nice to have a home and family that's so solid, so permanent, like that big rock in the park."

Perplexed, Hannah cocked her head and chuckled, "I guess."

The Jeep slowed and veered right onto Poplar, climbing the hill above Randall's sleepy downtown. A few blocks went by and Hannah pointed out a low-slung, Frank Lloyd Wright Prairie School home, nestled—out of place—within the town's line of classic Victorian and Queen Anne gems.

"That's Claire's house where she grew up; famous," she explained. "It's in all sorts of architecture books and stuff. Her niece and her niece's husband live there now. Architecture majors come here to tour the place."

Charley turned and admired the very different home as they passed.

A block or so on, Hannah turned left at Prairie Hill Lane, downshifted, then stopped at the security gate.

"If you have to drive, I have a remote for the gate here on the visor," she breezily told her companion.

"No chance, not coordinated, can't drive a stick," Charley replied.

"You, not coordinated? Ha! The way you play a piano?" she asked, teasing. "You should take up juggling!"

"A piano or organ's different," he said.

She punched the remote and the big gate slowly swung back. The street wound to the left, past several McMansions, then around to the top of a wooded hill. Where the street curved right, Hannah slowed, then went straight onto the Bentley driveway, parking in front of a sprawling, mostly windows, gray and white, flat-roofed, mid-century modern home.

"We're here!" she chirped as she turned the key.

Charley sat, stunned, as he looked at the impressive house through the windshield. First, she points to that Victorian castle, then a Frank Lloyd Wright original—and now this. And what's that about giving away money for ball fields?

These people had money, really serious money. He gulped.

"Livin' the dream," he muttered.

Just then, Hannah's parents came out to greet their daughter, mom through the carport and dad from the front door. Hannah jumped out and skipped over to her dad and gave him a hug.

"Welcome home, sweetheart, have a good drive down from Columbia?" Tom Junior asked.

"Fine," she answered as Judy Bentley walked up and hugged both of them, then kissed her daughter.

Her brother, Chad, came out the front door and smiled with a "Hey, big Sis!"

"You're home for the summer already?" Hannah asked her younger, but considerably taller, brother.

"Yep, wrapped up finals yesterday, got out of the dorm in Rolla this morning, freshman year done! I'll let you guess where I got a summer job," he said.

"Hmmm, any chance it's with the Bentley Hardware Company— '*America's top choice for quality tools and supplies*?'" she asked, her eyebrows arched in fun.

"Now, how did you know that, and you've seen the new website too?" the brother replied. "Seems to be something to do with having the CEO for a father."

Everyone laughed.

"Well, maybe you'll get to sit in Grandma Linda's chair at the reception desk!" Hannah replied to more laughter. "See what college did for me? Answering daddy's phone!"

"No, no, I think Pop stuck it in the closet as a souvenir," Tom Junior added. "Our office furniture isn't that old! And remember, Ladybug, I had you help with all those financial forecasts and budgets, you did a lot more than handle the phone!"

"I know where it is, big kid, if you really want to sit in it," mom said as she gave her son a good-hearted noogie.

Chad snickered.

The foursome went on in joyful banter, laughing, swapping high-fives and joking, happy to have the family's two college students home, glad to be together again.

Charley sat in the Jeep with his hand over his mouth, watching nervously, soaking in the happy reunion and the big house, amazed, shaking his head.

"What am I getting into?" he mumbled to himself.

Chapter 3
Charley

Hannah interrupted the happy chatter.

"Hey guys, you need to meet Charley!" she said as she pointed back at the Jeep.

Charley took a deep breath, opened the door and stepped out, politely nodding.

"Hi," he said quietly.

"Well, come here!" Hannah urged as she waved him over.

"Everyone, this is Charley. Charley, please meet my mom, Judy; my dad, Tom Junior; and my brother, Chad," she added.

Tom Junior extended his hand.

"Welcome, young man, we're glad to have you," the father said pleasantly.

Charley nodded and smiled.

"Thanks, uh, pleased," he said nervously.

"Well, everyone come inside!" Mrs. Bentley said brightly, waving come here. "I have the pizza ready and I made a salad. We can unload after we eat."

Charley quietly looked up and around, in awe of the big house, as they walked in the front door. Floor-to-ceiling windows made it bright, airy, spacious.

Maybe entering the Sistine Chapel would feel like this.

Do people really live this way?

"Wash your hands and come and eat," the mom commanded down the hall.

The fivesome gathered in the dining room as she brought out a gigantic pizza and set it in the middle of the table.

"I told them an extra-large supreme, but I had no idea," she added. "Look at that thing, I won't have to fix breakfast tomorrow!"

Everyone laughed, Tom Junior said grace, then added "dig in."

They all grabbed slices and shoveled salad, polite conversation started as the meal began.

"So remind me, how did you two get acquainted?" Judy asked, looking at her daughter.

"Sure, well, let's see: We met at Cross Members, that Christian student group on campus," Hannah explained. "We have an accounting majors study circle. We met there, sort of, for the first time more than two years ago."

"But we didn't *meet* meet, you know what I mean, 'til January," Charley said, interrupting.

Hannah giggled.

"Yeah, so funny! We went around the circle to introduce ourselves as this spring semester began and it came my turn. I simply said, 'I'm Hannah Bentley, I'm from Randall, near Springfield," she added.

"So then I asked, 'You mean *Bentley*, like that old couple on radio?' Then she says, 'Yes, he's my grandfather,'" Charley said.

Hannah laughed.

"Then, here came a Greek chorus! Everyone in the group said, together, '*Really*?' she added.

So I had to explain things. Charley stopped me after the meeting and started asking all these questions about Grandpa Tom and Claire. I bet we stood there at the door talking a half-hour."

"Yeah," a hungry Charley said as he reached for a second slice. "What an odd name: *Actionable Anecdotes with Tom and Claire*. That's weird, but I got hooked the first time I listened to it. Everyone remembers their wedding."

"So, well, we just sort of connected, I guess," Hannah said with a shrug. "We'd go out for coffee or whatever after study circle, Charley always wanted to discuss the latest show."

"I catch the podcast," the boy explained. "They make you think when they talk about their lives. They throw in all these nuggets from the Bible, Thomas Aquinas, Brené Brown, Mark Twain, Erma Bombeck, Norman Vincent Peale, Dale Carnegie—you know.

"I don't think they know how much good they do people like me."

"So, all he ever wanted to talk about was *them,* Grandpa Tom and Claire," Hannah added, just a tinge of frustration in her voice.

"Whatever," Charley added. "I bought her a lot of hazelnut lattes."

"Yes, you did! Anyway, so I told him a couple weeks ago, 'I'm going home for their anniversary the first of June, you'll have to ride down to Randall with me and meet them! And, you should meet my parents," Hannah said, shaking her finger at Charley. "My whole family's nice."

Charley hung his head.

"Yeah."

Tom Junior smirked and winked at his wife, then glowered at Hannah's male companion across the table.

"So, young man, just what do you admire about my daughter? Her grandfather does not count."

Charley turned red.

"Uh, well, uh, sir, well, she's always upbeat, happy, joyful. She's fun to be around."

"And do you favor her *physically?*" the father asked, leaning toward Charley and squinting.

The boy slid down in his chair.

"Oh my," he mumbled.

All the Bentleys laughed.

"Okay, Dad, put the bullwhip away. I think he's harmless," Judy said.

Charley stared at his plate, puzzled.

"No, wait, I mean that! Well, like, you see…" Charley trailed off, embarrassed. "And, well, and, uh, well, I'm not saying this for you, no really: She has a nice family!"

"No harm, no foul," Tom Junior replied with a playful smile. "So, tell us about your family."

Charley put down his pizza and sighed.

"Well, mom lives in Neosho," he said.

"So, do you plan to take Hannah there for a visit?" the father asked.

Charley thought for a minute.

"Don't know."

"Any brothers or sisters?"

"No."

"And your dad?"

Silence hung in the air, a very awkward and long silence.

The ice machine in the kitchen made a loud "CLUNK!" as it dumped more cubes.

"Uh, really don't know my dad," Charley said, shifting in his chair.

Awkward.

"So, uh, you grew up in Neosho? Nice town," Tom Junior asked. "They had that big Army base there, that missile plant."

"No," Charley replied, very ill at ease, "started high school my junior year."

"Where did you move from?" Judy asked.

"Cairo, Illinois."

"You grew up there?" Tom Junior asked.

"No."

"And before then?" the mom asked.

"Bowling Green, Kentucky."

Obviously, Charley did not want this conversation, change the subject! Tom Junior turned to Hannah and continued the playfully tough questions.

"And, young lady, tell me what you like about Charley?"

Hannah knew her father, they had done this just-for-fun third-degree many times. She knew the gag.

"He's cute—and he plays a *mean* piano," she replied brightly. "He's a prodigy!"

Charley shrugged.

"Is that so?" Judy said, sitting back. "We bought a second-hand piano and force-fed both of these kids lessons, not that it did any good."

"That's right," Chad said. "I did fine until the teacher made me play the black keys too."

"Ah, but you have other redeeming qualities, so we kept you!" his mother answered with a wink.

"Name one!" Hannah added playfully, pointing at her brother.

"Well, he's going to load the dishwasher when we're done," mom answered.

"Sure," brother replied.

The four Bentleys laughed.

"And the rest of us will adjourn to the living room for an inspiring recital," Tom Junior added with a smile.

The banter, the laughter, it baffled Charley.

What to make of these people?

Was he in trouble?

Was this a joke?

Was this a test?

Do some families really work this way?

Maybe they wanted to run him off.

Probably just play, but maybe not, he had to go along with it.

Hannah and her mom helped Chad clear the table as Tom Junior and Charley went into the front room to inspect the piano.

"So, is he the one?" Judy asked quietly as they carried dishes into the kitchen.

"Mom!" Hannah answered with an edge. "He's just a nice guy, that's all.

"You know your methodical daughter, I have my life all planned out: graduate high school, graduate college, get a job, find a guy, then get married—someday.

"I just turned twenty-one, it's too soon!

"Charley's really sweet, a friend. He's nice and all, I do kind of like him, you know, as a pal, a bud. I'm not ready for anything serious with any boy.

"Honestly, he sees more in me than I see in him—I think—but he's very shy. This weekend's just a way for him to actually meet Grandpa Tom and Claire, he loves their show.

"If they have groupies, he's one of 'em!"

Mrs. Bentley put down her load of dishes and looked at her daughter with a smile.

"Okay, didn't know where things stood. Your sweet daddy rattled his cage," she replied.

They both laughed.

"But remember, Hannah, when opportunity knocks…."

The table cleared, they joined Tom Junior and Charley around the piano as Chad took over in the kitchen. An old, cherry wood spinet sat in one corner, out of place in an ultramodern room obviously laid out by a professional interior designer.

Charley mumbled, "Okay, what would you like?" as the women walked up.

Charley opened the keyboard and quickly played scales up and down the keys.

"Begging pardon, out of tune," he said meekly.

"No doubt," Judy said. I don't think we've had it tuned since Chad's eighth grade recital, five years?"

Charley thought for a moment, then launched into a zippy rendition of the first movement of Bach's *Brandenburg Concerto No. 3*.

The Bentleys stood enthralled.

Charley finished, turned to Hannah and asked quietly, "How's that?"

His little audience applauded enthusiastically.

"He can do so much more, he does music for the group devotions in Columbia," the daughter added. "He can play anything!"

Judy scowled and smugly asked, "Play *Misty* for me," confident a twentyish boy wouldn't get the joke. She loved Clint Eastwood.

"Sure," and Charley launched into the old standard as he sang a thin tenor, looking up at Hannah.

"Look at me…"

She smiled.

He finished the tune and Tom Junior muttered, "Wow!"

"I told you, he's good!" she said.

"How do you get that out of an old second-hand piano?" Judy asked, incredulous.

"Don't know, just do it," Charley said with a smirk.

"So, who's your favorite pianist?" the father asked.

"Leon Russell," Charley replied.

"Who?" Chad asked, as he walked in the room.

"He did innovative blues back in the Seventies."

"Hmm, I'd say 'before my time' but not quite, kindergarten about then, I guess," Judy said.

Tom Junior scowled.

"So, let me get this straight, you are an accounting major? Why not music?" the father asked, arms crossed, leaning against the piano.

"Because musicians, overall, don't make much money," Charley replied thoughtfully. "I got a job last year to play weekends at this Columbia steakhouse, had to walk over to Goodwill down on Grindstone and buy a suit. A couple nights and I could gross a hundred bucks in tips. That buys a lot of ramen noodles but it's hard to live on. I love to play, but I need something to support myself.

"I guess it's like the Apostle Paul making tents. He loved the ministry, but he had to eat."

The logic of Charley's explanation spoke volumes to a level-headed, MBA-holding, CPA-earning, corporate CEO—and very protective of his beloved daughter—father.

"Impressed, yes, you're entirely right," Tom Junior replied, nodding.

Chapter 4
Randy

"Great fun, but we need to get you two unpacked," Judy said. "It's almost dark."

Everyone headed out to the Jeep.

"You travel light for a girl," Charley said as he grabbed her bag.

"Thanks, but I'm home, if I need something, it's here," she replied.

"And quite a home," Charley replied, awed still. Spacious, open, airy—do people really live in houses like this? It stood in contrast to the small, dark trailer he called home.

"So, tell us about your day," Tom Junior said to his daughter as everyone walked down the hall.

"Guess who we ran into out at the park?" Hannah answered painfully.

"Randy Smith," Chad replied sharply.

Hannah stopped and looked back at her brother.

"You know he's in town?"

"Obviously, someone here does not read the *Randall Ledger*'s website," her brother replied. "You don't know what he did?"

"Guess not."

Chad sighed.

"Pure Randy: This happened just before spring break," he explained. "Randy and some of his lowlife pals got drunk one night, then went on a rampage around the campus in Springfield, turned over trash cans and benches, broke windows, set a dumpster on fire, other stupid stuff. The worst of it: They tumped over this statue of a famous professor or college president or somebody. It cracked and broke.

"The campus cops showed up and chased them to one of the guy's cars. The others got in the car and drove off. Randy, blotto drunk, didn't make it to the car before the police tackled him—good thing for him.

"How so?" Hannah asked.

"Of course, the police caught them, and when the po-po searched the car they found bags of pills and a kilo of pot under the seats. Bad stuff that made for easy possession-with-intent charges. Lucky Randy dodged that bullet—not in the car, the cops had no proof he had been.

"Ah, but they did slap him with public drunk, vandalism, destruction of public property, disorderly conduct and resisting arrest. He plea-bargained guilty to malicious mischief. He had to do some weekends in jail, now he has to work off a zillion community service hours.

"Somehow, he got the Greene County judge to allow him to do his community service over here in Limestone County instead, the weasel. The City of Randall Parks and Recreation Department needed a part-time park ranger.

"There you have it," Chad said with a grimace as he flipped on the guest room light.

"What is *wrong* with him?" Hannah asked in a serious tone.

"He could do so much, but he just keeps up the stupid stuff. What I didn't like this afternoon: a comment as we left that 'I'm watching you.'"

Tom Junior blanched.

"He did?" the concerned father asked. "Creepy, I don't like that. I better call my friend at the police department.

"Meanwhile, Ladybug, make sure you're with someone when you go out."

Hannah dropped against the door and sighed.

"I want to get rid of him once and for all," she said with a heavy sigh. "I wish he'd leave me alone."

The family's chipper tone had turned glum, something big had popped up.

"Can I help? What can I do?" Charley asked quietly.

"Probably nothing, and probably nothing to worry about since the two of you will head back to Columbia early Monday; quick little weekend," Judy replied. "But just in case, let's stay together, we can still have a good time tomorrow with Grandpa Tom and Claire."

"Okay, enough of this, here you are, the Bentley Hilton!" Hannah said as she waved her hand across the sparse room.

The room seemed bland, given the Bentley's grand home—double bed, nightstand, a chair and chest. However, a gaily painted flower garden, with birds and bees above the blooms, covered one wall that stopped, unfinished, just short of a bathroom door.

Charley looked at the artwork and shook his head.

"That's different," he said.

Tom Junior laughed.

"That objet d'art represents the artistic endeavor of my sister, Brenda," he explained. "She showed up minutes before Pop and Claire got married. We hadn't seen her in twenty years, she left Randall in a huff while Judy was pregnant with Hannah.

"Then, Aunt Brenda lived with us for a few weeks and, well, she occupied herself with this. My wife came home one afternoon to find a note that said, 'Back soon.' We haven't heard from her since, ten months."

Everyone stood quietly for a moment until Judy added, "Every family needs a little color."

The parents and Chad slowly walked off from Charley and Hannah.

"Would you like to see the house?" she asked.

"Sure."

The pair walked back up the hall to the immense front room, where the little piano sat. Charley noticed copies of *Architectural Digest* and *Bon Appétit* on a coffee table. He'd heard of them. Also, a glossy publication, still in a polybag mailer, called *Family Office Magazine* with a picture of a Rolls-Royce on the cover. He hadn't heard of that one.

They went out in the hall, down a couple doors and walked into Tom Junior's souvenir- and photo-filled office, with floor-to-ceiling windows opening to the heavily wooded lot. The father sat at his computer and offered a friendly "Welcome!" as they walked in.

"Dad uses this office a lot nowadays," Hannah explained.

"Yep, ain't the Internet grand?" Tom Junior said as he leaned back in his chair with his hands behind his head. "Beats suiting up and going in—when I can get away with it, and my wife's coffee's better," he added with a chuckle.

Charley noticed a black-and-white photo of a smiling young woman on a shelf near the door.

"Now that's a different pose for you," he said with a glance at Hannah, as he motioned at the photo.

"Uh, that's not me," Hannah said.

Charley stared at the picture.

"No?"

"That's Hannah's grandmother, my mom, Pop's first wife, Linda," Tom Junior explained. "See the resemblance? Note the '60 DeSoto in the background, that's what Pop drove when they met.

"Somewhere I have a pic of the two of 'em standing behind that car. Someone had written JUST MARRIED on the trunk lid in shoe polish, between the tail fins. There are all these tin cans and old shoes tied to the bumper. Corny, but they did that back then.

"Pop's twenty-nine years old," Tom Junior said with a sigh. "Think about that when you meet that old fella' tomorrow, we'll all be there someday."

"You're right, I see the resemblance, you mentioned that," the boy said to Hannah, looking intently at the picture, then the girl next to him.

He turned to Hannah's father.

"If you don't mind, everyone calls you Tom Junior. Are you a junior, or a nickname?" Charley asked.

"No, I am Thomas James Bentley *Junior*, Pop's Thomas James Bentley *Senior*," he explained. The father then leaned forward, propped his elbow on his desk, and placed his chin in his palm.

His bright mood changed.

"I asked her one time," he added as he pointed at the photo, "'Why did you guys name me after dad?' I may have been eight or nine, about when kids start asking profound questions.

"It must've been summer, home from school, we stood in the kitchen while she drank her morning coffee. I guess we had talked about stuff over breakfast, don't remember.

"Mom stopped, thought for moment, sat down at the table, and looked at me with those same smiling brown eyes Ladybug has.

"'*We* didn't name you after your father—*I* did,' she said emphatically. 'When I gave birth to both of you kids, your father asked me to name you. I named your sister after my sister, we're close.

"'And you?

"'Well, Tommy, I named you after the finest man I have ever known, he totally changed my life for the better. Why he picked me to love I'll never know, I couldn't offer him anything. A Bentley man could have married any girl in this town with his family's reputation and money.

"'Why me?

"'Son, always remember: What you do, and what you say, can change peoples' lives for good, or for bad. Make sure you change lives for good.' Then she hugged me," Tom Junior said thoughtfully.

"Me? Just a goofy kid, I probably went out to kick my soccer ball around, don't remember. I knew she had something really special, really important. It stuck with me. Mom didn't get serious very often, she lived her life bright, cheerful, lovingly teasing—sort of like your bouncy friend here," Tom Junior said with a nod at Hannah.

"Pop's a good man, no doubt about it, and it's a challenge to fill his shoes sometimes."

Tom Junior sighed.

"I try."

It moved Charley.

Hannah interrupted the moment and asked, "Do you want to see the rest of the house?"

"Uh, sure."

She took Charley through the mid-century modern home's kitchen with its stainless steel appliances—Sub-Zero, Wolf, Cove—he'd never heard of those brands. Then they went in the media room with a jumbo TV screen, a well-stocked library, a game room with a pool table beneath a deer head, and a mostly empty wine closet.

"This certainly looks different than your grandfather's Victorian house," Charley replied as they went down the back hall.

"I think my folks wanted to make some kind of statement or something," Hannah explained. "But we love it, bright and airy: the open concept, the big windows, and up here on the hill you get great views.

"You can watch thunderstorms roll in."

"Here we find Chad's room, which tonight seems unusually neat," she said with a wink.

"Alright, already!" he complained, sprawled on his bed, looking up from his iPad.

A nicely framed, blue jersey hung on the wall with BENTLEY 54 in white, which caught Charley's eye.

"Played football?" the visitor asked.

"Yep, that's how I met our old pal, Randy," Chad replied.

"We played linebacker together his senior year, my sophomore. He's pretty much a lost cause—except at football. He could absolutely change a game, more than any single player I've ever seen. He just has a gift, a sixth sense.

"He'd read the keys, watch the triangle, just like me, and come up with a completely different defense instantly—and he nearly always guessed right.

"Randy, somehow, knew where the ball *would* be, and he got there first. It's like he knew the other team's game plan. The offense would run away from him, they double-teamed him. It didn't matter, he'd still make the play.

"Handoff? Bang! He'd tackle the ball carrier at the line," Chad continued. "They'd pass and Randy would have his fingers on the ball and tip it away an instant before it got to the receiver. Draw play? Never worked, he'd drop the quarterback for a loss."

Tom Junior and Judy walked up behind Hannah.

"Don't forget that time he flipped the ball away on a pass attempt, then you caught it in the air for an interception and ran back for a touchdown," the father said. "Your mom went wild."

"Ha! Indeed, I did," Judy added, laughing. "Look at my kid run!"

"I thought she'd had an attack. Pop worried about her, lost his cane under the bleachers as he held her up," her husband said.

"Yeah, the pinnacle of my football career," Chad replied with an ironic smirk. "Linebackers don't score much.

"But even Randy guessed wrong sometimes, we worked well together—on the field," he added. "Somehow, I seemed to make plays when he didn't, he made me look good, he made all of us better.

"Randy and I made all-conference that season, he made all-district and all-state. I never played the same after he graduated. A few also-ran teams offered me scholarships but I gave it up.

"He's good, very good, at football. The rest of life? Not so much. He has so much talent but it's wasted."

"Randall went to the semis that year, thanks to him. Our offense muddled along all season, like always, but when your opponents don't score, you win.

"You want to tell Charley why we didn't go to state, to the Jones Dome in St. Louis?" Tom Junior asked.

"Oh please, no," Hannah said with a moan, covering her eyes.

"I guess I have to now," Chad answered with a grimace. "They threw a pass, the receiver ran straight down the sideline, I came up behind him as Randy hit the guy, just as he caught the ball, knocked it loose. I thought he hit too soon, pass interference, but the ref ruled it incomplete."

Chad sighed.

"Play over, right? Oh no!

"Randy, well, Randy sped up and ran right on out of bounds and straight into Hannah, cheering on the sidelines, knocked her flat. Sis waved that little piece of picket fence the cheerleaders have, next to the girl with the big 'D', as they did their 'DEE-fense! DEE-fense!' cheer.

"Well, that could happen, except he just stayed there, lying on top of her."

Hannah looked away and sighed.

"I felt like I got hit by a truck. I don't know how much he out-weighs me. I'm bruised and cut, my uniform's all messed up, he did it on purpose. I'm on my back, his face guard's right in my face, and he whispers, 'I got you! I got you!'"

"I saw what happened and ran off the field and yelled at him, 'Get off my sister!'" Chad said. "He jumped up and we started to shove each other. Two guys on the same team in a fight! Things got out of hand, the refs kicked both of us out of the game."

"Our sponsor helped me over to the stands, mom ran down to help me, frantic," Hannah added. "Here came the ambulance paramedics, they checked me over, nothing broken but lots of bruises and cuts. I had bandages all over, sat out the rest of the game. He twisted my knee, I hobbled around, stiff, for days. We went to the drug store and bought a crutch."

Tom Junior took up the story.

"Alas, the mighty Randall Rams, in their biggest game in decades, shall we say lost their concentration. This happened late third quarter, only ahead by a field goal," he added. "The team got a bad case of the jitters.

"The fourth quarter? Disaster: we gave up three touchdowns. It made for a long, quiet drive home."

"One of the coaches put Randy in his car for the trip back, didn't dare let him ride in the team bus," Chad said. "The whole team would have beaten him to a pulp, and I would've helped!"

"Oh well, Randall made the state semis; pretty good year. But if it hadn't been for Randy, what if...." the father added.

"The big schools—Oklahoma, Notre Dame, Southern Cal—called on him," Chad said. "Then they'd get a look at his grades and his record with the cops. *Çiao!*

"Missouri State took a chance. Well, the Bears got two good seasons out of the idiot before he goofed up for good. The vandalism proved the last straw after who-knows-what else—showing up late for practice, mouthing off to coaches. He got kicked off the team and expelled from classes, plus the court verdict."

Chad sat quietly for a moment, thinking.

"You know what they say about sports, they help you learn how to work with people, to be part of a team? That's true," he said.

"But Randy? No way, any other guy would've had splinters in his bottom from the bench. He just did his own thing. But he played so well, he's so good, he got away with it," Hannah's brother added.

"Always the showoff, get his stupid ego out of the way, and the guy would be fantastic."

Chapter 5
A Bump In The Night

"Well, enough of this, let's go out on the patio," Hannah said.

The pair sat down in the dark on patio chairs to admire the town, twinkling below the night's first stars. Judy's little greenhouse sat to one side, a big Jacuzzi hot tub sat on the other.

In the distance to the left, the Limestone County Courthouse poked its clock tower and weather vane above the downtown square, framed by First Presbyterian's soaring steeple and the bank, Randall's one "skyscraper" at eight stories. To the right, the bypass and its string of fast food joints and big-box retailers shimmered in the late spring evening, either side of semis whining along the four-lane. A wooded hill straight ahead split the view.

"Wow, nice," Charley said

"Yes, we have just enough woods down below to make it kind of back to nature, then the town on either side."

Charley reached across and nervously took her hand.

"Thank you for this opportunity."

"You're welcome," Hannah said as she turned to him.

"I meant that about your family, you are blessed," he replied.

"I guess, maybe I take them for granted sometimes. Not everyone has the family I do."

Charley snorted.

"Yeah!"

They sat quietly for a while. Down on the bypass, some trucker hit his jake brake with a pop-pop-pop-pop. Crickets chirped in the woods.

"Tomorrow night we can fire up the hot tub—without the hot, of course," Hannah said, nodding back to the covered redwood box. Charley glanced admiringly at it.

"Honestly, figured a house like this, you'd have a pool."

"Oh, we did, I loved it!" Hannah replied. "But daddy got tired of it, always some headache—leaves, chemicals, pump. We found a dead 'possum floating in it once. Randall has no pool service so we had to do it all ourselves. We had an early freeze several years ago, busted the pump, and daddy said, 'That's it!' He had the pool filled in and bought the hot tub."

Charley shook his head.

"First World problem," he said.

Hannah laughed.

They sat quietly for a moment, listening to the crickets and semis.

"I guess this Randy thing must be hard," Charley said. "It surprised me how you acted at the park, I'd never seen happy, cheerful Hannah so curt. There's more?"

"Yes."

Bubbly Hannah turned quiet, drew her hand back and folded her arms, then sighed loudly.

"So long ago, it started our junior year," she explained sadly. "Then it ended in one night. He is the worst-possible guy for me but, somehow, we clicked. We both wanted it to click. I guess I still see something attractive in him, even now, behind so much that's revolting."

Hannah stared into the night and slowly shook her head.

"Randy already had become the big-shot, all-everything football star. Girls swooned when he walked by—and he does look pretty good—tall, muscular, shaggy blond hair, and that sneer. He oozed sexy bad boy.

"I had just made varsity cheer, so I guess we had kind of a Ken-and-Barbie thing, the football star and the cheerleader.

"Suddenly, I get all these texts: 'OMG! Randy Smith likes U! OMG!' 'Randy luvs U? 2D4!' 'U? Randy? SMH!' Then came smileys with their tongues hanging out.

"He said something to somebody, they spilled the tea. Every girl I knew envied me. I'd go in the girls' restroom and hear squeals: 'Oh, Hannah, you lucky thing!'

"Hey, I knew his reputation and, well, I'm a goody two-shoes, proud of it. I'm not going to let some guy use me. He'd done that to other girls—and I knew it.

"But my friends just went nuts, so I said okay to some easy stuff. We went to the drive-in for burgers and such, nothing serious. They turned out fine, he could be fun to talk to, joked around a lot, a big tease.

"I'd sit there munching, he'd pop off something funny. I spewed chewed-up French fries all over the dash once.

"My oh my, we were the talk of the school for a few weeks," she said with a distant sigh.

"Then our church had a Halloween hayride for the youth group out at some farmer's place, I invited him. We roasted wieners and marshmallows, then hopped on this hay wagon and sang songs as we rolled along; good, clean fun.

"Okay, so we're behind the tractor, headed back to the barn, things got quiet, it's a pretty night…" Hannah stopped and took a deep breath. "He stuck his big, meaty hand under my sweatshirt and touched me, he groped me.

"I made a scene: 'Stop that!' I yelled and slapped him. He sat up and drew back his fist.

"'No girl has ever slapped me!' he shouted.

"So I said, 'Then maybe it's time one did!'

"'Girls don't treat me that way! Don't you know who I am?'

"One of the adults stepped in, I rode home with a girlfriend.

"He passed me in the hall the next day and shook his finger at me, 'You'll regret that!' I went straight to the office and told the dean. I don't know what she did, but he didn't bother me again until that football game, a year later."

Charley shook his head.

"Sorry."

"I appreciate you, you're a gentleman," Hannah said sweetly. "You treat me well."

She sighed.

"We better call it a night. We've had a long day, tomorrow will be long too."

They stood up and walked back inside. Hannah shut the patio door, then looked up at Charley.

"Good night," she said, smiling. He nodded at her. Charley turned right to the guest room and she turned left to her bedroom.

The doors closed.

Hannah did her usual head-for-bed routine, showered, put on her long pink nightshirt with a big heart on the front, turned out the light and wrapped herself around the little stuffed hippopotamus she slept with every night. Ah, great to be back in her own rack for a night or two.

Thoughts, bad thoughts, lingered: Randy.

She wanted to forget him. Oh, how she wanted to forget him! But he did have that certain something.

Could it all come back?

Why couldn't all boys be like Charley? He's thoughtful, considerate, courteous—that's what a girl wants. Okay, right, he could be a little more exciting, a little more pizzazz.

Randy: tall and handsome, funny, a thug.

Charley: plain and dull, quiet, a gentleman.

She rolled and tossed a long time before sleep finally overtook her.

Dreams came—agitated nightmares. Randy leered at her with a lecherous grin, he loomed out of an inky night. He grabbed at her, she ran, screaming, through empty streets to get away from him.

She woke to the neighbor's dog barking loudly.

How odd, the old boy didn't make much noise, maybe a raccoon wondered in the yard?

But the barking—loud, intense barking—went on, then she heard the neighbor open a door and yell, "Pierce, you dumb dog, be quiet!"

The dog stopped the racket for a few minutes, then started again.

Suddenly, a chair bumped and scraped on the Bentley patio. Hannah jerked up from her pillow and looked toward the window. She could faintly make out a shadow moving across the curtain.

No raccoon: Someone loomed out there on the patio, just feet away.

Panic!

Ohmigosh, Randy!

Her heart jumped in her throat.

Hannah dove under her covers in abject fear.

"Oh, God, help me!" she whispered.

Wait, covers don't give much protection from an intruder, what to do? She could not bring herself to get out of bed.

Shaking, she reached out from under the covers and nervously grabbed her phone on the nightstand, then called her dad.

She could hear his phone down the hall before Tom Junior sleepily answered after several rings.

"Hey hon', what's goin' on?"

"Daddy! Someone's on the patio! I'm scared!" she nervously whispered, her head buried beneath her pillow.

"Do what?" the father answered, coming awake. "Who?"

"I don't know, it may be Randy!" she said, scarcely able to speak.

"Stay there, don't move!" Tom Junior replied sharply as he ended the call.

The dog barked, the chair scraped again.

Hannah peeked out, she could barely hear a drawer open in her parent's room, then a metallic slip-snap. She knew that sound: A magazine sliding in the grip of a Glock 19.

Dad's pistol.

She knew it from when daddy took his kids to the shooting range on Saturdays, great fun, even if Chad always proved the best shot.

But she'd never heard that sound at home, in the middle of the night. It sounded different, very different, threatening.

She shivered in fear but managed to get herself out of bed and open her door a crack.

Her parents whispered to each other, then she heard bare feet tip-toeing down the hall. Still in their pajamas, they stopped at the patio door. Tom Junior stood to one side of the door as Judy grabbed the doorknob with one hand and placed her other hand on the patio light switches.

Hannah could dimly make out her dad nod.

Her mother jerked, flipped on the patio lights and threw open the door in one quick move. Her father jumped through the door, aimed the gun into the night and yelled "FREEZE!"

The chair bumped the patio, she could hear someone mumble.

"What the....?" Tom Junior gasped as he lowered the pistol.

"What are *you* doing here?" he asked in frustration. "You nearly got yourself shot!"

"Oh, hi," she heard a woman's voice say.

Aunt Brenda!

Hannah put on her bathrobe as Chad and Charley both ran into the hall.

She peeked outside and, indeed, Aunt Brenda sleepily walked in, wearing her usual T-shirt, ragged jeans and flip flops, then turned on the hall light. She had a new tattoo of a pelican on her arm.

"Hello, everybody. Well, I came in town for dad's anniversary tomorrow, or I guess today by now," she said with an indifferent yawn. "Where's the guest room?"

"How did you get here?" Tom Junior angrily asked his sister.

"Oh, climbed over the gate," she replied.

"I mean from Louisiana or wherever—oh, never mind. So, why didn't you ring the doorbell?"

"I knew you'd be asleep, didn't want to bother you," Brenda replied with a shrug.

"Well, you certainly *did* bother us!" her brother answered in exasperation, still holding his pistol.

"Okay, whatever, let's go to bed," Brenda said nonchalantly with a wave of her hand. "Good night."

"Brenda, we have a problem," Judy explained. "Hannah's friend, Charley, has the guest room this weekend. You'll have to sleep on the couch."

"Fine," Brenda replied as she turned and shuffled toward the front room.

The agitated group broke up without noticing Charley in awkward dishabille, standing in the hall in gray Boxerjocks and a hairy chest, facing a startled Hannah.

"Uh, need some help?" the concerned-but-dumbfounded boy asked.

Shocked Hannah, getting an eyeful, quietly shook her head.

Charley looked down, realized his undress, then mumbled "excuse me."

"It's okay."

She closed and locked the patio door, turned off the lights and headed back to her bedroom. She took off her bathrobe and got back in bed with hippo, trying to un-see Charley.

How can you sleep after all that?

But she finally did, sometime before dawn.

Chapter 6
Mark

The family stirred later than usual Saturday morning—no surprise after the night's excitement. Hannah shuffled into the kitchen in her bathrobe and fuzzy slippers with a yawn to find donuts and juice, plus her mom's rocket-fuel coffee that filled the room with a rich aroma.

Aunt Brenda's snoring across the hall threatened to jar loose the pots and pans.

"You went out for donuts?" the daughter asked sleepily. That rated a surprise, given her mother's take-your-vitamins-and-eat-your-veggies dietary habits. Company for breakfast usually meant quiche or huevos rancheros.

"Sure, I certainly don't feel like cooking, easier to just buzz through the drive-up window at Donut Heaven. I took the Jeep, hope you don't mind," Judy said.

"Oh, not at all."

Hannah picked out a donut to accompany her coffee and had a seat in the breakfast nook. She stirred in two sugars to help wake herself up.

Charley stumbled in as he rubbed sleep out of his eyes, thankfully with a T-shirt and bluejeans ensemble this time. He needed a shave.

"Oh, hi," he said, groggy.

The mom grabbed a donut and sat down with her daughter as Charley poured himself some juice.

"It's the big day, do you two plan to go with us, and I guess my sister-in-law, or on your own?" Judy asked.

"Oh, I think we'll go out early, Mom. Charley wants to visit with grandpa and Claire. I know they'll have lots of visitors today, beat the rush."

"Yeah, talk," the boy added as he reached for a donut.

Tom Junior and Chad came in and both headed straight for the coffeemaker. Aunt Brenda continued to snore.

"I guess we better move along, isn't lunch at 11:30?" Hannah asked.

"Think so," her father answered.

Hannah and her tall friend readied themselves, a pretty dress and white shirt/Dockers, respectively.

The Jeep rolled through Randall's empty downtown, past the country club, and turned into Hickory Bough, offering "solutions for senior living," according to its big sign. Here, the famous, old couple had met again after six decades and married in a ceremony that made international news because, frankly, it occurred on a slow news week and the media didn't have much else to talk about.

Hickory Bough had to hire a guard to keep out the tourists.

Hannah led the way through the lobby and day room, populated by its usual assortment of sad and disheveled characters. But things seemed festive by Hickory Bough standards—the first anniversary of its finest hour.

The young couple stood out as they passed the big nurses' horseshoe and veered right toward C Hall, headed for Suite C 4. Hannah turned into the room, which to her surprise stood empty.

Stunned, she looked back out in the hall at the room number and the "Mr. & Mrs. Bentley" tag had disappeared. Puzzled, she looked around as Clémence, a nurse and Cote d'Ivoire native, came by.

"Oh, do you look for monsieur et Madame Bentley?" she asked in her thick accent. "You are the granddaughter, non?"

"Yes, have they moved?"

"Oui, to C 8," the nurse replied, pointing down the hall. "Plus gros!"

Hannah cupped her hands and timidly walked down the hall, Charley followed closely in anticipation.

Sure enough, C 8 had "Mr. & Mrs. Bentley" on its sign. She peeked inside and saw them: her dear Grandpa Tom in a blue suit with his hand on his ever-present cane, and next to him sat Claire in her wheelchair. Claire wore a flowery dress, her beautiful gold-and-silver hair in its usual bun. They chatted with a Hispanic man Hannah didn't recognize.

"Well! Look who's here!" Grandpa Tom called out brightly as he spotted Hannah, standing and reaching for his beloved granddaughter. "I didn't know if you'd make it."

"Hi, Grandpa, just a quick weekend, then back to campus on Monday morning, summer term," she said, hugging the old man.

"José, meet one of my kids, Hannah. Hannah, meet José Pérez, the new manager."

Hannah greeted Hickory Bough's boss and asked, "Hello, and Mrs. Stevens?"

"Oh, big promotion for the former manager," the manager explained. "Headquarters just went nuts over how well she managed the wedding last year. They moved her to headquarters in St. Louis, then transferred me up from San Antonio. Quite an honor, these two made Hickory Bough the star property of Bird Creek Senior Living," Pérez said.

"Come here and hug me!" Claire called warmly up to Hannah, "and introduce your gentleman friend."

Charley stood frozen at the door, enthralled, with a There's-The-President! look on his face.

"This is just so awesome," he mumbled.

"Oh, I'm sorry, meet my friend Charley from Mizzou, he's a big fan of your program."

Awestruck Charley could scarcely speak.

"Hi," he managed with a polite nod.

"Come in, come in, we don't bite!" Grandpa Tom said with a wave.

The men shook, then Claire leaned forward to take Charley's hand.

"What an honor," Charley said slowly, "I listen to all your shows."

"I'm glad somebody does," the grandfather said with a chuckle. "We put a lot of work into them. You know, 'cast your bread upon the waters....'"

"I appreciate them so much," Charley added. "You talk about things I want to do with my life, but I don't know how. I learn a lot."

"So, you moved?" Hannah asked.

"Yes, that's our big news, just a couple weeks ago," Claire explained. "See, we have a side door right here, directly into C 10— twice the room. We use C 8 as a lounge, den, office—name it—and next door's our bedroom. We have writers and producers with the show come in, and other guests now that we're big-shot famous."

"I guess we really do have a suite now. We love each other, but one room? Too cozy, this way she can get away from me for a while," Tom explained with a smile.

Claire laughed.

"Not on your life, you crazy man! After what I went through to get you back, Tom Bentley? I'll chain you to my chair!"

"Well, guess what? We tracked down your initials on that big rock at Hoot Owl Hollow yesterday," Hannah said joyfully.

She pulled her phone out and scrolled until she found the shot of the weathered TB+CD, then handed the phone to Grandpa Tom.

"Well, I'll be!" her grandfather said. "That brings back memories. Look, hon," he said, as he handed the phone to Claire as she put on her glasses.

"Oh, what a lovely afternoon, I remember it well," she said. "Tom talked about it on the show a few weeks ago."

"Yes," Charley said, still in awe. "I asked Hannah if we could look for them."

"Thank you, thank you," Tom said with a glance at the phone. "My oh my, the memories. Can you get the drug store to print it for us?"

"Sure," Hannah replied.

"Well, let's see: *Actionable Anecdotes with Tom and Claire*. So, you enjoy the little tidbits we put together?" Tom asked Charley. "The stations love it, upbeat little item for morning or evening drive times. Five minutes: thirty seconds for a national sponsor, they get to sell thirty seconds locally, and we have to come up with topics to fill the other four minutes."

Charley pulled up a chair and plopped down in front of the old couple. His questions flowed: How do you pick topics? How do you record the shows? How many listeners do you have? Do you make any money? Do you get fan mail? What's the demographic?

Hannah never had seen quiet Charley so talkative. He hung on their answers.

Claire explained Wheatley Davis & Harrison, the St. Louis PR and marketing firm that herded around the reporter mob there for the media-event wedding, pitched the big radio chains on the program while their names lingered in the news.

For a few weeks, Tom and Claire booted British royalty, space aliens and Hollywood stars out of the supermarket tabloids. Hannah painfully flashed back to a checkout line, leaning on her cart, stunned by a cover with fuzzy, blown-up photos of her dear grandfather and his new wife and a headline that screamed:

NYMPHO NURSE LURES TOM!

DECEMBER BRIDE DECIDES DIVORCE!

Ugh! Her own dearest people victims of made-up garbage!

The family-friendly show proved a surprise hit, thanks to the couple's endearing wit and thought-provoking topics. They bantered, they lectured, they discussed, they laughed, they argued—most of all they loved each other.

You could tell, and ratings soared. Advertisers fought to buy the show's commercial spots.

"They're the best thing on radio since Paul Harvey… good day!" one media trade magazine crowed.

"She didn't tell you her nephew and PR whiz, Bobby Dearborn, works for us," Tom said with a wink.

"Well, yes, that too," Claire said nonchalantly.

Hannah sat on a sofa by the door as José greeted Josefina, another nurse, as she came in the room. The two stepped off to one side.

"¿Qué onda?" he asked.

"¿Nada, y tú? Josefina replied, and the conversation flowed in Spanish.

There sat the accounting-major Charley, all business to talk serious stuff with the old couple. Hannah found the trio's moment sweet.

But it went on and on. After a few minutes, a thought popped in her head: Could this be too much? Did Charley stiff her just to meet Tom and Claire?

Focused, she hadn't noticed a quiet shuffle beside her.

"Hey, baby, lookin' for a hot date?" a male voice whispered in her ear.

Startled, Hannah jerked and looked to her side: Tony, grandpa's best friend, had rolled his wheelchair up next to her.

"Oh, hello, Mr. Di Burlone," she replied with a laugh. "I guess so, aren't you a little old for me?"

"I am, but he isn't," Tony answered, pointing back to the door.

Hannah turned back and looked up—and her heart skipped.

"Ohmigosh," she whispered.

There stood just the absolutely most strikingly attractive guy she had ever seen in her life, who simply defined tall-dark-handsome. Dark wavy hair, brown eyes, and ramrod-straight posture, all held together with a perfectly tailored gray suit, white shirt and red tie with tiny white dots. He had dimples and a Kirk Douglas chin—a living, breathing *GQ* model!

He smiled, and the room lit up like a lightning bolt blasted through.

Smooth.

Her jaw dropped.

"Hi, I'm Mark Wade," he said softly as he nodded and flashed his Bert Parks smile again, dazzling her. "Please excuse my grandfather."

Hannah nervously laughed.

"Oh, I know all about him, Grandpa Tom tells stories."

"You don't know the half of it, tootsie," Tony said. "Remember, your grandfather's a co-conspirator, we're partners in crime."

Tony turned and looked up at his handsome grandson from his wheelchair.

"Okay, Markie boy, I've done my part. The rest is up to you! Be sure and mail me a save-the-date when you lovebirds get things set," Tony said.

Hannah blushed, the grandson didn't twitch.

Tony looked around and winked at Grandpa Tom, who winked back. Then he wheeled his chair around and pushed himself out the door, backwards as always.

"Uh…" Hannah could find no words.

"Sounds like you know my grandfather as well as I do, the mischief maker. Isn't he Hickory Bough's self-appointed manager of snarky remarks?" Mark asked with a chuckle as he took a step past the open door and leaned against the wall.

She sat there, bug-eyed.

Good golly, this guy looked good! She could scarcely breathe.

The man had presence.

Hannah nervously coughed.

"Well, uh, uh, this has been a, a set-up?" she stuttered. "So, tell me a little about yourself."

"Former Navy officer and pilot, now a defense-contractor aeronautical engineer, church lay leader, live in St. Louis," he answered briefly.

Navy pilot? "Tom Cruise" flashed through her mind; impressed! She could play Kelly McGillis to this guy! And he must be six-six, how did he fold himself into a cockpit?

"Still pilot a little for fun in a flying club. I suffer guilt, I don't get down here often enough to see my grandfather and parents. They retired and bought a place south of town.

"Grandpa urged me to come for your folks' anniversary, said I would find a little extra excitement.

"He's right."

Mark smiled and lit up the room again.

"Ugh, a bit much," Hannah thought to herself as she continued to cheerfully smile.

Ah, but Mark's smile: Different than hers.

Hannah grinned, chipper and happy.

Mark sported a blinding sunrise.

Whoa, she felt dizzy, here came a crush!

"Stop it," she thought. But what a cute guy!

"Now, the information relayed by my grandfather, received from a reliable source believed to be a certain elderly gentleman across the room from us—the one with the cane, thick glasses and gray moustache, married to a retired federal judge—you happen to be an accounting major at Mizzou, a former top-flight cheerleader, softball phenomenon, and avid outdoorswoman.

"And at this point in your life, you badly need suitable male company."

Hannah coughed and fidgeted.

"Mostly, but that's not entirely the case," she replied politely. "I do have a gentleman acquaintance here with me," and she nodded toward Charley.

"Not a surprise," Mark said, the teeth gleamed again. "May I take a number and wait my turn? Or, do you have any numbers left?"

What a line!

Hannah smiled an embarrassed smile. Charley, her buddy, sat across the room. She owed him something.

"Okay, well, so what else did your grandfather told you?"

"Only that you are pretty, upbeat, like to laugh, smart as a whip, and a joy to hang around."

Her jaw dropped. "I need to put on galoshes," she thought.

"Well then," Hannah said, "I guess with those two old guys in cahoots, neither of us needs a dating app."

"Not that you would ever need one," Mark replied.

Gosh, the pickup lines!

"Thank you."

This guy dumped it out by the shovel full, yet made it sound believable. He had practiced with other women, obviously, not a good sign.

She sat smitten, in spite of herself.

The conversation continued: He earned his engineering degree and Navy ROTC commission at Oklahoma.

Yes, lots of sea duty, he'd flown jets off aircraft carriers. Where? Iraq, he'd done missions from the *Constellation,* he chased Somali pirates from the *Dwight D. Eisenhower.* He recently resigned his commission and took the defense contractor gig back home in St. Louis—excellent pay, home most nights. "Great position, they put me on the fast track, expect to make vice president in a couple years."

Mark had a certain arrogance, a swagger. She didn't like it—or did she?

He wanted to know more about her, "Grandpa Tony didn't tell me everything."

Hannah described herself modestly: Straight-arrow Girl Scout who achieved the Gold Award, church volunteer, reads her Bible daily, sports and outdoors enthusiast. Yes, she shot a deer one fall, filled the freezer that winter.

"I'm not a party girl, kind of a tomboy, pretty dull I guess. I act goofy sometimes," she volunteered with a shrug. "I'm Psi Sig at Mizzou."

"Navy jets? Maybe that'll cool his romantic jets," she thought—as she continued to pleasantly smile.

"Psi Sigma Eta? Really? I'm Alpha Upsilon, OU," Mark said. "The Psi Sig girls were our little sisters!"

She grimaced. Oops, should've left the sorority thing out, but she continued to describe herself and her life.

God blessed her with a successful and loving family that had lived in Randall for decades. And now-famous Grandpa Tom and Claire, there across the room, made her life even more special.

The conversation continued, they had a lot in common:

Hannah loved the outdoors. Mark did too.

Hannah followed the St. Louis Rams. Mark did too.

Hannah loved to dance. Mark did too.

Hannah worked with teens at church camp one summer. Mark had too.

Hannah drove a Jeep. Mark did too—well, a Grand Cherokee, but that counts.

They matched very well, maybe Grandpa Tom's buddy saw it? Could he be worth checking out, despite the cheesy lines?

"Mesmerized" came to mind.

"Stop it," she thought to herself: Charley's here! And hey, this guy had to be really old—maybe thirty!

Chapter 7
Banter

Hannah and Mark had talked for quite a while. She glanced across the room to see Grandpa Tom, Claire and Charley still visited. Claire caught her gaze and smiled back sweetly.

"Listen, I've enjoyed this but I have some people here I really need to see," she said politely.

"Maybe I can call you later?" Mark asked, and the room lit up again.

Good gosh, she could hear a choir sing when this man smiled!

"I guess, I get back to Columbia Monday afternoon, I start summer classes Wednesday. Let me give you my number."

"I have it," Mark said confidently, "I'll call you Tuesday."

"I guess our old friends thought of everything," she answered with a chuckle.

"Looks like, talk to you later."

Mark stood up, winked at her, and started to leave just as Tony rolled back into the room.

"Any luck, Markie? Does she want a princess cut or a marquise?" Tony asked.

His grandson just smiled that big smile again as he strolled off.

Just then Hannah's parents, Chad, and Aunt Brenda walked in, nodding at Tony and his grandson.

"I'm hungry, when do we eat?" the aunt asked loudly as Hannah's parents went to greet the couple of honor.

"Well, Brenda, you're here!" the old man said warmly, raising his hand to stop Charley's questions. He stood to hug his daughter. They embraced and Grandpa Tom sat down again next to Claire.

A familiar, all-black sphere rolled into the room—the rotund, effervescent Rev. Gaylene Gillogly, Hickory Bough's part-time chaplain and fulltime Episcopal priest, in her clerical collar.

"Hello, everyone! Three cheers for the happy couple!" she chirped with her usual gusto.

"Thanks, Gaylene, good to see you," Tom replied. "I guess you did a good job on us, one-year out and we're still hitched."

Gaylene laughed and struck up a conversation with Hickory Bough's manager.

Suite C 8 had a crowd by now as Claire's niece, Martha Dawson, came through the door toting a travel bag.

"Well hello, Marty!" Claire called brightly.

"Hi, Aunt Claire, and congratulations," her niece answered as she bent over to give her aunt an affectionate hug. "Happy anniversary, you knew I wouldn't miss your party."

The two ladies had a lively chat, then Martha plopped her bag in Claire's lap and declared, "I brought you a little anniversary gift" as she reached in the bag and pulled out a battered black, oblong case.

"Look what I found," the sixtyish woman said as she handed the box to her aunt.

Claire gasped.

"My flute! Where did you find it?" she asked, turning over the beat-up case. "Look, Tom," she added, touching his hand and pointing to a badly tarnished brass plaque under the handle, engraved "CED."

"Claire Elaine Dearborn: Ha! More initials, looks like we left a trail," Tom said.

"Quite, my parents gave this to me for my birthday as our freshman year began," Claire explained fondly. "We met a month later. It got quite a workout in its day. Dad paid more than a hundred dollars for it, a lot of money in those days. You couldn't find them because of the war, mom and dad knew I loved to play in the school band."

"We're making your old bedroom into a theater room," the niece explained. "The workmen pulled the shelves out of your closet to install the projector and sound gear, so guess what they found stuck up in the corner on a top shelf, out of sight? They pulled the shelf off the wall with crowbars and, Plop!, this fell on the floor.

Claire gingerly opened the latches and looked at the silver instrument's badly tarnished parts. She shook her head as she sighed.

"The last time I played it, let's see, would've been Easter weekend my sophomore year at Cottey College, 1951. Someone put together a high school band alumni party, we had a grand time that Saturday night.

"Tom? Off in the war, and me lonely beyond words. I needed something to do."

"I bet that thing brings back lots of memories," Grandpa Tom said as Claire carefully looked at the flute, lost in thought.

"Indeed, it does," his wife replied with a smile. "Guess what I had under my feet on that midnight bus ride?" she said, winking at her husband.

"I wasn't looking at your feet," her husband answered.

"Oops!" Claire said, her hand over her mouth.

The crowd shared the same blank look: What midnight bus ride?

Tom laughed, dropping his cane as he slapped his hands.

"I know! I know!" Tony called as he waved his hand.

"Don't tell!" Tom cautioned his friend as he bent over to pick up his walking stick.

"Honey, you better get us out of this," Claire added, punching Tom with her elbow.

Tom thought for a moment as laughter tittered through the room.

"Let me see, what can I tell in mixed company?"

The laughter grew louder.

"You do not help things!" Claire replied, joining the levity.

"Well, let's see: November 1945, it was a dark and stormy night! We rode home on a packed school bus from a football game over in Springfield, a big Randall Ram victory!

"Claire didn't have anywhere to sit—so she invited herself onto my lap. Let's just say, how to put it, the relationship started."

More laughter.

"A first kiss?" Judy asked her father-in-law, raising an eyebrow.

The old man sat for a moment, thinking, with one eye closed.

"You could say we bussed on the bus," Tom said dryly.

Claire bent over laughing with the rest of the crowd.

"I still love to kiss you, but I found it more exciting the first time!" her husband said brightly.

"Same here, you made a shy girl's dream come true that night," Claire replied.

The old couple kissed and held the pose for a moment as "Aaahhhh!" went through the crowd.

"Little did we know," Claire said as she gazed at Tom fondly. She turned back to the case and lifted the cleaning rod and cloth, a few long, blonde hairs came up with them.

"Hmmm, now to whom do those belong?" Tom asked.

Claire winked at her husband and they hugged.

Charley sat, enthralled: more banter!

Nearly seventy years had gone by, the people and places remained in place; good-natured laughter. They teased each other.

How could that be? Do families really do things like this? Can people really be so affectionate, so supportive?

"Listen, this has been wonderful, but we need to move along to lunch," Claire said warmly as she took Charley's hand and they shook. "I've enjoyed our visit."

"Good to talk to you young man," Grandpa Tom said as he stood. "Let's see, Charley, I believe. Sorry, didn't catch your last name?"

"Trottel, properly Charles Trottel," the boy replied.

The old man felt a sudden chill hit the room.

He could tell by the way Claire's eyebrows furrowed. Hardly noticeable, no one else would see it, but he did.

He knew this woman.

Tom Bentley first saw that look sometime before that midnight bus ride.

Claire Dearborn—that tall, thin girl crowned with beautiful long, blonde hair and piecing blue eyes, the one with that funny, pouty smile.

He fell for her, "crush" didn't tell the story. Then only to find out—wonder of wonders—she had secretly adored him for years. They became inseparable.

He found her a tough read. She could be any one of three girls: intense and quiet, friendly and fun-loving, sneaky and scheming. He read a book once that described a girl as "like the moon, part of her is always hidden."

That's Claire.

Tom learned he had to watch her faint expressions closely. That look meant something just happened.

But what?

Something had just made her sad or mad—or both.

But what?

The thoughtful, quiet, reserved Claire suddenly came to the fore, replacing the friendly, chatty Claire that had been seated next to him.

Well, he'd find out, time to move along the party.

Tom Junior announced, "Everyone, let's go eat!"

Grandpa Tom handed his cane to Claire, who glumly placed it across the armrests of her wheelchair as he stepped back to push her to lunch.

Hickory Bough's dining room looked unusually festive with table cloths and flowers as assembled residents and guests greeted the couple of honor. A big cake with a single, large "1" sat in front of their usual dining spot.

Mr. Pérez welcomed the crowd, then invited Gaylene to say an invocation.

Gaylene, chipper even by her always-bubbly standards, began a prayer for the ages. She finally got around to "Amen!" after several minutes and Grandpa Tom leaned over to Tom Junior and whispered "Genesis to maps."

The son burst out laughing.

Everyone enjoyed a lively meal.

Then the manager stood and made a short speech about how Hickory Bough appreciated its most famous residents. Polite applause followed, and as it died down, Tony blurted out, "Don't let it go to your head Tommy, we knew you when!"

More laughter.

Waitresses busily cut the cake and passed out slices amid noisy visiting.

Hannah demurely sat next to Charley, a couple seats down from Grandpa Tom.

She could see Tony and Mark across the way. Mark discreetly smiled and nodded at her.

Oh, that smile!

She smiled back.

Gifts waited to be opened, then Grandpa Tom stood to thank everyone.

A too-quiet Claire said nothing, despite the room's levity.

The party slowly broke up and Hannah hugged the old couple as Charley shook hands with Grandpa Tom. Claire held her hand to her mouth and looked away.

"So what do we do now?" Charley asked Hannah.

"I vote to go back to the house and take a nap," she replied.

"Great idea, rough one last night," he answered, yawning.

Chapter 8
Claire's Call

Hannah changed into jeans and a top before she plopped on her bed. She had a good nap under way, curled around hippo, as her phone rang.

"Phooey!"

She sleepily reached to answer. A 513 area code? No one she knew. She yawned and slipped the phone back on her nightstand; scam.

A minute passed and the phone suddenly played *In the Mood*— Grandpa Tom's ring!

She grabbed the phone and answered a bouncy "Hi, Grandpa!"

"Hannah, this is Claire," came a serious reply. "I just tried to call you, I guess you didn't recognize my number."

"I'm sorry, I didn't. I'll put it in my contacts."

"That's okay, I still have my old Cincinnati number," Claire replied. "Listen, I have something very important to talk to you about."

"Sure, what's up?" Hannah answered, now wide awake. She pushed hippo aside and sat up.

"Can you come out, right now?"

"I guess, let me ask Charley, I know he'd like to visit some more," Hannah replied.

"NO! I want you to come *alone*," Claire said firmly.

"Uh, everything alright?" the girl replied, puzzled.

"I'm not sure. Please, Hannah, come see me," Claire said. "It's important."

Hannah had never heard that tone in her step-grandmother's voice. Claire could be cold and aloof, or warm and friendly, but this time she sounded shaken, scared.

"Okay, give me a few minutes. 'Bye," Hannah answered.

What on earth?

This sounded odd, but she knew level-headed Claire wouldn't do stuff like this without a reason. Everyone else had come home and started naps. Aunt Brenda snored loudly on the sofa again, so Hannah slipped on her shoes, grabbed her purse, left an "At Hickory Bough" note on the kitchen counter, then tiptoed out to her Jeep.

Yes, Grandpa Tom and Claire, so sweet, remained a mystery of sorts. Their story, long and tangled, glowed beautifully in her mind.

What fantastic people! Would she get to hear a new chapter?

The neighborhood's big gate opened and she headed down Poplar, still puzzled by it all.

Then it hit her: Randy!

Ohmigosh, no! Randy!

Her parents had cautioned her to not go out alone—and for good reason.

Fear: Should she go home, or go ahead? Look around you!

Did that blue car in her rearview mirror follow her?

Who stood at the corner while she waited for a red light?

Paranoia: She made sure the doors locked. She thought of the old dad joke her father told: "You're not paranoid if they really are out to get you."

Yes, Randy really was out to get her.

Well, you're in broad daylight, should be okay. She'd call home when she got to Hickory Bough.

And more than likely, the city had Randy at the park gate, leering at other girls, on a late-spring Saturday afternoon.

But she looked around more than usual. She noticed the trucks and construction equipment at Grandpa Tom's house again as she passed. Oh, she'd ask about that.

Hannah parked near Hickory Bough's front door, looked around, then briskly walked in, crossed the lobby and day room, headed for C Hall. Multiple gifts and a big balloon bouquet still cheered Suite C 8.

"There you are," Claire called. "Please come sit here with me, sweetheart. Tom, shut the door."

Shut the door?

Grandpa Tom took his cane, shuffled over, hung the Do Not Disturb sign on the doorknob and closed it, then made his way back to the women.

"Have I done something wrong?" Hannah asked, her eyes big, curious.

Claire shook her head.

"No. Hannah, my sweet darling, you seem to do everything right," came the answer. "Please keep what I am about to tell you between us."

Claire took a deep breath.

"Hannah," she began, "when Tom and I married I purposed in my heart to make his family my own. I love all of you, although that can be a challenge."

"Aunt Brenda?" Hannah asked.

Claire smiled briefly. "You said it, not me."

"But Hannah, I especially love you: I have found your bright, animated personality a true joy—I want you to know that. You are a delightful young lady, a beautiful young woman. And, I say this in love, maybe you can be a bit naïve sometimes. Maybe that makes you even more charming.

"I do not want anything to happen to you," Claire added firmly as she reached to take the girl's hand.

"Yes?" Hannah replied, puzzled.

Claire looked at her intensely.

"What do you know about that boy, Charley?"

Interruption: Hannah's phone suddenly buzzed with her mom's ring.

"Excuse me, I better get this," Hannah said.

"Hi, Mom," she answered apologetically.

"Hannah, where *are* you? I thought we agreed you are not to go out alone!" her mother replied curtly.

"Yes, I know, very sudden, but I'm fine. I'm at Hickory Bough with Grandpa Tom and Claire."

"What's going on?"

"They wanted to talk to me, I'm sorry. I'm fine, everything's fine. I'll explain later."

"Okay, but stay there, we'll come get you. Please, please, we're worried about you!"

"Yes, I'll keep you posted. Again, I'm sorry, I'm fine, love you!" and she hung up.

Hannah turned back to Claire.

"Where were we? Uh, yeah, Charley.

"He's nice, we're friends, buddies, I kind of like him as a pal, I guess. He seems more into me than I am in him."

"Have you dated long?" Claire asked.

"No, I guess we've only had one real date—and I asked *him* out," Hannah answered. "Mostly, we just go out for coffee after our Christian student group meetings, then talk about your show—he's fascinated with what you two have to say. We go out to eat with the gang after church on Sundays. We hang out some, nothing serious."

"And the date?" Grandpa Tom asked.

Hannah leaned back, clapped her hands and laughed.

"It did not go well!" the girl answered, eyebrows furrowed.

"I invited him to Psi Sig's Sisters of Spring garden party, on the lawn behind our chapter house. You know how these sorority things go, everybody stays in their little groups, their cliques, so he didn't fit in, he's independent.

"We sang for our brother fraternity, did a skit, and some other stuff. Charley wandered off, then came up to me and asked, 'What's a *kigh-oh*?' I said I didn't understand.

"He explained he'd heard two girls talking about another girl they didn't like and one said, 'What do you expect, she's a *kigh-oh*!'

"I stifled laughter and told him 'Chi Omega, she's a Chi-O—that's another sorority—like Tri-Delts and Delta Gamma. He shrugged and walked off. Let's just say he's not into Greek life.

"Oh, but he really got into the band! We danced several times, he's a great dancer! Charley loves music.

"He helped the band set up, the frat boys just stood around drinking beer, so afterward I got him one of our 'Psi Sigma Eta Brother' polos to thank him for the help. He wears it a lot, really proud of it."

"What about his family? Where does he come from?" Claire asked sharply.

Hannah shook her head, perplexed.

"Well, he has a single mom, she lives in Neosho. I know they moved there a few years ago from Illinois, or someplace. Beyond that, not sure," she answered.

"He rarely talks about his mom, don't think he has a happy home life. I think they argue a lot, but he respects her. He made the comment last night at dinner that he appreciates our close family."

"Good," Tom said.

Claire sighed.

"This is very hard for me, my dear."

She took a deep breath.

"Many years ago, before I became a federal judge, I met a terrible man, the sharpest operator you can imagine. He could talk paint off a wall.

"Oh! He defined smooth: poised, confident, incredibly good looking, sharp dresser, a real heartthrob for any young woman. He posed as a big-time banking lawyer.

"I fell head over heels for him, Hannah. Thoughtful, careful Claire let her emotions take over. I didn't know about his crimes at first.

"They called young women like me 'career girls' in those days: single, sophisticated, chic. I could manage for myself—or thought I could. I lost your dear grandfather here years before this happened through a terrible mistake I made.

"I decided, after I lost Tom, to never let another man in my life. I would go it alone.

"Then I met this man, this awful man. He knew my type, he knew what to say and do, he caught me.

"He talked me into things I should not have done. At one point, because of him, I seriously contemplated suicide. Later, I feared someone might kill me because of him."

Hannah's mouth dropped.

"Why?"

"He worked for the mob," Claire added as her hands shook. "He ended up murdered in prison, and I feared whoever killed him might come after me."

Claire leaned forward in her wheelchair.

"His name was Bert Trottel."

Hannah set upright, startled.

"And you think Charley..." her voice trailed off.

"I have no way of knowing, my dear, but you don't find that unusual name often, and he looks a bit like the man I knew. If your Charley is a grandson or nephew or some such, I want you to know. I do not want you hurt too.

"I do not want you to have anything to do with that boy!"

Hannah shook her head, bewildered.

"I met Bert in Washington, D.C., when I lived in the capital, he spent a lot of time there. He had lots of government contacts that his criminal associates needed. He lived in Cleveland, and also spent a lot of time in New York City. Has Charley ever spoken of those places?"

"No."

"Talk about a rake, he used and abused women—that included me," Claire said forcefully. "He had personal women, like me, besides prostitution rings, drugs, money laundering, abortion mills, and I don't know what other evils he did. Find a racket, Bert did it.

"He had contacts so that when a shady pal got in trouble, things suddenly worked out. Evidence disappeared, witnesses forgot what they saw, that sort of thing. FBI agents suddenly got transferred from Washington to, say, Butte, Montana, their files got lost in the move.

"I didn't know all this at first, I thought myself his one and only, someday we'd marry."

Tears rolled down Claire's cheeks and she sniffed loudly.

"Okay, I've had a bad experience with a boy too, although nothing like that. But why suicide?" Hannah asked innocently.

Claire cried.

"I'm sorry, I'd rather not go into it," Claire sniffed. She wiped her eyes and shook her head. "It still hurts."

Tom handed her a Kleenex.

"I had it all planned: We'd have a big wedding at the National Cathedral, then I would be a socially prominent sophisticate, the wife of a big-time Washington lawyer and lobbyist, who took me to swanky parties and galas.

"Bert vacationed at Hyannis Port with the Kennedys, he knew the Johnsons and Nixons, I figured we'd dance in the East Room someday.

"Then, by accident or God's intervention, I found out Bert *was* married. He had a wife!

"His only one? Ha!

"It crushed me, it devastated me. Smart Claire got outsmarted.

"Suddenly, the blinders came off, I really saw him: a fake, a money grubber, a self-centered criminal, a liar. He used me."

"So how did you find out?" Hannah asked, hanging on Claire's words.

"His wife sued for divorce. It turned into a show trial: All his evil deeds, all his work for organized crime, spilled out in the press—all these awful details of multiple other women he kept. Then came criminal charges, convictions, he went to prison. Like I said, they found him dead in his cell."

Hannah listened in disbelief.

"What did he say, what did he do, that made you go for him?" Hannah asked.

"Darling, I don't know. It wasn't what he said and did, but the way he said and did things, and that's very hard to define," Claire said, dabbing at her eyes.

"The one good thing he did for me? He called someone, that got me the nomination.

"The Senate approved my judgeship and I went off to Ohio just as he went to prison.

"But God has a way of working things out when we trust Him. What Bert meant for evil turned into good, I believe. My first Sunday in Dayton, I went to this Presbyterian church down the street from my apartment, I hadn't been to worship in months.

"The pastor preached a sermon about the Babylonians from Habakkuk, that little book in the Old Testament. It didn't mean much to me, but one verse from the scripture reading that morning popped out, like someone threw a brick at me from the lectern:

"'*Therefore the law is slacked, and judgment doth never go forth: for the wicked doth compass about the righteous; therefore wrong judgment proceedeth.*'

"I memorized that verse, Hannah. I had the opportunity to do something about wicked people like Bert. I would make sure good came out of what happened to me," Claire added.

Hannah felt dazed, her eyes watered.

Could all this be true?

Could this be the same Claire, the prim and proper professional woman she looked up to and admired, the federal appeals court judge who had been on a shortlist for a Supreme Court nomination?

This successful woman who brought honor, and yes fame, to her and her family?

This wonderful, very special person hung out with a bigtime mobster?

No, it couldn't be.

Maybe Claire created this story, a ruse, some kind of sick joke, a hallucination. After all, the lady had passed eighty. Did she have dementia, maybe Alzheimer's?

Wait a minute: Maybe Grandpa Tom and Claire put this story together as some sort of plot to get rid of Charley—for Mark's sake.

Surely not, but what if?

"Okay, excuse me, Grandpa," she asked, turning to Tom. "But does this have anything to do with Mr. Di Burlone's grandson? Apparently, Tony and you have talked to him about me."

The question startled her grandfather.

"Absolutely not, no, not at all, sweetheart! I wouldn't do that," Grandpa Tom answered firmly.

"True, Tony's a big fan of his grandson and he thought the two of you might make a match. You made a big impression on him the few times he met you, and he got to thinking out loud one day: 'Let's have some fun, Tommy! Maybe we can match up our grandkids? Wouldn't that be great! Hey, if they get hitched, won't we be uncles or cousins or something?'

"You know, he's a real a cut-up.

"And from the looks of things this morning, you two did connect. Maybe Tony's right. Honestly, I didn't know about Charley, didn't know he would be here, I know it turned awkward for you."

"It's not that I'm serious about Charley, it made things, well, difficult," Hannah replied.

"No, Mark's not involved in this. Claire told me about the guy she knew back when, but I didn't connect the name until we talked after lunch," Grandpa Tom continued.

"I told Claire that you're one of my dearest possessions and maybe we need to warn you."

"So this Charley, a smooth talker?" Claire asked.

Hannah shook her head and laughed.

"Hardly! No, he's polite, courteous, good-hearted. But I wouldn't call him smooth. He's a little clumsy, unsure of himself.

"He can be a klutz," she replied, thinking of poor Charley standing in the hall in his underwear.

"I think he sees me as a girlfriend—that is a friend who's a girl."

"How did you meet him?" Claire asked, probing.

Hannah relayed how they met at Mizzou, how he stopped to ask about Grandpa Tom and Claire, then how a friendship blossomed.

Yes, in fact, Grandpa Tom and Claire brought them together.

"We met at a Christian student group, we go to church," she added brightly.

"Well! Now that does not sound like the Trottel I knew," Claire said. "The only reason he'd go in a church would be to steal the chalice.

"Still, I'm worried, sweetheart. I don't want you to be hurt, you understand?"

Hannah sat and stared at Claire, absolutely numb.

"Thank you, but it seems unlikely. He's from Neosho, that's a long ways from Washington. How would Charley end up there if they're related?" the girl asked.

"I don't know, I don't know," Claire said.

"But I have to add to all this that God answered my prayers for forgiveness. My life worked out, and this dear man came back into my life again," she said as she patted Tom's leg.

Just then came a loud knock on the door.

Claire jerked.

"Sssh! Say nothing, don't get hurt, love you," Claire said quickly to Hannah.

Tom Junior, Judy, Aunt Brenda, Chad and Charley came through the door in a rush.

"Are you okay?" her father hurriedly asked.

"Yes, I'm fine, we're okay. Sorry I scared you," Hannah replied meekly.

The visitors looked at the tear-stained faces of Claire and Hannah, and the thousand-yard stare on Grandpa Tom's face.

"My word, what's going on, are you *sure* you're okay?" Judy asked, puzzled. "You don't *look* okay."

She and Tom Junior shared that special glance that married couples have when something with their kid isn't right.

Claire managed a smile.

"Tom and I wanted to share some special things with your daughter," she said, reaching to pat Hannah.

"I'm sure she enjoyed our little talk, didn't you?" Claire asked.

Hannah nodded.

"Here, please, come in, sit down," Claire added.

Chapter 9
The Stalker

Everyone found a seat. The usual television babble out in the hall made the only sound.

Tom Junior cleared his throat.

"Well, uh, that lunch today proved special," he said. "The staff did a good job, great to see everyone."

"I guess," Grandpa Tom replied. "We'd like to spend more time with the family, maybe we could all do something special this evening?"

"Good idea," Judy replied suspiciously. "You two need to get out of this place more. Maybe we could go out to eat? Just us? Just the family, for fun?"

"I'd like that," Grandpa Tom replied. "Claire?"

"Well, yes, of course. I know it's a lot of trouble to haul me around in this thing," she said with a pat on her wheelchair. She wiped her eyes again and sniffed.

"Let's go to Rio Bravo," Hannah suggested. "I told Charley how much I like their taco salads."

"Nah, not that!" Aunt Brenda moaned. "Those Mexicans put MSG in their food, that's bad for you, causes cancer!"

Options?

"Well, there's that fried chicken place down the street, Bea's Hen House," Tom Junior suggested. "Would that be okay?"

"Do they serve free-range chicken?" Brenda asked curtly.

Maybe, no one knew, shrugs and headshakes, seems like they would mention it on the menu, whatever.

Brenda launched into a monologue about how poultry farms leave chickens unhappy and depressed. No one likes depressed chickens. Her diatribe seemed to get the group's attention off whatever Claire and Hannah had talked about.

"Do they use vegetable oil?" she asked. "Canola works best, the plants have pretty flowers. Better yet, do they have baked chicken?"

Tom Junior hemmed and hawed, surely they use vegetable oil to fry their chicken. Judy added that she thought they had a baked chicken option too, "and I know they have catfish."

Brenda recoiled and gasped in horror.

"I can't eat catfish, it's a bottom feeder!"

The wayward aunt jumped up and waved her arms.

"Why don't you people talk about *important* things? I can't go around eating carcinogenic chicken!" she said loudly.

She began another monologue, this time on the health benefits of canola oil, peanut oil, olive oil ("But chicken tastes funny when you cook it in olive oil!"), and—worst of all—animal fat.

A taste of lard? Instant death!

"I'm sure they have salads too," Chad offered, trying to move things along.

"But are the vegetables organically grown?"

No one knew, maybe, could be.

"Okay, but I don't want to have to wait long for a table," Brenda replied. "I have better things to do."

Tom and Tom Junior both shook their heads and sighed. We'll risk cancer and unhappy chickens, Bea's Hen House it is. Chad pushed Claire's wheelchair and off they went.

"Did I do something wrong? I'll apologize," Charley nervously whispered to Hannah as the group headed to the parking lot.

"No, not at all, I'm not sure what this is about," Hannah replied grimly.

It took some shuffling to get the party of eight in two vehicles, assuring that Claire could ride in the front of Judy's big Nissan Armada, which Tom Junior affectionately called "the Beast." Claire could manage one shaky step up or down, anything else required troublesome lifts by a couple people.

Grandpa Tom arranged to get in the Jeep's front seat. He loved Hannah's Wrangler.

Judy and Hannah dropped off their riders in front of Bea's—which already had a line out the door. They had to drive around to find parking; busy Saturday. Hannah and her mom came around the corner together to the end of the line, joining the rest of the Bentley crew, enqueue.

Friendly chatter filled the time as they edged toward the door, enjoying the restaurant's enticing aroma.

Charley came back to stand with Hannah, they chatted.

So they have great chicken here, you like fried chicken?

Sure, except that stuff in the dorm cafeteria my freshman year.

They laughed.

Well, it has been quite an afternoon, hope you had fun.

Yes, and you?

I did, thanks.

Did the Cardinals win this afternoon?

No, rainout in Pittsburgh.

Are you ready to go for your summer classes?

Think so, and you?

Yep, I want to roll so I can graduate next spring.

Tom Junior stood in front of her and as they talked Hannah affectionately wrapped her arm around her father's waist. She felt a lump.

"What's that?" she said, looking up at her father.

He leaned to her and whispered "concealed carry."

"Daddy!" she gulped.

"Hey, have to take care of my Ladybug, don't I?" he said, hugging his daughter. "You-know-who goes too far, I'll double-tap at center mass, don't want to lose you."

She hugged back.

More Hannah-Charley chit-chat, they inched along.

When's church tomorrow?

Depends, 8:30 and 10:30.

Hannah didn't look behind her as she absentmindedly ended up at the back of the line.

"I love eating out, and I love breasts and thighs," she heard a familiar, low voice say right behind her.

Startled, she turned around: Randy!

Hannah gasped.

"GET AWAY FROM ME!" she yelled.

The shout, and its panicked tone, caught the attention of all four men in the party. They quickly turned around and stepped back to the girl.

"Young man, get out of here!" Tom Junior ordered, grabbing his back.

The quick response and a line of stern-looking faces circling the girl, surprised Randy. The big, blond kid staggered back.

"YOU'RE MINE, HANNAH!" he shouted, pointing at the girl, as he took off running.

It left Hannah and her family shaky.

"Should we call the police?" Chad asked.

"I called them earlier," the father replied. "I think he's gone for now, but let's stay together. Obviously, we're being followed."

"Where does he live?" Grandpa Tom asked. "Maybe the police should go see his parents or something."

"I have no idea. That kid may live under a rock with other vermin, for all I know," Tom Junior replied. "I suspect they'll be out there, though."

Judy stepped back to her daughter.

"Honey, he's gone. We're here with you, let's try to have a good time," the mother said, consoling her.

The hostess poked her head out the door and called "Bentley, party of eight!" Tom Junior pushed Claire and the group found its table.

The family-style dinner proved delightful as tensions eased, topped off by peach cobbler a la mode.

Now, to get home. Judy and Brenda would take Grandpa Tom and Claire back to Hickory Bough. Tom Junior would drive the Jeep with Hannah, Chad and Charley.

Nothing happened, but normally chipper Hannah sat glumly in the tight back seat, her hand over her mouth, next to Charley.

"I'm sorry, it hasn't turned out to be much of a weekend," Charley whispered as they rode up Poplar past Grandpa Tom's old house, silhouetted behind a nearly full moon.

She glanced nervously at her now-suspect seatmate—what had Claire said?

"You don't know the half of it," she answered.

Chapter 10
The Keyboard

Mother Bentley got out of bed early Sunday morning to fix a big breakfast. Judy had guilt about donuts the day before and figured, this time, a big meal would perk everyone up.

It did.

Randy's presence made plans to drive Hoot Owl's Jeep trail moot. So, Hannah and Charley decided, a spontaneous thing, to do a hike after worship instead.

"I guess that's okay," the still-worried mom said. "Randy probably has to work today, but you two stay close, stay together!"

Meanwhile, Claire's warning troubled Hannah, but bland Charley just seemed different, harmless, especially in contrast to loathsome Randy. Trottel? The name must be a coincidence, that's all.

Church proved great, some of Hannah's old high school chums happily greeted her, glad to see her again.

Charley stood quietly to one side as the gaggle of girls talked and laughed.

Aunt Brenda even went to church, but mostly sat and stared at the bulletin, even as the congregation stood to exchange the traditional handshakes and greetings.

After the final amen, the Bentleys and Hannah's tall guest shuffled out of the sanctuary in the middle of the throng headed to the parking lot.

"Let's move along so we can get on the road," she said to Charley.

He nodded.

"Wow, great music!" the musician answered. "They really make those Hillsong numbers rock!"

"Yes, they do," Hannah answered with a laugh, "and they did *your* song this morning."

The boy brightened and stopped, looking down at the grinning girl.

"Yes, shall we dance?" Charley chirped.

"But of course!"

The couple turned to each other, Hannah giggled. Charley smiled and bowed, she curtsied. They joined hands and started a broad waltz in the middle of the crowd as they sang an impromptu duet:

"Who am I that the highest King
Would welcome me?
I was lost but He brought me in
Oh His love for me,
Oh His love for me."

They paused, faced each other, and laughed as the crowd around them, dressed in Sunday best, stared. The waltz resumed as they sang:

"In my Father's house
There's a place for me,
I'm a child of God
Yes I ammmm!"

Charley and Hannah stopped and hugged as the puzzled onlookers applauded.

"Hannah Bentley, you amaze me!" her dumbstruck mom said, shaking her head.

The daughter bent over laughing.

"Perfect triple time! Now, how often do you get to waltz in church?" she asked.

The crowd joined the laughter as they shuffled on.

Puzzled parents.

"There's a story inside all that somewhere," Tom Junior whispered to his wife. "He changed suddenly, did you see that?"

"Yes, I'm just glad she's back to her bubbly self after yesterday, poor kid," Judy replied, shaking her head. "Isn't dancing in church like something she'd do?"

"Yeah, and you love her for it," Tom Junior said.

"You know I do!" Judy answered.

Hurry! Hannah and Charley changed into jeans and T-shirts, Charley sported a Neosho Wildcats baseball cap. Hannah pulled out her backpack and Chad loaned Charley his pack. The pair started a sandwich assembly line on the kitchen counter.

We just have whole wheat, no, here's some rye. You want that?

Mustard or mayo?

Ham or turkey?

Cheese? We have provolone and Swiss.

You want more lettuce?

Mom, do we have any tomatoes?

Pickles, I like lots of pickles.

Judy grabbed some snack-size potato chips in the pantry, they found raisins and nuts and made trail mix.

"You'll never have to talk my daughter into camping or hiking— the tomboy!" she laughed.

"Whatever she wants, she gets," Charley answered firmly.

"You do know M&Ms in gorp are better for you than regular M&Ms!" Hannah assured Charley.

"I feel healthier," he replied.

Judy set out several bottles of water for the pair.

"Well, that should be enough, won't be gone long," Hannah said as they stuffed their packs. "Now, you know where we're going, up Turley Hill, that short hike over the creek south of town? We'll be back late afternoon."

"Oh yes, I went with your Girl Scout troop that time, have fun, sweetheart!" Judy replied.

A hike?

Great, let's go!

Maybe today would make up for the bad things, for thoughts about—and confrontations with—Randy.

Yes sir, it would be a great day!

But what about Claire's warning?

Hey, Charley's just a pal, okay? They'd been alone in her Columbia apartment watching TV and nothing happened. What, me worry? Charley's nervous smack on her cheek Friday afternoon was as racy as things ever got. Don't be serious!

Forget all that—let's just have a fun time.

Whatever! "You sound like Grandpa Tom and Claire's radio show when you start thinking like that," Hannah said to herself. Be positive, encouraging, make life great!

A half-hour or so in the Jeep would give them time to talk. Likeable, good-natured Charley would tell her all about his family, he'd lay things out, just a coincidence, you know? She could put Claire's worries to rest.

They headed south, where the Missouri prairie melts into the Arkansas Ozarks. What a beautiful day, just a few puffy clouds in a crystal blue sky.

"You want to listen to Sirius or you want to talk?" she asked as they passed Hickory Bough on their way out of town. It felt funny not to stop.

"Talk," Charley answered. "You perk me up when we visit, you're so upbeat."

"Thanks, again I'm sorry for all the confusion this weekend."

"That's okay," Charley replied.

"Well, hey, you've spent so much time with my family this weekend, maybe you need to tell me more about your family," Hannah said.

Charley shrugged.

"Not much to tell."

"So, where were you born?" Hannah asked.

"Washington, D.C.," Charley replied.

Hannah gulped.

"Well, really just over the line, Maryland, PG County."

"So, your father's name is Trottel?" she asked cautiously.

Charley sighed, sat his elbow on the door's armrest and rested his cheek in his palm.

"No."

"So, your mom divorced and remarried?"

"No."

"So, I guess I don't understand."

Charley shook his head.

"My parents never married," he replied quietly.

"Like I said Friday night, I don't know him, never met my father," the boy added flatly. The Jeep rolled along quietly.

"I saw my birth certificate once, mom had to get it to put me in school. She caught me looking at it, yanked it away. 'Forget you ever saw that!'" she yelled, then she threw it in a drawer.

"His name is something like Bridger, Baker, Barker, Bannister, Blagojevich—that's all I know."

Hannah sat silently, trying not to react to her awkward questions and his uncomfortable answers.

"So, your mom's family name is Trottel?"

"Yeah."

"So, uh, um, what about that family, you have any aunts or uncles, cousins?"

"No, just the two of us. Well, my grandmother, she came to visit a few times."

"Where does she live?" Hannah asked.

"Cleveland."

Hannah shuttered.

Oh! My! Gosh!

"See why I like your family? You have something I've always wanted—an extended, loving, supportive family. You have a loving and caring mom, a loving and caring father, a good-guy brother, plus, your grandfather and Claire. You talk, you support each other, you tease, you do things together.

"You don't yell at each other. Hannah, that's your gift from God," the boy said seriously.

Stunned, she stared out the windshield.

"Maybe, maybe I have more than I know," Hannah replied.

"Mother's running from something," he explained with a heavy sigh.

"Uh, who's your male role model?" she asked as she thought to herself: "If he says anything about the mob or prison we're turning around."

"Not much to talk about there," Charley answered.

"I guess a male role model has to be a pastor I met when we lived in Bowling Green, a Rev. Daniel Rankin—older guy, finest man I have ever known. Your Grandpa Tom makes me think of him."

A minister? Ah, now that's more like it.

"Tell me about him," Hannah asked as she slowed for a curve.

"We went to Kentucky like we moved everywhere. Mom came in and said 'We're moving!' We lived in Huntington, West Virginia. We moved in the hottest days of summer, our Bowling Green house had no A/C, so I wandered into this city park and sat down in a picnic shelter, bored out of my mind.

"This older man comes by, walking his dog, looks at me and says, 'You look bored.' I said, 'Yeah.' He sat down and introduced himself.

"Rev. Rankin pastored a little church and asked me to mow the churchyard for ten bucks. Sure, something to do, and the money didn't hurt. I went over to a Dairy Queen afterward and blew part of the money on the biggest Snickers Blizzard they had. I was hot, it was cold, I had a sugar high like you wouldn't believe. Life got better."

Hannah laughed. "So how old were you?"

"Twelve."

Charley brightened and sat up.

"He took an interest in me, the first adult to do so. He gave me other odd jobs. He had a really sweet wife, sometimes she'd make me lunch. Their children, grown and gone, guess they liked having a kid around again."

"What did your mom think about this?" the girl asked.

"Nothing, she liked to have me out of the house. She's worked for years doing eight-hundred number, website customer service, social media monitoring, stuff like that, doesn't want to be disturbed.

"My grandmother has some business contacts in New York, they got her into that sort of thing," he added.

Bingo: Washington, Cleveland, New York! Hannah grimaced.

That's it, turn around, Hannah—now. Charley unknowingly rambled on.

"'Don't get in trouble,' she'd tell me as I left, extent of her parental guidance."

"That sounds cruel." Hannah answered nervously.

Charley sighed.

"More than once she said things like 'I wish you would go away, I don't know why I kept you.'"

Hannah winced.

"Really?"

"Yeah."

"Pastor Rankin? Different.

"He wanted to know what I did, how's school? I got to know kids in his youth group, I had friends—something I didn't have other places we lived. He gave me this kid's Bible to read. It had this reading plan in the front, I like to read, so I read most of it. I'm a big reader.

Hannah, I figured out life offered more than what little I had, what I had seen. It's like the song:

"'In my Father's house
There's a place for me…'

"I had a school choir concert one night. He and his wife came, mother didn't.

"A turning point in my life came the day I helped him clean out his garage. I pulled this old electronic piano keyboard, seventy-six keys, out. I asked, 'What's this?' He told me and added, 'You can have it, our son used to play it in the services.'

"I took it home, big thing, heavy, all I could do to carry it. Mom got mad and yelled at me, said I stole it. I assured her no, I had been helping this old couple and they gave it to me.

"'Okay, but keep it low,' she said. I went back in my bedroom, shut the door, and plugged it in. It worked! I plinked around, I could sit and play that thing for hours.

"Hannah, I found my gift. Family's your gift, mine's music.

"I can hear a song once—and play it. I have some kind of ability, I don't know what.

"It's like I get in the author's head, I know what's coming next. And the crazy thing, it works in accounting too. I look at a company's financials, say, and I know what the next numbers in the table will be.

"It's weird."

A puzzled, and nervous, Hannah hung on Charley's story as she drove.

"The hard part of music for me came with the written notes and stuff.

"Pastor Rankin's wife dug out some of their son's old music books and gave them to me. They had an upright piano, she worked with me, gave me lessons, explained how to read music.

"I thanked her one day and she replied with a big smile, 'You know what they say, Charley: Every good boy deserves favor!' I knew just enough about music to get the joke and I laughed. 'And Charley,' she added, 'Always be sharp!'

"Hannah, I got hooked." Charley said. "It's like anything else, the more you work with it, the more you learn, stacking chords—whatever."

"Indeed, I envy you," she replied. "So what happened to your friend, the pastor?"

"Same ol', same ol'—we moved." Charley continued. "This time: Middle of the night, she came in, poked me and said, 'Wake up, we're moving!' She had this clunker, '83 Oldsmobile station wagon, barely ran. We went out and packed up our belongings in the dark. I grabbed my keyboard and she said, 'Leave that thing, we don't have room.'

"I replied, 'If you leave it, you have to leave me.'

"She answered, 'Don't tempt me!'

"Well, we agreed I could take it if I held it between my legs. I could just barely get it in between me and the dashboard."

"That's cruel," Hannah said, shaking her head.

"You get used to it."

"So where did you move next?"

"Cairo, Illinois, I wrote Pastor Rankin a letter. I wasn't sure about his address, I didn't have a phone number. I never heard from him, but the letter didn't come back either. I stole a stamp from mother, still feel bad about that.

"I don't know, Hannah, maybe he's an angel. You know what the Bible says about 'entertaining angels unaware?' He might be one. He popped into my life right when I needed him, gave me what I needed, then disappeared. He flew off to wherever angels go."

"I've heard about things like that," Hannah said.

"Then we moved to Neosho and, well…." Charley said with a shrug. "I had good grades and a strong SAT, good enough to get the scholarship, that's how I ended up at Mizzou. You know the rest."

"So why did she want to move in the middle of the night?" Hannah asked.

"Don't know. Like I said, I think she's been running from something her whole life.

"Somewhere, somehow, along the way I showed up."

Chapter 11
Take A Hike

The countryside became hillier, forests replaced fields, as the Jeep hummed south. The road began to curve and climb up and over hills. They slowed as Hannah carefully followed the little highway as it hugged a creek for a mile or so. She turned off and parked on a wide, graveled shoulder.

"Here we are!" she said. "We can go down this bank, make our way across the creek—lots of rocks so we won't get our feet wet—and then climb up to that rocky knoll on the other side; maybe a mile. Very easy, very pretty, my Girl Scout troop did it a couple times."

"Perfect," Charley replied.

"Great! Let's go!"

They climbed out and Hannah pulled a paper pad out of the glovebox and carefully wrote a note and slipped it under a windshield wiper.

"Just to be careful," she explained. "If we're not back by this evening, whoever can call my dad's number."

Charley looked surprised.

"Good idea."

Charley reached in the backseat and grabbed their packs.

"Okay, while you're back there, grab my floppy hat. And where's the bug spray?" she asked as she dug through her console. "There are deer here, that means ticks."

But she couldn't find bug repellant after looking through her pack and the glovebox too.

"Darn! I must've left it at home, haven't done this in a while. Oh well, just avoid brush and we can check our legs when we get back."

Off they went.

They had a steep climb down the path from the road, sliding on gravel. Sure enough, stepping stones in the creek allowed them to jump across the clear water, except once when clumsy Charley slipped on a rock and stumbled. He got a wet shoe.

Up they went on the other side around big boulders. Birds sang in the trees above.

The forest cleared at the hill's crest and they turned out onto the knoll, huffing and puffing. Green mountains rolled to the horizon beneath a blue sky and yellow sun.

"Look," Hannah said, pointing south.

Her tall friend stood, entranced by the fabulous view. "This is just so awesome."

She laughed.

"Let's eat, enjoy the scenery!"

And they did. They found a little patch of shade behind a big rock. Off came the packs and out came the sandwiches and potato chips, washed down with a couple bottles of water.

"Save the trail mix for later," Hannah advised as they munched.

"Why?" Charley asked.

"I keep it as an end-of-hike reward," she explained. "Success! Or if you get lost, you have a snack to keep you going until you get back on the trail."

"Makes sense," he answered.

A hawk circled in the distance.

"This is just so awesome," Charley said again as he ate, leaning against the rock, looking at the mountains.

"You're a nemophilist," he added solemnly.

"A what?" Hannah asked.

"Don't get to use that word much, it means someone who loves the woods."

"That's true," she said, puzzled. "Anyway, I'm glad you like it. This has been more fun than when I hiked up here with a bunch of giggly girls."

"I bet," he said, leaning toward her. He took off his baseball cap, bent her floppy hat's brim back and they shared a quick kiss, just a smack.

"You taste like mayo!" Hannah replied, wiping her mouth.

She laughed, her eyes smiled. He smiled back nervously.

Had he done something wrong?

"Oh, you wonderful, beautiful girl," Charley said with a sigh. "You're the best thing I've found since that keyboard."

Now, that touched her.

Charley, quiet and rather dull Charley: He didn't throw off lines like Mark.

But remember Claire's warning! Stay alert!

"Thank you," she said softly. But hey, Charley's a pal, right? That's all, right?

What Claire said haunted her, maybe he isn't what he seems.

And Mark: Wow!

Hannah had rolled it over and over in her mind: *It wasn't what he said and did, but the way he said and did things.*

Charley seemed sincere, but really? He seemed affectionate, but hardly smooth. Anything romantic came nervously, a jerk, a swipe, unsteady, unsure of himself.

No Casanova he.

Then again, what could this poor guy offer her?

Claire's Bert Trottel had wealth, power, prestige.

Hannah's Charley Trottel had a keyboard and ramen noodles.

Should she be wary? Time would tell, she could take care of herself.

Besides, she had the car keys.

Charley could tell something bothered her.

"You okay? I, uh, hope I haven't done anything wrong," Charley said, worried, as he opened a bag of potato chips.

"Oh no, just been a crazy weekend," the girl said as she wiped her sweaty face with a napkin. "You have all these expectations, some happen, some don't. Let's take a break and then we can head back down."

They leaned against each other.

"Thank you for being here, whoever you are," she said softly.

What did that mean?

Charley found the comment odd, some kind of joke? He smiled at her, then pulled her floppy hat down and put his baseball cap back on.

The exercise and lunch made both groggy. They dozed off, against each other and the big rock. The distant roar of a jet, miles above, ended the quiet, along with the occasional chirping bird.

Heads nodded, naps began.

Hannah woke, she didn't know how long they had been asleep, to find herself in bright sun, their shady patch gone. She looked up and yawned, then noticed the sky now had lots of puffy clouds. The wind had come up.

"Hey, Rip Van Winkle, wake up!" she said, punching Charley in the ribs.

"Huh?" he responded with a yawn. "I went to sleep."

"We both did, better head back," she replied, standing.

"It's still early, why don't we go down and across that draw over there, then climb up to the other hill?" he asked as he pointed in the distance.

Hannah thought for a moment, staring at the far hill.

"Gee, I don't know, that's a lot of walking, a lot of ups and downs."

"Hey, I want this to last, I don't get to do stuff like this. But you decide, you're the expert, you make the call," Charley replied.

Hannah thought for a moment.

"Okay, we can do it, then we can follow the creek back to where we crossed it below the road. The trail's pretty clear there."

They put their packs back on and threaded their way down and around. It turned into a far tougher hike than they expected. First came heavy brush, then thick timber. They scrambled through the hollow's dry wash, then wound their way toward the rocks that topped the far hill.

They broke out in a clear meadow with more huffing and puffing.

"Water break!" Hannah called. She pulled a bottle out of her pack's side pocket and noticed the sky had clouded over. Off in the distance she heard low thunder.

Uh-oh.

"Hey, looks like there's a storm coming, we better head back," she cautioned.

Charley looked around.

"You're right."

Down they went but somehow, somewhere, they turned the wrong way, away from the creek. The thunder grew louder, bright light shimmered across the dark forest floor from lightning above. Cool gusts of wind whipped the trees above them as they stepped out into a clearing.

Big rain drops smacked them.

"I don't like this at all!" a worried Hannah shouted as she looked up. "I don't want to be outside with lightning around. We better find somewhere to get—fast."

Chapter 12
Rock of Ages

First came a powerful wind gust, then rain slammed them in a blinding sheet.

"This way!" she yelled as they stumbled up to the bottom of a low cliff with a rock outcrop. It offered a scant few feet of dry ground below an overhang—just enough, barely, to get them out of the downpour.

But running through the deluge left both soaked.

"Yuck!" Charley said, taking off his pack so he could make enough room to scoot below the narrow ledge above them, out of the wet. He helped Hannah get her pack off and they both sat down with their backs flat against the rock wall, legs scrunched up, as the sudden storm pounded the forest in front of them.

BLAM!

A blinding flash of light, deafening thunder, the ground shook: Lightning hit a tree, maybe a hundred feet away. The trunk shattered, chunks of bark flew at them.

Hannah screamed, Charley jerked and banged his head on the rock wall behind them.

Flames leaped from the bare tree's skeleton for a few seconds before the rain doused the blaze. The couple sat, wrapped around each other, watching, shaking, petrified.

"We, we, stood right there just a minute ago!" Hannah said, trembling.

"I know," Charley said in wide-eyed wonder. "What do we do now?"

"Not a thing, we can only wait it out," she answered, shaking.

Charley sat, glumly looking at the storm.

"Okay, I'm a musician," he said with a shrug. "What do I think of?

"*Rock of ages, cleft for me,*
let me hide myself in thee..." he sang.

"I guess that's appropriate," Hannah said, doing what she could to dry herself off.

"More than you know," Charley replied over the storm's roar. "The author got stuck out like us. I took a hymns and sacred music elective last year. The story goes he got caught in a thunderstorm and hid under a big rock.

"What's his name? Toplady, Augustus Toplady wrote it. He got inspired by the idea of God's protection in the storms of life. Quite a rabble rouser, I think, but he wrote great music."

Lightning popped, thunder boomed, above them.

Rain cascaded off the hill above, over the cliff that created their narrow shelter, in a jerky waterfall. They sat, backs against the rock on their few feet of dry ground. The storm raged on, but they managed to stay out of it—barely.

"Oh thank you, Lord!" Hannah said. "This isn't much but at least we're not out there," she added. She stretched her hand out to catch drops of water that fell in front of them.

Pea-size hail fell from angry, gray-green clouds with a loud roar.

They sat, knees under their chins, terrified. Wet clothes gave them shivers as the hail chilled the air.

"Well, the worse the storm, the shorter it lasts," Hannah said, trying to be upbeat.

But it didn't.

The rain continued—hard—as the lightning and hail finally ended.

The alternatives: scrunch on this narrow sliver of dry ground or run for it.

Run for it?

No.

Leaving offered no option since they weren't exactly sure where they were, and it might be a mile or two of hard walking to the Jeep, maybe longer, in heavy rain.

Time ticked away. Conversation proved slim as they hypnotically stared at the onslaught. Boredom brings random thoughts. Hannah recalled her eighth-grade geography teacher telling her students the English "Ozarks" comes from the French "aux arcs-en-ciel," meaning "to the rainbows." Whenever had she thought of that?

"We could use a rainbow about now," she mumbled to herself.

More idle thoughts, an earworm started to crawl. The old hymn's lyrics slithered on through Hannah's uneasy mind:

"Could my zeal no respite know,
Could my tears forever flow,
All for sin could not atone;
Thou must save, and Thou alone..."

Talk about sin, Hannah, the supposed outdoors expert, had allowed them to walk into a terrible mistake.

Here she sat, lost in a thunderstorm with some guy she'd been warned to avoid. Hannah sat scared, really, really scared. All her out-in-the-woods experience suddenly proved worthless.

She shook her head, in tears.

"This is all my fault, my blunder," she said. "I've been outdoors enough to know to check the weather forecast—and I didn't. I just didn't think."

"Don't beat yourself up," Charley said. "I pushed this."

"I better start to think now, we could be here all night," she replied.

"Thanks to you, at least we have something to eat."

"Trail mix? Yeah, but not much, and I'm down to one bottle of water."

Charley checked his pack.

"Same here."

"Let's not get hasty, we may be hungry and thirsty for longer than we know," she cautioned.

A couple hours ticked by. The rain eased into a shower but continued to fall, the waterfall in front of them dissolved to a steady drip.

"Want to make a run for it?" Charley finally asked.

Hannah mulled the idea.

"No, if I knew where we are, yes, but I don't. We could get even more lost, and it'll be dark soon. The map app on my phone won't be much help—even if I can get it to work out in this mess. But let me try, maybe I can get a signal."

Hannah dug her cell out of her pocket, turned it on and waited: "No Service" flashed on the screen. She punched her father's number and tried, just in case. She got one brief ring, then dead air.

"So much for that," she said, turning off the phone.

The sky slowly darkened as the sun, somewhere above the heavy gray blanket above, sunk under the horizon. The rain slacked to a drizzle.

Tedium.

Both took discrete potty breaks, as the companion looked away, as far from where they sat as possible without getting out in the rain. Slowly drying clothes helped but the night ahead meant more chill. It would be cold out here.

"So how can we sleep sitting up?" Charley asked glumly.

"We can't," Hannah answered. "We'll have to spoon."

"What?"

"Spoon: We lie on our sides and curl around each other to preserve body heat. It's saved peoples' lives when they got caught out in bad weather.

"That's how you live: stay close."

"Well, doesn't sound so bad," Charley said.

"Hmmm, okay," she said with a grimace.

To get up close with a guy, any guy—touching—made her uneasy. Would Charley try something? She thought back to Randy on that hayride.

Could Claire be right?

Well, you gotta' do what you gotta' do. Whack him with a rock, sugar, if he tries anything.

Dark slowly fell, they found the least-rocky spot they could, then put their damp packs down for pillows. Charley kicked loose a few rocks and moved them out of the way to soften their dusty sleeping spot. He did what he could to make her comfortable.

Her phone's flashlight provided the only light in the black night.

Hannah laid down on her side, took her floppy hat off and laid it on her pack. Charley took his cap off and eased down behind her, wrapping one arm around her waist, then laid the other under her neck. He pulled himself up closely against her back and legs.

They both felt better in minutes, wrapped around each other, as they shared body heat.

"If I must, it's nice I have to do this with you," he said to the back of her head.

"Oh, you hopeless romantic, just don't get any mud on me!" Hannah replied, snickering. "Seriously, I'm just so sorry about everything."

"It's okay," Charley said quietly. He leaned forward, moved her damp hair aside and lightly kissed her cheek.

Hannah sat up on impulse and turned back to him. Charley sat up, surprised.

They stared at each other for a moment in the dim light. Charley leaned forward to take her cheeks and pulled Hannah to his face. They kissed, mouth to mouth, the first passionate kiss they had ever shared.

"Thank you," she said as their lips parted, an inch from his face.

He hugged her tightly as he whispered, "Hannah."

"Hang on, we'll get out of this!" she answered.

They kissed once more, then laid down again, wrapped even closer around each other.

She felt humiliated.

Instead of she being scared of him, maybe he should be scared of her. If he could forgive her for this....

Maybe the two of them shared something, maybe Charley had something she wanted, or needed, in a guy. Maybe she should look at him a different way. Could he be more than a buddy?

She felt safe with Charley wrapped around her despite Claire's warning. No, more than just safe: secure.

"Who is this guy?" Hannah thought to herself. A few minutes passed as they quietly listened to the drizzle. Hannah asked softly, "Charley, did you use deodorant this morning?"

He snorted.

"Yeah, thought the same about you," the boy answered. "I'd take my shoes off but that would make it worse."

Hannah giggled. "Good idea, maybe we both sweated off our de-stinker dancing at church."

They laughed, then got quiet—seriously quiet.

"That seems so long ago," Charley said as they snuggled tightly, "very long ago."

"Lord, we need help," he muttered. "We're doing what we can, please get us out of here."

"Amen to that," the Hannah replied. "It'll happen!"

"Do you think your folks miss us yet?"

"No doubt, they're frantic!" she answered. "Their little girl's so dependable and predictable—something's badly wrong if she's not home, if she hasn't called."

"Good," Charley replied. "Must be nice to have people worry about you."

Hannah started to say something but caught herself. Did no one care about Charley? And if not, why not?

Sleepy, but things churned in her mind.

Behold, Hannah Bentley: Afraid, cold, scared, stuck in the dark—and sleeping with a boy Claire warned her to avoid.

Wait: *sleeping with a boy* sounded all wrong.

But, well, she was. She could feel his chest rise and fall against her back as he breathed.

Charley, the gentleman, did nothing to take advantage of her—not that tonight proved very sensual. He did what he could to make her comfortable. She appreciated that about him, so different than Randy.

Randy!

Oh, if Claire only knew about Randy! She didn't need a warning from a woman in her eighties.

Why did she have to think about that scoundrel now? She had enough misery at the moment—cold, wet, muddy, lost—stuck out in the mountains in a storm.

Maybe Claire worried about Charley for nothing?

Hannah hoped so, but she appreciated Claire's concern.

"Bless her, Lord," Hannah whispered to herself.

She thought of the sweet couple in their nice, warm bed at Hickory Bough, the old folks probably had been in it an hour by now.

Little did they know....

She could only imagine, again, things at home: Hannah should have been home hours ago, what happened? Why hadn't she called?

The storm?

A wreck?

Randy?

They both drifted off into uneasy slumber, sleeping about as well as anyone can, lying in damp clothes, on rocks, in a storm, with an empty stomach. The old hymn's lyrics continued roaming in her head as her heavy eyes closed:

"Naked, come to Thee for dress;
Helpless, look to Thee for grace;
Foul, I to the fountain fly..."

Chapter 13
Unexpected Help

A bird's twitter roused Hannah at first light. She could tell Charley continued to sleep behind her. One side of her body had gone numb and she wanted to roll over. But she didn't want to wake him, poor guy.

She fidgeted, which did wake him.

"Huh?" he mumbled, yawning. "Morning?"

"Finally, how are you doing?" she asked.

"Not very good," Charley answered with a groan.

"I can understand that, I've had a rock in my ribs all night."

"No, I mean, like, sick or something."

Hannah rolled around and indeed, Charley's face looked puffy and flushed in the dim light.

"Maybe we just need to eat, we still have the trail mix," she said, sitting up to open her pack.

"No," he whispered, "nauseated."

She felt his forehead: hot.

"You have a fever," she said, concerned. "We better get moving, can you walk?"

"I guess," he replied. He panted as he got up.

They stood, knocked dirt off their clothes and put on their packs and hats.

They slipped and slid down the muddy hillside. They passed the lightning-hit tree, standing bare and scorched.

Charley shuffled and stumbled along, weakly following Hannah. The walk downhill to the gully proved the easy part, then what? Which way to turn? Did the little gully bend, and where did it meet the big creek?

No dry gully now, it roared, filled with brown water.

A few watery beams of sunlight spiked through the misty woods as the sky slowly cleared with the sunrise. That helped their attitude, but the muddy, gunky ground made the going slow. They slopped into heavy woods when a low roar and chop-chop-chop came in the distance.

A helicopter!

"They're looking for us!" Hannah cried, running back up the hill to a clear spot, but the helicopter had disappeared by the time she got out of the trees.

"Have a seat, let's stay here in case they come back over," she called down to Charley.

He glumly slumped down on a rock and held his head in his hands, breathing hard. The helicopter did come back in a few minutes, headed the other way, but so far away her jumping and waving went unnoticed.

"Oh well, let's move along," Hannah said as she came back to him.

No way could they cross the stream now. They followed the gully's twists and turns through the woods for maybe a half-mile until it ran into the big creek.

That creek, no surprise, roared bank-to-bank. Trees bumped along in the raging current.

Hannah stood, helpless, as she watched the brown flood on two sides of them. Charley leaned against a tree, groggy, as she thought. They had to cross the big creek to get to the road and the Jeep, but how? They could hear the helicopter again, somewhere, in the distance.

"Stay here, I'm going to check things out," she told her friend.

A pale Charley quietly nodded and slumped on the muddy ground.

"Oh God, how much worse can this get? Help us!" she prayed, looking back at her very ailing friend, who sat against a tree, holding his head.

She rounded a big rock, just above the surging water, when to her surprise a young man in a white T-shirt came out of the trees.

"May I help you?" he called politely.

"Yes, we need to cross the creek," she answered, out of breath.

"Go back and get your friend, then follow the creek up another hundred yards or so. You'll find a tree lying across a couple high rocks, just above the water. You can cross there. Be careful, it's slippery."

"Thank you, I'll be right back!" she called, figuring the man would radio the sheriff or something. Hannah ran back to get Charley, back against the tree.

"Someone's here, we can cross the creek!" she said, panting.

Charley nodded, pushed himself up, then vomited.

She watched, horrified.

They waited a minute, then repeated her route along the roaring creek and, sure enough, what had once been a huge tree had fallen across the rocks, just above the water. She looked around, the young man had disappeared. Oh well, must've gone for help.

"This will be tricky, you go first," she said.

Charley nodded, then slowly crossed the trunk on all fours, stopping twice to catch his breath. Hannah followed him carefully.

They slumped on the opposite bank to take a long rest.

"You need to drink some water, maybe that'll help you feel better," she asked.

Charley shook his head and gasped, "water gone."

Hannah offered him what little water she had but Charley shook his head no. She drained the last drops in her bottle as she thought about what to do next: Should they take off straight ahead and maybe find the road, or follow the creek downstream to where she knew the Jeep sat? She had no idea how the creek and the road twisted and turned, the road might be a mile from where they sat, or fifty yards.

What to do?

"Let's follow the creek, it can't be that far," she said.

Charley nodded, painfully got up and they started moving again. High water covered the creek bed, so they had to climb over and around multiple rocks and trees. The helicopter flew overhead again but they couldn't be seen under the trees.

The boy had to stop every few minutes to rest, puffy and pale. He slumped against a rock and mumbled, "Don't know if I can go on, leave me here."

"I can't, Charley! Please, I still don't know for certain where we are. Let's take it easy and get as close to where we parked as we can," she replied, frantic.

Charley slowly stood up.

"Here, let me help you," Hannah offered, wrapping his arm over her shoulders. "You can do it! C'mon!"

A five-foot girl didn't help a six-foot-plus man very much, but at least they kept shuffling. He stumbled and fell twice, rested for a few minutes, then gamely got up and started with Hannah's help.

"Keep going, it won't be far!"

The rah-rah didn't convince her, and she figured it did nothing for him either.

The creek twisted and turned, how many hours had it been? The sun now beamed from above. Could it be noon?

Then she saw it up ahead: the faint path up the steep slope they had joyfully gone down the day before.

"That's it! We've made it!" she said, "We're here!"

"I… can't… go… on…" he mumbled as he stumbled and fell sideways into a clump of poison ivy.

Hannah gasped.

"Please, please, roll over this way!" she pleaded, bending over to try and move him. "You don't need a case of poison ivy now!"

"Go on, leave me," he whispered as he painfully rolled onto grass and muddy gravel.

Charley's pale body bulged out of his clothes, red splotches popped out of his face and arms. He gasped for every breath.

"Okay, it won't be far, stay put—I'll be back soon," she said. Tears streamed down her muddy, sweaty face. Hannah could not bear to think of leaving him, but what else could she do?

She sighed, said a quick prayer, then went on alone.

Hannah turned away from the swollen creek and started the steep climb up the trail. Yesterday's loose dirt and gravel had turned to slick mud. She grabbed tree limbs and weeds to pull herself forward as she finally broke out onto the highway.

There sat the Jeep, dinged from hail. The soggy remnants of her note hung over a wiper blade. She stumbled forward and hugged a fender, as though the car could help.

Hannah looked up and down the empty road: nothing.

"HELP ME! HELP ME, PLEASE!" she screamed at the top of her lungs to no one. Her voice echoed in the emptiness, the only other sound the roaring creek below. Then she leaned wearily against the Wrangler as she gasped for breath.

"Hannah!" came a faint call, maybe a quarter-mile away.

Chad came over a rise in the road at a dead run.

"Sis! Are you alright? Where's Charley?" he said, out of breath, as he hugged his sweaty, muddy sister.

"I'm okay. But Charley passed out, he's not far from here, by the creek, he's sick—bad sick!"

Chad grabbed a walkie-talkie off his belt and yelled, "I found 'em at the Jeep!"

A metallic voice crackled "On our way!" In a minute, two sheriff's cars roared up the road, lights flashing.

The deputies jumped out.

"Never mind me, Charley's down there!" she pleaded as she took off her backpack. "Do you have a rope? The trail's mud, you'll have to carry him up, he can't walk."

"Sure," a deputy said as he opened his car's trunk. He tied one end of a heavy rope to a tree and threw the rest down the slope.

A siren wailed and an ambulance roared up. A paramedic jumped out and trotted toward Hannah.

"Are you alright, miss?" he asked.

"I'm just okay, really need a drink, I'm nauseated, exhausted. But go get Charley, he's down this trail, very sick," she explained frantically. "Turn left, then stay just above the water, maybe two- or three-hundred yards."

The ambulance crewmen grabbed a basket and headed down the trail, hanging onto the rope. Hannah focused on them and didn't notice her dad and Grandpa Tom had pulled up.

"Ladybug!" her father called, He jumped out of the car and ran toward her.

"Daddy!"

She turned around, then bawled loudly as her dad gave her a bear hug. Grandpa Tom came up behind him, as fast as his cane could tap across the gravel.

"Are you alright?" Tom Junior asked as he took off her soaking-wet floppy hat.

"I could use a drink, we ran out of water. But I'm really worried about Charley, he passed out!" she said, crying.

"I'll be right back," her father answered as grandpa came up and hugged her.

"I'm filthy dirty, you sure you want to touch me?" she asked.

"I don't care, sweetheart, we're just glad to have you back, didn't know if we'd find you dead or alive. Claire's prayed up a storm for you back at Hickory Bough, she'd be on her knees if she could get out of her wheelchair," he said.

Grandpa Tom helped Hannah back to her father's Lexus, opened the passenger door and she sat down, her dirty clothes on the leather seats and muddy hiking boots on the carpet. Tom Junior handed her a bottle of water. She chugged it, greedily, then sat, panting.

"So, what happened?" the concerned father asked.

"That big storm hit as we headed back," she explained. "We took shelter under this cliff someplace up there," she explained, pointing out in the forest. "At least we stayed dry all night."

"I'm really worried about Charley," Hannah added, biting her finger.

"I'm sure they'll do all they can," Grandpa Tom said.

"So, did you try to call last night?" her father asked. "My phone rang once with your number, then quit. That didn't help ease our worries."

"Yes, I did," Hannah said, catching her breath. "I tried, but got a no-service."

"That's when we started making calls," her father explained. "We almost came last night but it rained so hard. We got out here before dawn, the sheriff and the highway patrol have been great. They have a K-9 unit and horses on the way, guess we won't need them."

"I'm glad you had that guy out in the woods, he helped us cross the creek," Hannah told one of the deputies.

"What guy?" came the answer.

"Back over there, upstream," Hannah explained, pointing up the creek.

The officer shook his head.

"We don't have anyone in the woods yet, we're waiting for the dogs."

"But I saw...."

Hannah sat, panting, could it be?

The helicopter flew above the party, wagged once, and headed off.

Grandpa Tom shook his head.

"We had just gone to bed, the rain fell in buckets outside," he explained. "Claire suddenly sat up and gasped, 'Hannah's in trouble!'

"About then, your dad called," he added. "I told him I had to come, although I'm not much of a hiker anymore," the grandfather added, shaking his cane.

There came much grunting and shouting from the trail as the ambulance crewmen and a sheriff's deputy labored to pull Charley up. Hannah jumped out of the car and ran toward them.

"How is he?" she asked, worried.

"To be honest, ma'am, not very good, anaphylaxis," came the reply. "He's in some kind of toxic shock. We gave him an epi injection, we need to get him to the hospital—fast. Wish that helicopter had medical gear."

A desperate Hannah looked down at Charley. Pale, his eyes swollen shut, he breathed in labored gasps.

"Let's take you too," the paramedic added.

"Go ahead, hon', Chad can drive the Jeep," her father said with a wave. Grandpa Tom hugged her.

"You're okay now," he whispered in his granddaughter's ear.

Chapter 14
Visitors

Depression.

Hannah, the always-happy, upbeat girl everyone loved to be with, ever cheerful, sat glumly in her hospital bed, cheek in hand.

"Funk" came to mind—she needed a stronger word.

She thought of the Winston Churchill biography she read in high school English and the great wartime leader's troubles with his "black dog"—terrible, paralyzing depression.

The black dog had bit her. The perky girl didn't perk.

What went wrong?

She, the experienced, adventurous nature lover.

She, who hiked, camped and hunted a hundred times.

She, who had done the Tour de Mont Blanc trail in the Alps, and eighty miles of the Appalachian Trail in Tennessee and North Carolina.

She, who treasured that big photo of herself on her bedroom wall, hands on her hips, a smug smile and a huge pack on her back, as the mighty Matterhorn peeked out of the clouds behind her.

She, crouched in a blind in camo and safety orange with her dad and brother on their deer lease at first light, the .30-06 on her shoulder as the buck wandered out of the trees.

She knew this outdoorsy stuff!

Nothing ever, ever, happened like this, and on a stupid, little Sunday afternoon jaunt. They took sandwiches and potato chips, no MREs. Hey, no Lewis and Clark thing here.

She knew the drill: Why didn't she check the weather? Why did she forget bug repellant? Why didn't she bring more water? Why didn't she bring a jacket? She had her doubts when Charley suggested going to the second hill, why didn't she say no?

The whole hike had been spontaneous, and when you don't think things through, stuff happens.

She knew that. The accounting term: due diligence.

Hospital tests found her okay, dehydration and other minor stuff—cuts, bruises, a muscle sprain. The doctor wanted her to stay a night for observation, though, just in case.

Ah, but down the hall: poor, sick Charley.

Think about that, Hannah: Your negligence might kill someone.

But then again, they did plan a simple, short afternoon hike on a route she knew.

"Don't kick yourself," she mumbled.

It didn't help.

Charley, alone in ICU, family only: She couldn't see him, as badly as she wanted to. Hannah, after all, didn't do very well herself right now—tired, exhausted, queasy. All this mess, and summer classes start tomorrow. Well, so much for that.

She closed her eyes and shook her head, that horrible ambulance ride back to the hospital yesterday afternoon flashed through her mind again: The paramedics frantically worked on Charley, just a foot away. She watched one's stethoscope swing from his neck as he pounded on Charley's chest.

Spread out on the stretcher, poor Charley, pale white with a red rash, fingernails and lips blue, his body puffy as a marshmallow, an oxygen mask on his face.

They cheered when his blood pressure struggled back up to ninety. A shallow pulse zoomed well past a hundred and stayed there.

The worst moment came when one of the crewmen shook his head and sighed, "I don't know if he's gonna' make it."

The old hymn came back with its threatening last verse:

"While I draw this fleeting breath,
When mine eyes shall close in death…"

No!

She had prayed with everything inside her as tears ran down her cheeks: "Please, God, no, heal him! I don't want to sit here and watch him die!"

And it would be her fault.

Her parents walked in her room just then, both hugged her.

"How are you doing, sweetheart?" Tom Junior asked.

"Not very well, I'm still stuck in a storm, this time in my head," she answered with a frown.

Her father reached under her neck, kissed her forehead and hugged her.

"Look, does a dark and cloudy sky mean the sun's gone? Does night cancel out the day? Of course not," he said softly. "Look, just because things seem dark for you now, it doesn't mean the sun will never shine again. You went through a storm, but the sun came out today, right? Look outside, see it?"

"Yes," she said, sniffing, gazing out the window at a blue sky.

"Just like when the sun disappears, God can still be working even if you don't see it. This will work out, you'll see great things come out of this. Trust me, you will."

"Oh, Daddy, thank you!" she said. They hugged.

"Listen, this isn't your fault," her mom added. "I know you, you're a pro, you did the best you could. Anyway, the good news: Charley's been moved out of ICU."

"We have to run now, Aunt Brenda and I will be here this afternoon with Chad. Maybe we can sneak in some pizza, or would you prefer more of that great hospital chow?" her mother asked, teasing.

"You know," the girl answered with a weak smile as her parents walked out.

The good news about Charley helped.

A friendly voice called "Knock! Knock!" and interrupted her melancholy.

What? Who?

Mark—of all people—walked in with a big bouquet.

"How are you?" he asked as he flashed his neon smile. "I brought you a little gift, hear you like yellow roses."

Hannah gasped. Two dozen? Three dozen? Huge!

She loved yellow roses.

"Oh, thank you! Here, please, put it on the nightstand, thank you!" she replied with surprise, sitting up in bed. "Uh, I thought you went home to St. Louis?"

What a happy surprise but, oh gosh, nothing on but a thin hospital gown, her hair a mess, and zero makeup. Okay, Hannah Bentley never wore a lot of makeup but, hey, she might scare him off looking like this! She pulled the covers up to her neck.

"Well, I did, Sunday afternoon as planned," Mark explained. "Then Grandpa Tony called me early Monday morning, told me you and your, uh, acquaintance," Mark coughed, "went missing: 'Tommy's out there lookin' for 'em. Hope that old coot doesn't get lost too, I'd go nuts without him around!'

"He called again last night to tell me you had checked into the hospital. 'Get yourself down here, Markie, Tommy's grand-gal needs you real bad!' he added.

"Two phone calls in one day! You know, it's tough for him to make calls, numbers mean zilch to him after his stroke, has to have a nurse dial the phone. He still shouts when he calls long distance."

Hannah smiled. Mark: what a happy surprise, she felt better!

"I promised at the lunch Saturday I'd call you Tuesday, so I guess this is just to keep my word. It's Tuesday, I'll call in person," he said.

The Cheshire Cat grinned.

Hannah smiled up at him, still stunned.

"Thank you, I really appreciate this. Sorry, I guess I don't look very presentable," she said, rubbing her face.

"Not to worry, your natural beauty shines through," he said.

Mark and his lines!

"So, what can I do to help?"

"I'm not sure right now," she replied. "My acquaintance has been in ICU, he really needs prayer. The ambulance crew thought they might lose him on the way in."

"He has mine," Mark said, "you can count on that. I wish him a speedy recovery."

Hannah shook her head in disbelief.

"My apologies, I just don't know what to say. I, I'm shocked, I'm flattered. Isn't it a long drive?"

"Two hundred-seven miles from my driveway, to be exact," Mark said, "three hours-plus. And worth every mile, I might add, just to see that beautiful smile. I burned a personal use day."

"Well, again, thank you, I'm speechless," she added, dumbfounded. "Please, please, have a seat."

Mark pulled a chair over to her bed and the enjoyable conversation they shared Saturday picked up where it left off. They talked for two hours.

What a really, really neat guy. Okay, he had dumb pickup lines, but they fell away in a serious conversation about personal interests, challenges and life. She sensed something special in him.

He too, loved the outdoors and yes, he had been caught in a thunderstorm on a hike as a Boy Scout, only made Life rank.

"You know what they say, 'There's nothing worse in life, than to be a Life Scout for life!" Mark said, and his smile radiated again.

The talk rambled on, his time in the Navy, her family, spiritual things. What should we do with our lives? Then, he repeated particularly bad jokes told by Grandpa Tony, real groaners, that left both in wild laughter. "You know, our grandfathers are a real pair!"

Rev. Gillogly, Hickory Bough's rotund and ever-chipper chaplain, fizzed into the room as they visited with a cheery "Hello, Hannah!" She bent over and gave the girl a quick hug. The cross necklace around her clerical collar caught on the girl's nose and they struggled to get it loose.

"I just had to come and see you! Claire and Tom worry about you so!" she said excitedly. "They love you so much! I told them I'd come tell you 'Hi'—just for them!"

"Oh! And I'm so pleased to see you!" Gaylene said to Mark. "You're Tony's grandson, he brags on you!"

"Don't believe all you hear," Mark answered.

The trio enjoyed a lively conversation that Gaylene dominated, mostly about the grandfathers, "wonderful men, and I just love that Claire so much, we're so lucky to have her!"

Gaylene excused herself with a lively "Gotta' go, I have congregants to see!" then bent over and gave Hannah another hug and a happy pat.

"May you be healed in Jesus' name!" Gaylene said cheerfully as she laid her hand on the girl's head. "You are on the parish prayer list!"

Mark watched the reverend walk out, then turned to Hannah.

"Well, much as I hate to say it, I need to go, long drive back," Mark said. The smile glowed.

Oh, gosh, that smile, above that dimpled chin!

She had to put her shades on when this man smiled!

"Anyway, I'd like a hug too. Do you have one left?"

"Of course," Hannah answered, reaching up modestly from under her covers.

Mark bent over and they embraced. After shave? Cologne? Not Old Spice, not Versace, not Giorgio Armani, something else, sort of a refreshing woodsy scent, she liked it.

Hey, this guy even smells good!

Mark held the embrace for a moment, and so did she. They both put a little extra squeeze into it—they both knew it. It became more than a simple "get well soon/best wishes" greeting—they both knew it.

"Do you have your phone? I'll call you later," he said as he headed slowly to the door.

"Right here," Hannah said, reaching behind his roses. "Maybe you can call tonight when you get home?"

"Count on it, uh, I hope you're up and around soon. Keep me posted," Mark said with a little wave. "Good-bye."

"'Bye!" Hannah called out with a feeble wave.

Wow, what a shock!

Let's see, she figured: This guy burned a vacation day, drove more than four-hundred miles, something like seven hours total, just to spend an hour or two with her? And all those roses ain't cheap!

"Wow," she muttered, surprised.

She stared into space—Mark thoughts—as a middle-aged woman with wavy, salt-and-pepper hair and a crooked frown came briskly in her room. Poorly dressed, she could have been attractive if she fixed herself up.

"What have you done to my son?" she demanded loudly as she marched up to Hannah's bed. "You nearly killed him!"

Startled, the girl looked up.

"And you are…?"

"I'm Kristi Trottel," the woman said sharply.

"Oh, Charley's mother? Well, pleased to meet you," Hannah answered sweetly.

"Forget the niceties, dearie, this is a helluva mess. I want an explanation!" she demanded, shaking her fist at Hannah.

It caught the girl dumbfounded.

"I, uh, well, we did a hike Sunday afternoon and a thunderstorm caught us. The ambulance medics say Charley had some kind of allergic reaction, a tick bite," she explained. "I know you're worried, we all are."

"What I'm worried about is Charles hanging out with little hussies like you! I know all about your kind!" the woman snapped.

Anger flickered inside Hannah, an emotion she rarely felt.

"Excuse me, but I am not a hussy," she said slowly as she restrained her emotions. "If I may say so, what I did may have saved your son's life."

Charley's mom snorted.

"Ha! You expect me to believe that? I just saw him—what's left of him. He's so swollen we'll have trouble stuffing him in a casket. Looks like some idiot tried to kill him!"

"Ma'am, I'm telling the truth. Believe what you want, but please, this hurts me as well. I got caught out there too," Hannah said with all the sincerity she could muster. "Charley's a really sweet guy, a good friend. I would never, ever, want to hurt him."

"I ordered my son to leave you alone! You stay away from him, you hear me?" the angry mother shouted, pointing at Hannah. "I'm gonna' get him out of this outhouse of a hospital as soon as I can, and I don't want to hear your name ever again! Ever! Do you understand me?"

With that, the woman stomped out before Hannah could answer. Her jaw dropped.

That's Charley's mother?

That explains some things.

What a situation:

Claire cautioned Hannah to stay away from Charley.

Charley's mom ordered Charley to stay away from Hannah.

What did they see that the two of them couldn't?

Depression.

The black dog bit again.

She sat, numb, in silence, for an hour before she drifted off to sleep. Scary nightmares of screaming people, lightning and thunder, a moaning Charley devoured by gigantic poison ivy plants, terrorized her.

"…When mine eyes shall close in death…"

"You okay, Sis?" a voice said, she felt her arm shake.

Huh?

Chad.

She looked up to see her family around her bed, concerned.

"Oh, hi," she said with a sleepy yawn.

"I guess it's good you're getting caught up on your sleep," her father said. "How are you doing?"

Hannah shook her head. "Up and down."

"Let's go see Charley since he's in a room now," her mother offered. "Let me find your bathrobe."

The girl sat up, put on the robe and slippers Judy brought. Her brother and father helped her stand.

"Sorry, I'm a little shaky," she said apologetically.

"The poor guy, the worst may be yet to come, tick paralysis. He's going to be here a while. He could have permanent injuries," her mother explained.

The little group shuffled down the hall at Hannah's slow pace to Charley's room. He looked awful.

"Are you okay?" Hannah asked.

"Don't know," Charley whispered.

The Bentleys stood silently. A nurse stuck her head in the door.

"Excuse me folks, this patient's limited to one visitor at a time," she said.

"Oh," Judy said, turning to Hannah. "Here, you two visit, we'll wait in the hall."

They shuffled out, Hannah and Charley were alone. Charley looked at her with a blank stare, eyes glazed.

What to say?

"I'm glad you're doing better," Hannah said quietly.

Charley nodded.

They stared at each other, she forced a smile below worried eyebrows.

"Please let my parents know if you need anything, they'll be happy to help," Hannah offered.

Charley nodded again.

"I'm sorry about things," she added.

"Okay," he answered with a hoarse whisper.

This did not go well.

"Well, I'm a few rooms down, maybe we can talk later?"

"Okay."

"Uh, I guess I better go."

"Okay."

"Maybe I can come by tomorrow?"

He shrugged.

She smiled at him weakly and turned to go.

Charley did not smile back.

Okay, he's sick. But where had the affectionate Charley she had passionately kissed less than two days before go? What happened to the boy who tightly hugged her and whispered her name in the dark?

Chapter 15
A Change In Plans

"Miss Bentley?"

Hannah rolled over in bed and there stood a nurse with a meal tray.

"Good morning! I brought breakfast early, you're supposed to check out right away, thought you might want to go ahead and eat," the nurse added.

"Uh, thanks," Hannah said with a yawn. She sat up and took the cover off the plate.

"Hoo boy, another mystery meal," she mumbled. Pancakes, a fruit cup and milk—not too bad. But oh, could she use some coffee.

Hannah ate, showered and dressed. The nurse came back and checked her vitals, everything pretty much back to normal.

Her mom came in, they gathered personal things, then headed to the business office to handle all the paperwork, or computer work, or whatever they call it nowadays.

They walked out to the parking lot and climbed in the Beast.

"Do you mind if we go out to Hickory Bough? Grandpa and Claire want to see you first thing," Judy said.

"Oh, that's fine, but let's stop at a C-store and get me some coffee," Hannah replied.

"I'll do better than that," her mom said as she reached into the rear seat. "Here," and she handed the girl a Thermos.

"Perfect, thank you!" the daughter replied as she opened it and poured a cup in the Thermos' lid. Mom's hundred-octane coffee, perfect!

"I know my kid—I know what you want!" her mother replied.

Off they went across town, turning into the Hickory Bough parking lot. They ambled through the lobby and dayroom to C 8, her mother walked in first.

"Good morning, look who I found!" she said brightly.

Tom and Claire answered with an "Oh!" duet as Hannah walked in.

"We are so glad to see you!" Claire said lovingly. "I've prayed for you nonstop since your father called."

Hannah shook her head.

"I'm okay, but I don't think Charley's very well. They moved him out of ICU and we went by to see him last night. He's, how to put it?, not himself."

"That's a shame, give him a few days," Grandpa Tom said. Claire said nothing.

"Didn't you plan to do summer school?" her grandfather asked.

"Yes, my classes start this morning. Guess I need to call the registrar, I'll pick things up this fall. It won't work to start a summer term late, classes get scrunched anyway," Hannah said with a sigh.

"So what do you plan now?" her grandfather asked.

"Don't know, just hang out with the fam' in Randall for a few weeks," the girl replied. "My roomie's home for the summer in Parkville, so I'd have our apartment to myself; lonesome. I'd rather be here."

Claire laid her hand on her husband's leg.

"Tom, listen, she could help with the move," she said, "the girl has free time."

"Another move?" Hannah asked.

"No, not us, the family office," Grandpa Tom explained.

"Family office? That's something new for my folks," Hannah said.

"Yes, it's a private investment firm owned by members of a successful family," Claire explained. "In our case, of course, that's the Dearborns. The family turned over its investments, real estate assets and other activities, such as benevolent contributions, to a trained staff. The company, in turn, distributes earnings back to the family members.

"My late father, Campbell, started our family office back in the 1970s, a new idea back then, when he retired," she added. "He finally eased up. If the man had a fault, he made workaholics look lazy.

"Then my parents built this beautiful house on a mountain above Whitefish, Montana, the family office still manages it.

"He finally let someone else do all the number-crunching and he took up fly fishing. My oh my, we had some great times there. We'd have trout he caught, mom made huckleberry sundaes for dessert; wonderful place. My brothers, their families and I did Christmas there a couple years.

"The man had a gift. He could look ahead and see how things would work out, particularly when it came to business and finances, so the family office always has had, shall we say, a lot to work with.

"We had the staff in downtown St. Louis, right on Olive Street, since my dad set the office up. My brothers oversaw things for dad when it started, they lived out in the County. Then I served as the CEO until I had my first stroke, my niece oversees things now. But the rent kept going up and St. Louis, hate to say it, isn't the same.

"So, we considered options. With the Internet, they can work from anywhere, don't have to be down the street from the bank.

"Also, our chief investment officer, Yusuf Wiesen, grew up here," Claire continued. "His parents and grandparents owned Wiesen's Jewelry, if you remember it. He wants to move back to help the little Randall synagogue stay alive. He's a brilliant investment strategist, Penn and Wharton School, we certainly want to keep him around."

"So, I had an idea," Grandpa Tom added. "Why not convert our old house, which never sold, into an office and move the staff down here? They all loved the concept—especially Joe. And meanwhile, we decided to roll the various Bentley investments into the Dearborns' office since we *are* joined now," he added as he winked at Claire.

"Ah, the other primal desire: money!"

"Tom!" Claire gasped. "What am I going to do with you?"

"Seriously, what a great idea," Claire added, "combining what your family has achieved over the years with our Dearborn holdings, all of us come out ahead. We can do a lot more charitable work. Your father has pushed that, Hannah. We have grants we pay to sustain orphanages in Central America, that sort of thing."

"So, we did it, the Bentleys' investments joined the Dearborns'," Tom said. "Card players have a term for this: spit in the ocean."

Everyone laughed.

"Oh now, you Bentleys have done quite well for yourselves!" Claire replied.

"Perhaps, but you can't beat your father as a business genius," Tom said.

"You know, he also had a pretty good eye for guys that his drop-dead gorgeous daughter should date," he added, then coughed loudly.

"Now, don't get into that!" Claire answered with a grimace. "It did work out, my love, it just, well, took a little longer than daddy expected."

"You two amaze me!" Hannah said with a laugh. "What do you want me to do?"

"The contractor will finish the renovation by Friday, then the movers will start to haul the office files down here next week," Claire explained. "The staff plans to be here by the first of July.

"Get your clipboard: We need someone to check off items as they arrive, then make sure the movers get boxes to the right cubicles. Also, we need someone to make sure the phones and computers work, details, details."

"Can you handle it? Sounds pretty tough for a four-point Mizzou accounting student," Grandpa Tom said, teasing.

"I am up to the challenge!" Hannah replied brightly. "Now, speaking of money…."

"Well, of course we'll pay you, put you on as a temp," Claire said. "You should be done in a couple weeks, I imagine."

"Tell you what," Judy told her daughter, "why don't we stop by on the way home?"

"Great!" Hannah replied. "I'd noticed construction stuff when I passed by."

"Yes, we had to do a lot of work to make city code, fire sprinklers, a new fire escape in the back, that sort of thing. Zoning turned out to be no problem, the house has been in a transition area for years. My old bedroom has cubicles now," Grandpa Tom said. "Who would've thought?

"The only variance we asked for, and got? An inward-opening door on the porch, so we could keep that big stained-glass transom over it," he added.

"Let's go!" the girl said, bouncing up.

She hugged Grandpa Tom and Claire.

"Thank you, thank you so much for your prayers and support," she said. "This has been a tough few days."

"I'm sure it has, and we'll be in prayer for your friend, Charley," her grandfather said, standing up.

"Yes, I most definitely will say a prayer for Charley," Claire added quietly. "He needs it."

The beautiful old house, freshly repainted with new landscaping, looked snappier than ever, Hannah thought, as her mom pulled in the driveway and parked in a newly paved lot in the side yard. An elegant new sign stood in front of the ornate wrought-iron fence: THE DEARBORN INTERESTS LLC.

Inside, the house she had known all her life had changed, yet oddly remained familiar.

The historic gas light in the baluster at the foot of the big stairs' handrail—which had never worked in her lifetime—now twinkled with a decorative LED light. The dull brass chandelier above the front room—built to burn gas, converted to incandescent bulbs, and now LED fixtures—gleamed brightly for the first time in decades.

New rugs covered portions of the re-sanded and refinished hardwood floors. A receptionist's desk replaced a sofa in the front room that little-girl Hannah had napped on many times.

And wonder of wonders: A round, glass-enclosed elevator!

Claire's niece, Martha, greeted the pair.

"Aunt Claire called, said you'll work with us to finish the transition," Martha said. "That's wonderful, I need all the help I can get."

She showed them around: The parlor had become Mr. Wiesen's office, the kitchen would be a break room, the old servant's quarters became an overnight guest room. Upstairs, bedrooms became offices and the big attic had been opened as a third floor for more office space and storage. The stable-turned-garage in the backyard turned into a conference room.

"I can't believe it, it's just amazing!" Hannah said in awe, looking around. She stopped with her mom at the front door to take it all in as they headed out. She sniffed: The musty smell of an old home had gone away, replaced by fresh paint and new carpet odors.

Her phone buzzed and the girl awoke from a richly deserved nap, curled around hippo. Why do naps make phones ring?

Area code 314: St. Louis, she didn't recognize the number but answered anyway.

"Hello?"

"Hey, Mark here, hope I'm not interrupting anything," a warm voice responded. "Thought I'd call."

"How are you?" she answered wide-eyed now.

"I'm fine, and I hope you are too. Say, would it be a problem for me to come down this weekend? I'd like to see you again," he said.

"Oh, that would be wonderful!" Hannah replied, thinking dreamy thoughts of that electric smile. "But we don't have any place to put you."

"Your, uh, acquaintance, out of the hospital?"

"No, but my Aunt Brenda's here in our guest room."

"That's fine, I'll get a hotel room out on the bypass. I'm gold-level Hilton Honors, travel a lot for work, you know. I like to rack-up all those points for future special occasions, weddings, things like that," Mark said.

Bang!

Weddings? Whose?

Idle chatter—or a hint?

She had no way to know. If a hint, it came way too early.

"Oh, well, sure, that would be great," Hannah answered. "When do you expect to get here?"

"How about we meet and do breakfast Saturday?"

"Sure, uh, call me Friday night when you get in town; look forward to it," Hannah said.

"Fine, and I look forward to it as well. 'Bye for now," and the phone clicked.

Mark would come back? The thought left Hannah dizzy!

But this could get complicated. What if Charley got out of the hospital, say, Friday afternoon? Then what?

Time to talk to mom.

She found Judy in the front room, reading her iPad, and mother and daughter visited. Sure, should be no problem, we can find someplace to stash Charley if he's out by then. The neighbors have a spare bedroom he could use a day or two until he goes back to Neosho. Otherwise—have a good time, sweetheart.

"Tell you what, let's go over to the hospital and you can see Charley. Again, probably best if I take you, your father would have a fit if he heard you went out-and-about in town by yourself. We can't tell what you-know-who might be doing," the mother added.

"Sure, I'm still not a hundred percent."

It felt better to walk through the hospital in street clothes than a bathrobe. Mrs. Bentley took a seat in a lounge down the hall, a news channel shouted away on a TV.

Hannah sighed, thinking of the awkward visit they had before she checked out. Maybe drugs left the poor guy dopey, he'll be better now. She looked in the door of Charley's room to find him reading a Gideon Bible.

"Hi there! Thought I'd come check on you," she said cheerfully.

Charley looked up with a blank stare.

"May I come in?" Hannah asked.

He quietly nodded.

"So, how do you feel?"

Charley shrugged and closed the Bible.

"Anything I can do for you?" she asked innocently.

Charley shook his head.

"Hannah, look, this won't work," he said slowly.

"What do you mean?" she asked, puzzled. "I can call a nurse."

"No, you and me," Charley said with a sigh.

"I do not want to see you again."

Hannah looked at him, stunned.

"Why?"

Charley scratched his whiskered chin and stared out the window.

"Mom and I had a long talk," he said. "She can be difficult, we disagree about a lot, but she can be right sometimes. She's right about us.

"Mom made me think: We're too different, give it up, son. We're friends now, break it off before it becomes something more—and we both get hurt."

Hannah, stunned, grabbed the wall behind her.

"You're outdoorsy, I'm a piano-playing homebody.

"You're lively and outgoing, I'm quiet, an introvert.

"Your family's rich, I shop at Goodwill.

"It just will not work, we could never be happy."

Hannah stood shocked, mouth open.

"Charley, I... What's the word that I think describes you? 'Potential?' I see so much you can do, you will make something of yourself. Can't we at least be friends?"

"No," he said as he stared out the window.

"Just forget it."

"You know, opposites attract and all that," she replied. "Look at Grandpa Tom and Claire—very different. They complement each other. We can be pals, buds, just appreciate each other."

Charley sighed.

"No."

Hannah's eyes watered.

"Look, again, I'm sorry about the hike, if that's what's bothering you," she said nervously.

"More than that."

"But…" Hannah started.

"No buts," Charley said, "maybe I'll see you 'round on campus."

He turned and looked at her.

"I think you better go now."

Hannah stood there for a few moments.

Nothing.

She turned and walked out, tears streaming down her cheeks.

Mark? Perfect timing.

Chapter 16
The Temp

Friday night, out of the shower, and she slipped into her pink nightshirt. Aunt Brenda played Ravi Shankar in the guest room, just a touch too loud for this hour. Hannah ambled down the hall to the kitchen to get the usual glass of water she liked to keep on her nightstand. She made it a point to close her door on the sitar music— or whatever that racket might be.

She turned out the light and curled around hippo.

Her phone rang, just as she hoped.

She picked it up, the familiar 314 number flashed on the screen again.

"Hello, Mark," she cooed.

"Are you in bed already?" he asked.

"Yes, just got in, you in town?"

"Finally, big wreck on I-44 the other side of Rolla, got away from the office late, hard trip," he explained. "So, what wild excitement can we find in Randall this weekend? I'm sure whatever it is will include you."

"Oh, c'mon, stop it!" Hannah replied with a snicker. Mark laughed too.

"Well, anything you want, but let's not do a hike," she suggested.

"Uh, I guess we should go see my grandfather sometime," Mark said.

"That's fine. Why don't you come over for breakfast in the morning? Let me give you our address, you'll need a gate code to get in the neighborhood," she said.

"I have both," he answered—she could almost hear that smile.

"Oh my, those geezers thought of everything, didn't they?"

"How do you think I knew you like yellow roses?"

Hannah laughed.

"I don't know if I should be flattered or offended."

"Flattered, of course," Mark said firmly.

"They both think a lot of you, and me. Is that a bad thing?"

"You'll need to pay your grandfather a finder's fee," she added, laughing.

"Every penny will be worth it, what time?"

"Plan on eight, I guess."

"Great, see you in the morning, good night."

"'Bye."

Wow!

Hannah sent her mom a text to let her know Mark would join the family in the morning. She heard her mother's phone ding down the hall, then her phone dinged with a thumbs up.

She curled around hippo, smiled happily, and went sound asleep.

Saturday: Mark pulled up promptly at eight o'clock in his white Grand Cherokee. The guy looked like a million bucks in a golf shirt and Dockers. Breakfast, a visit to Hickory Bough, then nine holes at the club, lunch at one of those chain restaurants out on the bypass, and an afternoon with her family.

Tom Junior and Mark bonded.

Dad knew little about the Navy, asked lots of questions. Mark knew little about hardware, asked lots of questions.

Ah, but they both knew football!

That brought lots of talk about the St. Louis Rams. What's this rumor they might move? Tom Junior, Mizzou, and Mark, Oklahoma, didn't think much of the Tigers jumping from the Big XII to the SEC, and the eastern division of the SEC to boot. What's that all about? A great rivalry got thrown aside for Vanderbilt? Who? Ha!

Dad cooked steaks on his big patio grill, then came Netflix in the media room. She nuked a big tub of popcorn and made lemonade.

What a neat, neat guy.

If Charley wanted to be history, well, she could get used to this!

Sunday: Girlfriends at church teased her about a "boyfriend of the week." They didn't dare ask about last week's guy with Mark in earshot. Tom Junior fired up the grill again and cooked burgers for lunch. A few innings of the Cardinals and Mets on TV, then Mark announced he had to go.

She walked out to his Jeep and lingered after he got in, as they talked through the window.

"When can you come back?" she asked with a warm smile.

"Next weekend's out," he replied. "They have me headed out to California, San Diego, Navy project. Maybe two weeks?"

"Sooner the better!" Hannah replied. "Text me, call, whatever, uh, keep in touch!"

"Sure, and thank you for a wonderful two days."

He lifted up on the steering wheel, she leaned through the window, and they kissed for the first time.

He flashed his smile-in-Cinerama, started the car and backed out as she stood up.

Hannah waved slightly.

"A lot can happen in one week," she mumbled.

Monday morning: Hi ho! Hi ho! It's off to work we go!

Tom Junior dropped her off at the house/office and Marty came out to meet her on the big front porch. It proved a whirlwind day: details, details, details. Had this been finished? What about the damaged cubicle walls? Will we need a fax machine? The movers want us to make motel reservations for their crew.

Busy, busy, busy!

Whew! But what fun to be a part of it all.

They wrapped up at five o'clock and Marty ran her home.

Tom Junior didn't get home until late, walking in with a grimace.

"What's up?" Judy asked her husband. "You don't look happy."

"Let's talk," he said to his wife as he motioned Hannah and Chad into the front room and they sat down.

"We have a problem," he said seriously. "Charley got out of the hospital today, they tracked me down at the office."

"Why you?" Hannah asked. "I figured he'd go home to Neosho."

"He can't," Tom Junior explained. "The doctors want him to come in every few days for a week or two for tests. He has to stay in town. He remembered your offer to help, sweetheart, he has no alternative."

"And?" Judy asked.

"I could think of only one option: Claire and her niece had the contractor add that guest suite back behind the old kitchen in Pop's house for when family members come in," he explained. "Originally, that served as the servant's quarters when they built the house, but it's been used for storage all my life.

"We fixed it up, added a little toilet and shower after we cut off the back part of the hall. Anyone who stays there has access to the breakroom's kitchen.

"It's an odd deal, but it'll work when one of my cranky cousins comes in from Kansas City, or something. I'd just as soon not have them in my house.

"Anyway, a motel offered the only quick alternative, so I dropped him off at one tonight. I told him we'll put him on part-time at the warehouse if he wants something to do."

"But, I…" Hannah said, hesitating.

"I know, I know, you two are on the outs and you want to avoid him," Tom Junior answered, raising his hand. "We can make this work for a week, a few days. I'll keep him busy, you won't have to see him."

Awkward, but Charley wanted this, she thought.

The days flew by with lists to check, people to call, a cleaning crew to direct. Marty jokingly ran what she called "stray-bullet drills" every day to find what they missed.

Excitement! She watched the big project, something different, come together.

Hannah and Marty made a great team.

Thursday they broke for an early lunch, Marty drove Hannah to the Dearborn house to grab a bite, the first time the girl had been in the historic Prairie School home. She'd passed it for years, and more than once a tour bus sat on the shoulder while visitors snapped photos in the front yard. To get inside and see the places Grandpa Tom and Claire talked about—in person and on their show—proved extra special. They walked on the back porch, then out to the backyard gazebo.

What a beautiful place, a treasure, unique—like Claire.

Judy brought Grandpa Tom and Claire to the new office that afternoon for a visit. "I'm here to officially test the wheelchair ramp!" Claire explained, "Anything to get me out of Hickory Bough!"

A husky mover wheeled her up the ramp, onto the porch.

"Tom, they took out the swing," she noted as her husband tapped up the ramp behind her.

"I guess they don't let swingers work here," he noted.

The old, red mailbox at the curb had disappeared.

Marty gave the couple a tour, including a ride up in the elevator.

"Proof, right here: If you live long enough, you'll see everything," Tom said as the elevator opened and they went out into the upstairs hallway. As he had been told, his old bedroom now held two cubicles and filing cabinets. The old man shook his head.

Things pretty much had been done by Friday afternoon, just a little left for next week. Marty gave Hannah the key, then explained she had errands to run, just turn off the lights and lock the door when you go.

Sure, some paperwork to finish and she'd be ready to call her mom to be picked up, the girl responded.

"Have a good weekend and I'll see you Monday, almost done!" Hannah called brightly as Marty went out the door with a wave.

Chapter 17
Click

But the work orders and spreadsheets failed to match. What Hannah thought would be a quick chore turned into an hour-plus of line-by-line tedium. She spread everything out on the receptionist's desk in the front room-turned-lobby, either side of the keyboard. Now, to get what they had on paper to match Excel on the screen.

But ta-da, she did it!

She could have left it all until Monday but no siree, not hardworker Hannah! No way! That would throw things behind, finish tonight, girl!

She ran AutoSum—perfect—the numbers finally matched. Great, let's go home!

Ah, mom always made some extra-yummy dish on Friday nights. Put everything away, then call the house for a ride.

She heard an odd "click" and looked up.

Randy!

The sneering boy stood, back against the front door, his hand still on the lock he'd just turned. He stared at her under low brows, above an evil grin.

She panicked.

"What are you doing here?" she gasped as she stood.

"You *know* why I'm here, babe," he said as he shuffled slowly forward, leering, as he unzipped his jeans.

"GET AWAY FROM ME!" Hannah yelled as she frantically fumbled for her phone to call 911.

Randy jumped toward her and knocked the phone out of her hand.

"Finally, at last, I'm going to get to enjoy you, all of you, just like I always wanted!" he said, coming slowly toward the girl as she backed away in abject fear.

"Hey, relax hon', we can have a good time. I know how to make you feel real good."

"Leave… leave me *alone*!" Hannah demanded, desperate.

"No way, you luscious little thing. You are my desire, I'm gonna' finally get to enjoy you—and your stupid brother can't stop me.

"And if I can't have you, I'll see to it nobody else does!" Hannah screamed.

Randy grabbed her arms and they struggled. His hand broke free and he ripped her blouse. Buttons flew as the shirt gapped open.

Time slowed. Somewhere, somehow, way back in her memory, Hannah calmly remembered, in slow motion, Girl Scout lessons on how to fight off an assault. She slammed two fingers up Randy's nostrils as she kneed his groin. It slowed the hulking boy, he twisted and turned.

Blood gushed from his nose, pinpoint eyes inches from her face, glared at her.

"Yum! You're mine at last!" he huffed. "Drop your drawers!"

They lurched and struggled, tripping over a coffee table. Her adrenaline surged, she put up an incredible fight, but Randy, taller and heavier, won, pushing her backwards toward a sofa.

Hannah screamed again.

She heard a loud crash: Something happened.

Suddenly, Randy jerked and went limp, stumbled and fell forward, their foreheads banged together. Hannah saw stars. Randy's head jerked back, his eyes glazed over and rolled back in his head, his grip loosened.

He flopped, unconscious, on the floor.

She stood over him, screaming in utter hysterics, blood soaked her blouse and bra.

Huh?

Hannah, panting, looked up to see Charley standing over Randy's motionless body with the remains of a chair in his hands.

"Sounded like you needed help," he said calmly.

She leaned on a filing cabinet, gasping.

"Oh please, oh please, get him out of here!" she begged as she wiped her face, then slumped back on the sofa as she pulled her torn clothes together.

Randy groaned and moved. Charley whacked his head with a piece of the chair again and ordered "stay put!" He found Hannah's phone on the floor and called 911.

A patrol car roared up within a minute, siren wailing. The officer ran up on the porch, hand on his weapon, as Charley unlocked the door. Hannah curled in a fetal position on the sofa, crying in sobs.

"There's the guy," Charley said, pointing at Randy with a piece of the chair. "I saw it, bashed his head in."

More police and an ambulance came.

The officers handcuffed Randy, still woozy, before the ambulance crew placed him on a stretcher and hauled him out. An officer went along. Paramedics checked her over before they left. Charley brought a couple tea towels and a bottle of water around from the break room.

Questions, forms to fill out, pictures of the room, a lady cop interviewed Hannah.

Did he?

No, but he wanted to. *"And if I can't have you, I'll see to it nobody else does!"* rang in her head, and she made sure that went in the report.

And what of this other boy over here, the policewoman asked, how does he fit into all this?

He stays in the guest room in the back, happened to come home from work at the right time.

"He's innocent, more than that he's a hero," Hannah said between gasps.

Charley explained he heard a commotion and screams, then came out to find Randy assaulting Hannah. He figured the Dearborn Interests wouldn't mind the loss of a chair, he'd buy a new one.

"Sorry about that."

Tom Junior and Judy ran in the door, the police had called. The mother ran to Hannah, hugging her still sobbing daughter. Hannah curled up in her mother's lap as she cried.

The scene appalled Tom Junior: busted furniture, bloody carpet, and his blubbering daughter in her mother's arms; repulsed. Charley sat at the now ransacked receptionist's desk, calmly talking to an officer.

"Take me home! Take me home! I can't take anymore!" Hannah cried.

"Did he?" Judy asked.

"No, but I'm beat up. Please, just get me out of here!"

"Can she go now?" Judy asked.

Sure, we have what we need, we'll follow up.

The frantic mom helped up her daughter and they struggled out. Tom Junior turned to Charley.

"Thanks, thanks for what you did," he said as he shook the boy's hand.

"Welcome, I didn't do anything."

"Wrong, you may have saved her life," the father said. "Anything I can ever do for you, *ever*, let me know."

Charley nodded.

Things wound down. Someone called Marty to lock up. She rushed in and shook her head as she surveyed the mess.

"Well, I guess I can sign off the computer now."

Hippo never felt so cuddly. The ibuprofen began to wear off in the night and the bruises started to hurt again as dawn came. Judy slept with her daughter and, to no surprise, they both had a restless night. Hannah rolled over and hugged her mom, who held the girl.

"Why me? Everything's gone wrong!" Hannah whispered as she started to cry again.

"I don't know, honey, you have had a hard time of it," the mother said, wrapping her arms around her daughter.

Dawn finally came and mom got up to nuke a quick breakfast and brew some of her lip-tingling coffee.

Hannah grabbed her phone and punched her Bible app. She did this every morning and, always, the verse of the day fit perfectly with whatever she faced right then.

Funny how that works.

"Therefore, humble yourselves under the mighty hand of God, that He may exalt you in due time, casting all your care upon Him, for He cares for you."

Judy called and got her daughter into the doctor for a special, Saturday morning check. Nothing major to be found, bruises and cuts, a strained wrist. Here's a prescription for an extra-strength pain reliever.

Do you want Xanax, maybe trazodone? You've been through a lot, young lady, they'll help you calm down.

Hannah thought for a moment.

"No," she said firmly. "But I would like to talk to someone."

Fine, we can get you with a psychiatrist this afternoon. Would you like to see a minister or priest? Are you Jewish? We can call the rabbi.

"No, I want Grandpa Tom and Claire."

Mom called the old couple to see if they could see her daughter—what else would they be doing?—and dropped off Hannah while she went to get the prescription.

They greeted the girl warmly with hugs. Claire looked even more elegant than usual with her hair in a beautiful chignon.

"Please, tell us what happened," Claire said as Hannah painfully eased into a chair in front of them.

"To begin, Charley may have saved my life," the girl answered. She described Randy, the problems she'd had with him, and the attack, cut short by a chair to the head.

All this on top of the hike and Charley's odd behavior in the hospital. Then Mark, wonderful Mark, came along.

"Am I doing something wrong?" she asked plaintively.

"Doubtful," Grandpa Tom said rubbing his moustache. "You still have your wonderful parents, your brother and the two of us. This will work out. But I'm afraid this will be a long summer, a summer to remember.

"Hmmph, some quick weekend!"

They talked for an hour; positive, encouraging. You are a remarkable young woman, life has its ups and downs: Keep going. Let your sunny personality win. We're here if you need us, just call. We will help you whenever and however we can.

She hugged the old couple again and added a sweet, "I love you both."

"And we love you more than you know," Grandpa Tom said as he kissed her cheek.

She sat quietly as mom drove home and thought about what she would do this weekend: Nothing.

Chapter 18
'I'm Just a Father'

Monday morning, Tom Junior's monthly managers' review; dry as toast.

All Bentley Hardware vice presidents, directors and foremen packed the headquarters conference room, the field executives on the speaker phone in the middle of the table, all set to explain the company's latest developments to the CEO.

Sales looked fine, second quarter looks to beat targets—maybe a few stretch targets. The new stores opened in Frisco and Southlake, Texas, Memorial Day weekend and business exceeded expectations; lines out the door Saturday afternoon.

"We knocked two home runs!" the marketing veep crowed.

Cash flow remains strong, we paid down our revolver. Purchasing sounded glum. Port delays in California slow import deliveries. We plan to start moving through Mexican ports, NAFTA and all that.

Human resources droned through a PowerPoint on a proposed benefits package for next year. IT gave a report on the new web page. Traffic's up but we have a long ways to go, we're a gnat on Amazon's rump.

What about the warehouse and inventory, Tom Junior asked, how go things? The company leased that new space in Temple, Texas. It will help support our locations in Texas and the Southwest, lots of growth down there. Great location, if and when we start to move imports up from Mexico.

How goes the warehouse here?

"That's easy," the Randall warehouse foreman told the CEO. "Get me some more kids like that boy you brought in the other day."

"You mean Charley?" Tom Junior asked.

"Yeah, the one who comes to work with you," the warehouse boss replied. "Most of these summer hires seem to do nothin' but sit around and play with their phones, textin' dirty jokes to each other. Not him, he hits the ground runnin' and he's goin' until quittin' time. His drug test? No problem, clean as a hound's tooth!

"Does he have a brother?"

The room laughed.

"I don't think so, glad to hear he worked out," Tom Junior replied. "He won't be here long."

"Tom, look, don't be offended: I had my doubts. Your daughter's boyfriend? Hoo boy, here we go!

"I hope she hangs onto him, he's a good 'un. And I wouldn't mind a bit if you figure out a way to keep him."

Tom Junior smiled as he thought, don't tell all you know.

"Not my call, I'm just a father."

Everyone laughed again.

Charley came by later that day and stuck his head in Tom Junior's office.

"Excuse me, Mr. Bentley," he said politely.

"Sure, Charley, what's up?"

"The police want me for an interview, may I go tomorrow morning?"

"No problem, I'll drop you off at the station on the way, give them whatever they need," Tom Junior said, looking up from his desk. "And again, thank you for what you did."

"Uh, you're welcome."

Charley and Hannah saw more of the police station and the courthouse than they wanted. The police had questions, the prosecuting attorney had questions, the office's insurance adjuster had questions. Hannah had never been in the big courthouse before and had to roam the halls to find the prosecutor's office.

She opened the door to go in just as Charley came out.

They stopped and looked at each other.

"Uh, I don't know what to say," she mumbled.

"I didn't do anything," Charley said with a shrug.

"Yes, yes you did," Hannah answered quietly. "You did more than you can possibly know. I guess we'll see more of each other because of this, that okay?"

Charley nodded and walked off.

She watched him, puzzled.

Strictly business, Hannah, he's strictly business.

The prosecutor's office had both of them in later that week for one meeting to compare their stories, which proved awkward. They went over things again. "Like a total stranger," she thought, as she watched Charley across the table tell what he remembered. He would not look at her.

Hannah asked the prosecutor, what about Randy?

"Concussion, two nights in the hospital under guard, he's been in the can since," came the reply. "He can't make bail. Neither bondsman in town will touch him with his record, his family doesn't have the money."

Frankly, that came as a relief. She smiled at the thought of the brutish thug locked in a cell.

She helped Marty as she could between all the coming/going with the legal authorities, most everything had been done at the new office, with a replacement for the blood-stained carpet, and a new chair. The St. Louis employees started to drift in to check out the new digs.

At least she felt safe now driving herself around. Hannah knocked off early one afternoon to run out to Hickory Bough to see Grandpa Tom and Claire again, they always cheered her up.

She climbed in the Jeep to head home when her phone rang and the car announced "Mark Wade." She instantly hit the phone button on the steering wheel.

"Well, hello!"

"You certainly lead an exciting life down there, my grandfather told me about it," he replied.

"I know, my life thus summer sounds like *The Perils of Pauline*," Hannah said.

"Should I drive down this weekend?" Mark asked.

"I hope so, but hanging around me you might get hit by a meteor or tornado. It would be great to see you," Hannah answered brightly. "I just don't want to go to the police station."

"Count on that, want to meet Saturday morning again?"

"Sure, look forward to it."

"Uh, do I need to get a room again?"

"Oh yes, Aunt Brenda." Things had been so busy Hannah had scarcely seen her.

"Fine, I'll call you Friday night, 'bye."

Good news! Mark would be a welcome change from lawyers, policemen and the mechanical Charley.

The white Grand Cherokee pulled up at eight-on-the-dot again Saturday. The Bentleys and Hannah's gentleman caller had a lively conversation over omelets and muffins. Then the couple hopped in her Wrangler and they did the off-road trails at Hoot Owl Hollow— no need to worry about Randy.

Then they headed out to Hickory Bough and enjoyed a delightful visit with Tony, Tom and Claire. Tony proved in rare form with lots of hilarious stories and snarky remarks about Hickory Bough's foibles: "And 'ta think, people pay to live here!"

What fun!

The Jeep headed up Ninth Street and veered past the office afterward. Hannah noticed Charley, alone, on the porch. His head jerked as they passed.

She bit her lip and kept driving. Mark hadn't asked about her "acquaintance" lately, she wanted to keep it that way.

Tom Junior fired up the grill again Saturday night and the family and Mark enjoyed shish kababs, with Aunt Brenda eating veggie-only skewers after an extended lecture on the dangers of climate change from indiscriminate propane use.

Scrabble and pool in the game room followed, with Hannah and Mark wandering out on the patio after dark.

The hot tub finally got some use after Mark borrowed Chad's baggy swim trunks, with Hannah in her modest tank. A full moon drifted above, adding to the evening.

What a wonderful, wonderful guy.

He made their time together all about her: What do you want to do? That's fine, sure! What do you think about....? Do you like....? How do you feel....?

Sunday morning church, taco salads at Rio Bravo, and time came for him to leave again.

"I'm sorry Randall's not more exciting," she said as she followed him out to the driveway.

Mark stopped, lit up the neighborhood with his smile, and chuckled.

"Rather, I find this town very exciting: You're here," he said.

"Oh, you cad!" Hannah answered with a laugh. "Thank you for coming again, I enjoyed every minute. Will you be back next weekend?"

"Hard to say," Mark said. "I may have another business trip, lots going on."

"Make it soon."

"Of course."

He turned and got in and they shared a kiss through the window again. He winked at her, backed out, and drove away.

Mark meant more and more. Texts, emails, FaceTime, and phone calls—long phone calls—continued most weeknights. She would lie in bed, wrapped around hippo, talking to him. It just got better and better.

And Charley? Of course she thought of him, but why the rejection? What had she done? Could Claire be right after all?

Randy: Oh, she wished he would just disappear. Yes, they had been close, yes, she cared once. It seemed dreamlike, those happy few weeks in high school.

But now: the scum! How many years would he get? They should throw away the key. Whatever, life without parole, it would not be enough. Does Missouri have a firing squad?

Could she care again?

No, she could not.

She had wrapped herself around hippo again that Friday, just dozing off, when her phone rang.

Mark!

"Well, hello there, you're up late," she whispered.

"I've been working a deal for you, have anything planned tomorrow?"

"Nope, except anything that includes you," she cooed.

"Good," Mark said. She could see that smile. "I want to buy you a hundred-dollar hamburger."

"Do what?" Hannah said, sitting up.

"Think I mentioned I'm in a flying club, I get use of the planes. But as you might guess, Saturdays get booked months in advance. I got lucky, whoever had the Cessna for tomorrow had to cancel, I jumped on it."

"And?"

"And, can you be at the Randall airport, maybe ten o'clock? I'll take you for a spin and we can grab a bite someplace," Mark said. "It'll cost me a hundred dollars-plus to take you to lunch. See?"

"Sure!"

She had been to Randall's little airport only a couple times to pick up express packages for her dad. Hannah walked in the base operator's lounge just as the radio crackled.

"Here comes your boyfriend!" the lady at the counter said with a smile. Sure enough, the little Cessna landed and taxied up on the ramp—and out stepped Mark.

He walked up to her and they hugged.

"Ready for some fun?" he asked as he flashed that wondrous smile.

"Of course!"

He helped her in the co-pilot's seat, then explained the wall of gauges in front of her: VHF omnirange, turn and slip, variometer, artificial horizon (what's wrong with the real one?), altimeter....

Ah, altimeter! She caught that one! That's that thing that shows how high up you are. It looks sort of like a clock. He started the engine, taxied out, did the run-ups, then off and up they went into a beautiful summer morning.

Amazing, she had never flown in a plane smaller than a Boeing.

"Put on your headset!" Mark shouted over the engine as he banked over the little town. Down below: Randall High School and its football stadium, Bentley Fields, then the courthouse, the country club and dots—people—on its golf course spread along Quartz Creek. Straight ahead through the round blur of the propeller: Hickory Bough. Mark banked hard and Hannah looked through the window beside her—straight down at cows in a pasture. Whoa!

"Let's go eat," he said over the intercom as they headed toward Branson.

"Where?" she asked

"Vinita, Oklahoma, the airport's right next to the world's biggest McDonald's on the turnpike," Mark explained. "We can walk over."

The unique, arched restaurant passed them as Mark came in for a landing. She remembered a stop there once on a Brownie trip. Across the parking lot they walked, then up the escalator.

"My treat!" Hannah said as they waited in line. "You can get an apple pie for dessert for all I care!"

Burgers had never been so much fun. They talked and teased, seated next to one of the big windows, as they watched—and felt— semis roar beneath them. Mark told Navy stories. She found herself absentmindedly chewing fries as she stared at this wondrous guy who had come into her life.

What a lucky girl, thank you Mr. Di Burlone.

Mark, oh my, just seemed larger than her whole world. How could this amazing guy be interested in small-town Hannah Bentley? But apparently she caught his eye.

Could she love him?

Yeah, maybe she could, maybe he's the one. Not looking right now, mind you, that's not in the plan. But if the right one comes along....

The flight home got bumpy, she got queasy, they dodged puffy clouds. Mark swung over Randall again. Hickory Bough, Hoot Owl Hollow, grandpa's old house, Claire's girlhood home, her house—they all drifted below. She could make out the Bentleys' neighbor playing fetch with Pierce in the backyard.

Neat!

Mark banked and the little plane slowed. The runway with a big 14 painted on its end came in sight, they landed and Mark shut off the engine on the ramp.

"Guess I better get this thing back," he said as they took off their headsets. "I hope you had a good time."

"Did I!" Hannah answered. "Something new, I'd like to learn to fly one of these things."

"Stick around and I can arrange that," he said, seriously, as he looked her straight in the eye.

Mark did not smile.

What did that mean?

"Who knows? It could happen," she said with a grin.

"May I come back soon?" he asked.

"Any time—and any way—you want!"

Chapter 19
The Unknown Number

The Fourth rolled around on a Thursday and the Bentleys, along with much of the town, adjourned to Dearborn Park for Randall's holiday round of picnics, a bluegrass band, and yodeling contest, topped off with fireworks when it finally turned dark. Aunt Brenda loudly voiced serious social questions about underpaid Chinese workers who make fireworks.

The family enjoyed things anyway with the usual "oohs!" and "ahhs!" as the pyrotechnics boomed overhead.

After the last loud bang, the crowd shuffled toward the dozens of cars parked in the now smoky dark along nearby streets. Wait, did she see Charley? She caught a glance, some guy taller than others in the shuffling crowd.

Did she have another stalker following her?

Paranoia?

Another quiet weekend came and went, books to read and a couple movies. She looked up a few old high school chums, also in town for the summer. Did she have tales to tell! Monday, she decided to get things started on the fall term back in Columbia. Missing summer school messed up her plan, she'd graduate next summer instead of next spring.

She busily worked the Mizzou website on the computer when her phone rang.

Now who could that be? Area code 417, a local call, but she didn't know the number.

"Hello?"

Dead air.

She started to hang up when she heard a nervous voice stutter, "H-H-Hannah?"

"Who is this?"

"It's, it's Randy."

She froze.

"I thought they threw you in jail or prison or whatever. How can you call me?" she whispered fearfully.

"We have a phone."

Fear turned to anger.

"What do you want?" she snapped.

"Hannah, look, uh, I need to talk to you."

She sat, speechless.

"Are you out of your stupid, criminal, thuggish, ever-loving mind?" she shouted. "You tried to rape me, you dog! I hate you! You are the last person on earth I want to talk to! Good-bye!"

"No! Please, please, don't hang up!" Randy pleaded nervously in a voice she had never heard him use. He almost sounded, well, humble—not the sneering, brutish Randy she knew and despised.

"Okay, what?" She spat out the words.

"I want to tell you I'm sorry."

She pulled the phone away from her ear and looked at it, incredulous.

Huh?

"Isn't it a little late for that?" she finally replied.

"Maybe, but please, can you come visit me here at the jail?"

Her jaw dropped.

"So you want me to get in your cell with you or something? Crazy!"

"I want to tell you I'm sorry, in person."

Hannah laughed.

"This proves you are not just a criminal, but insane. There's no way I want to talk to you!"

"Please, please, I'm serious."

Hannah had had enough, she started to hit the end call button when she clearly heard a voice behind her say, "Go!"

Something eerie happened.

She thought maybe her dad had walked in the room, maybe Chad, so she turned and looked. No one in sight.

"Look, Randy, I have nothing to say to you! I don't know what scheme you're up to, whatever, it won't work."

"I know, but I have things I want to say to you. This is my fault, I know that. That's why I want to tell you, in person, I apologize."

Okay, this had turned into a bit much, Hannah thought. Time to hang up. She heard "Go!" again.

She looked around, no one in her bedroom.

"Let me think about it, what would I have to do?"

"Oh, thank you!" Randy said, relieved. His voice quivered. "Come to the justice center and follow the signs to the visitation room, weekdays, nine 'til noon. You don't have to get in a cell or nothin'. You'll have to have ID, and don't bring no weapons or nothin'."

Yeah, right, she thought. Most girls carry around Bowie knives, bazookas, and brass knuckles.

How odd for her, she thought, she didn't get snarky.

"Maybe," she said curtly. "I need to go."

"Please, Hannah, I mean it. I'm sorry, please come."

She hung up on him.

How positively weird, did she dream what just happened? She looked around again. No, the clock showed the time, the ceiling fan lazily spun above her, her computer made a soft whir—maybe he really did call her.

Leering, pushy, boorish Randy did not sound leering, pushy or boorish. He sounded contrite, fearful. His lawyer put him up to this, of course, some plot to weasel out of his charges. He'd done that before.

"Hey, Ladybug!" Tom Junior called as he came in her room. "What's up?"

"Oh, Daddy, didn't expect to see you," she answered. "You in here a minute ago?

"No, just got home," the father replied. "I left some files on my desk so I decided to zip home for lunch and pick them up."

"Well, I just had the strangest phone call," she said as she turned to her father to describe her conversation.

"I'd rather pick up a snake than talk to him, much less go see him, but somehow I think I should. I don't know why."

Tom Junior sat down on her bed, thinking.

"I agree," the father answered seriously.

"He can't hurt you and—if he's serious—I think it's the Christian thing to do. Who knows? Maybe Randy wants to turn things around. Let's hope.

"Maybe I can knock off tomorrow and I can take you over. Would that help?"

"Of course," Hannah said. "No way am I going there alone, even if they have a dozen cops and a tank."

The next morning, father and daughter headed through Randall's mostly vacant downtown and turned at the courthouse on the square. A block north, a drab, gray building stood behind a CAMPBELL DEARBORN MEMORIAL JUSTICE CENTER sign. They parked next to some squad cars and went inside. A plaque on the lobby wall said "Jail Visitation" with an arrow pointed upstairs.

The pair identified themselves, signed a form telling who they wanted to see, and a deputy and jail matron searched them.

Hannah, hands in the air, had never been frisked.

The deputy ushered them into chairs in front of a clear plastic window, sort of like a bank teller, she thought. A heavily tattooed young man spoke quietly to a woman at an adjoining window. A red sign warned KEEP HANDS BELOW COUNTER. Hannah nervously seated herself at the window while her father took a chair behind her.

A door opened on the other side and a guard came in with Randy, who wore a fluorescent orange jump suit with LIMESTONE COUNTY JAIL #5923 stenciled across the back, and sandals with white socks.

"Keep your hands behind you, thirty minutes, conversations may be recorded," the guard gruffly warned the prisoner, then stepped back.

Randy looked different, and not just because his usual shaggy mop of blond hair had been buzzed short. He didn't sneer.

The big boy sat down in front of her. Her hands jittered, her knees knocked. Tom Junior reached forward and patted her shoulder. "I'm right here," he whispered.

"Thanks," he mumbled through the window, acknowledging Hannah and her father.

"Well?" Hannah replied nervously, her arms folded to hide her nerves.

"I'm sorry, will you forgive me?" Randy mumbled slowly. He wouldn't look at her.

Hannah sat silently, glaring at him.

"Look, I don't know how to tell you how sorry I am for what I done, not only the office that night, but all the other times, other dumb stuff," he added, nervously rocking back in forth with his hands behind him as he looked down.

"Okay, so what are you up to?" she said with a grimace.

"I'm not up to nothin'," Randy answered as he glanced up at her and smiled briefly.

"Why the change of heart?" she asked.

"Well, see, look, uh, I had a long talk with the chaplain last week. I didn't have no cell mate, he came in, we sat on my bunk, talkin' for a couple hours.

"He talked a lot about the God thing, you know, Jesus and all that kind o' religion stuff. He pointed out Jesus never hurt nobody and loved people, we should all follow that example. Well, how to say it, I guess I decided to, I don't know, try somethin' else, give Jesus a try. I wanted to impress you and it don't work."

"No, it hasn't." she replied sharply.

"He gave me one of those easy-to-read, parabolic Bibles," he said. "It has pictures of Jesus and maps and stuff. Some of it's printed in red."

"Paraphrase?" Hannah asked.

"Yeah, that's it," Randy said.

"You know, there's some good stuff in the Bible."

"That's true," Hannah replied.

"Look, I've been doin' things all wrong. I really liked what the chaplain said to me. What I've been doin' ain't worked, that's why I'm here.

"I've changed."

Hannah listened.

"That's good," she said flatly.

"Can you forgive me, please? I really am sorry for everythin'."

"So what's your point? I forgive you and you expect to walk out of here? It doesn't work that way, Randy," Hannah replied.

He shook his head, still looking at the floor, rocking back and forth.

She thought for a moment.

"Okay, you asked me to forgive you and I guess I can. God has forgiven all of us and we should do the same, 'Forgive us our trespasses as we forgive others,' you know, we can go forward from here. You'll find that in your parabolic Bible. But that doesn't change things with the law," she added.

"That Bible also says, 'Render unto Caesar the things that are Caesar's,' and Caesar has laws about assault, rape and murder threats."

Randy flinched.

"Yeah, I know that. I gotta' go back to that stinkin' cell when we're done."

They sat quietly, Randy glanced up at her, grimaced, sort of smiled again, then looked back at the floor.

"You don't know how hard...," and his voice choked and he sniffed loudly. "Hannah, please, I don't know how to say nothin' but, well, you always been the girl I want, I dreamed of, maybe because you're so different than the slutty girls I hang around.

"You're different," Randy said with a loud gulp.

"I did some really stupid stuff to show you what a bigshot I am. I messed up, I failed. That's why I want to tell you how sorry I am."

Hannah listened quietly.

"True," she answered.

"Please say you forgive me, I want to make things right. I want to start over."

"What does that mean?"

Randy shook his head.

"I don't know. But somehow, some way, I want to show you how much I love you."

Randy Smith loved her?

Yuck!

Hannah's stomach churned.

"Yeah, right, like he loves all those other girls he's used and abused," she thought to herself. She'd heard talk of paternity suits and other assaults. She did not doubt them. Big, six-feet plus, well over two-hundred pounds, a muscled-up football star—he could overpower any woman.

No, this had to be a stunt, a trick: You see, judge? This poor, mixed-up girl thinks I'm wonderful, let's just forget the whole thing. Can I go now?

Hannah sighed.

"Look, okay, I said I forgive you, and I guess I do. But that doesn't get you off the hook. You know—and I know—what you wanted that night. You would have succeeded if Charley hadn't busted that chair over your head. Physically, I could not stop you. And what about that *'if I can't have you, I'll see to it nobody else does?'*"

Randy shook his head, his eyes got wet.

"Sure, okay, but can we try to make things right between us?"

"There is no *us*!" Hannah snapped through clenched teeth.

"You are you and I am me. We had some good times, true, I cared for you back then, I miss them too. But that all happened in high school, a long time ago. I've grown up and maybe, finally, you have too.

"I wish sometimes it had worked. But that night when you stuck your filthy paw up my shirt and felt me off, any kind of 'us' ended; finished! It's called respect.

"You want to know why I'm different, Randy Smith? I'll tell you why I'm different: I'm not a toy, I'm not a plaything you use to take care of your urges. I get interested in a guy who treats me like a lady—because I am one!

"There will come a day when I enjoy, when I welcome, a physical relationship with a man, and I'll let him touch me. But it will be because I know he loves Hannah Bentley, not because he wants to grab and fondle the body parts of whoever happens to be next to him tonight.

"And when I find him, I will love him enough to take his name, because I will love him the rest of my life. We will share a relationship that you can only imagine."

They sat in silence.

"He will be one, lucky dude. Can we start over, can it be me?" Randy asked, still rocking and looking at the floor.

"No," she answered flatly.

"If truly you want to start over, if you really care about me, you have taken the first step in a marathon—and I'm not convinced you do. It could happen, but you have a long way to go."

He nodded and sniffed.

"I can forgive you, but when they call me to testify I have to tell them exactly what happened," Hannah said firmly. "I am required by law to do that, I'll let the judge decide where things go from there."

Randy and Hannah sat quietly a while longer, separated by much more than Plexiglas. Tom Junior and the guard watched.

She continued to stare a hole in him, Randy looked at the floor. He glanced up at her again, then looked down.

"I better go," she said, standing.

Randy nodded.

"Thanks for comin', I mean that," he said. "I want to change, I want to make right for stuff, please let me. Please, let me start over."

Hannah stopped and stared down at him.

Did she feel anger, compassion or disgust?

She turned to her father and they walked out. She glanced back at the window as they went out the door to see the guard taking Randy, his head still hung down, back to his cell.

"Did you hear all that?' she asked her father as they went down the stairs.

"Yes," Tom Junior said with a sigh. "I hope he's sincere but somehow, knowing Randy, I see him doing high-fives and fist bumps with his lawyer as they laugh about now."

Chapter 20
The Ugly Duckling

Life settled into a dull routine, a routine that did not include Hannah. Dad and Chad got up and went to work every day, mom volunteered at the church or the library most days. Hannah tagged along to the library a couple times to re-shelve books, fun to spend extra time with mom. Aunt Brenda disappeared daily "to do artistic things that better the earth."

Whatever.

Hannah? Stuck at home, tough on a bouncy young lady who always had something to do, somewhere to go, someone to see.

She read books, she watched movies, she looked up high school gal pals home on summer break, she did a couple hikes with some besties out at Randy-free Hoot Owl Hollow. As always, it felt good to get outside.

Her phone buzzed one night, a text from Mark: "CU this wknd slpng bty?" She shot back: "4sure!" Mark replied with a thumbs-up—the most excitement she'd had all week.

Here came another day. She went in the media room and flipped on the Netflix menu. Nope, not a thing she hadn't seen or wanted to see. It would be more fun to sit in here with Mark, she thought. She could watch just about anything if she could cuddle up with him and a big bowl of popcorn.

Oh, forget the popcorn!

Curled up with Mark's arm over her shoulders, a quiet conversation—of such things dreams are made.

Maybe there are some DVDs in the cabinet she hadn't watched? She opened the door and spied an open DVD holder, what could it be? She flipped the sleeve over: Groucho Marx leered at her, cigar in the corner of his mouth, from "The Best of the Marx Brothers." Obviously, daddy had been there.

She puttered around the family library—bored to tears. She tried the game room, billiards isn't much fun when you play yourself. She surfed Facebook and Instagram, all her besties and sorority sisters had terrific summer jobs or exotic vacations.

Hannah?

Stuck.

Maybe she could go see Claire? Hey, that's an idea!

Hannah walked back to her bedroom, got her phone and punched Claire's number.

"Well, hello young lady!" came the bright answer.

"Hi, Claire, thought I'd come out and say hello if you're not busy."

"For you, I'm never busy. Tom's over in Tony's room."

Claire coughed and mumbled.

"Say, Hannah, don't you drive a Jeep?"

"Yes, well, the family's Jeep, daddy lets me drive it."

"Doesn't it set up kind of high, you know, it would be easy for someone, say, in a wheelchair to get in and out?"

Hannah laughed.

"Yes, do you have someone in mind?"

"Indeed, I know this little old lady out here who's plotted her escape. When can you get here?"

"On my way!" Hannah said.

She pulled up to find Claire at the front door with Josefina.

Hannah parked and the nurse rolled the wheelchair up to the car door and helped Claire in.

"I'll cover for you if Tom asks questions," the nurse said, laughing.

And off they went.

"¡Buen viaje!" Josefina called as she watched the *Silly Boys, Jeeps Are For Girls* tire cover disappear.

"Anywhere, drive around town," Claire said firmly, twirling her fingers. "I just want out for a while."

What a delight!

This afternoon? Just a couple of giggly school girls out and about, having a good time. Six decades separated them but they held so much in common: the same home town, the same high school, the same college—and the same Tom Bentley.

Poor Tom: They both shared funny stories about the guy.

Laughter, and if he were there he'd laugh too. They knew that.

"Just remember what that novelist, Margaret Atwood, once said," Claire told Hannah with her trademark half smile, "She observed once, 'In the end, we'll all become stories.'"

They sat at a stoplight giggling, Hannah didn't notice the light had turned green. Somebody behind her honked and she popped the clutch as they took off. Claire jerked across her seatbelt and laughed so hard she cried.

What fun!

Hannah drove out to Hoot Owl and idled up as close as she could to the big rock above the creek. Claire sat, enthralled, hands clasped at her chest.

"Oh my, I haven't been here in so long, decades, it looks just like I remember when we came here for our senior picnic. Tom disappeared, I went looking for him, then I finally saw him right over there, where our initials are, the ones you saw," she said.

But not all the Grandpa Tom stories turned funny, they shared the tender moments, the sweet times too, he had given them both.

"Say, can we go out by the cemetery?" Claire asked.

"Sure," Hannah replied, "I haven't been my grandmother's grave in a while."

She turned around and headed for Garden of Peace.

They drove through the big gate and Claire gave instructions: "Turn right at that tombstone with Jesus holding a lamb, then left at the big monument for the Peters family, then right again."

"We're headed for my grandmother's grave," Hannah replied, puzzled.

"Oh?" Claire said.

"See, right here," Hannah answered as she pulled to a stop and pointed at the tombstone:

Linda Kay Brown Bentley

1941-1980

Wife * Mother * Woman of God

"And there's our family's mausoleum," Claire said, pointing behind her grave.

DEARBORN

Campbell Robert

1898-1980

Jewel Mae Laerdal

1901-1990

Claire Elaine

1931-

But seek ye first the kingdom of God

The pair sat in silence as the engine idled.

"They'll open that door and slide me in someday," Claire said glumly, staring at the gray granite building.

"Okay, but think about this: The two women Grandpa Tom loved will end up literally a stone's throw apart," Hannah said brightly.

Claire smiled an ironic smile.

"I can hear her when I show up: 'There goes the neighborhood!'"

"Oh, I doubt that, I bet you'll be pals!" Hannah said. "Think of the stories you two could share!"

They both enjoyed another laugh.

Claire turned quiet.

"Life and death can be funny sometimes," she said with a sigh.

They both thought deep thoughts, like everyone does in a cemetery.

"Well, enough of this!" Claire finally said with a wave. "I'm hungry, does this one-horse town have a drive-in anyplace? I can't get out."

"Sure, on the bypass," Hannah said. "We can head over there."

"I want tater tots!" Claire said firmly. "I love those things, haven't had any in years, I'll buy lunch."

"Deal!" Hannah said firmly.

They drove around the courthouse square, then headed out to the bypass. Hannah turned in and found an empty stall.

"Do the carhops still roller skate?" Claire asked.

"Don't think so, what'll it be?" Hannah asked.

"Jumbo tater tots and a strawberry shake," Claire said. "Wait! Do they have chili?"

"I think so," Hannah said as she read the menu out her window. "Yes, but I never tried it."

"Okay, jumbo tater tots, strawberry shake and a chili, a rather odd order? I know I'll be disappointed but I haven't had any chili in a long time," Claire said. "That's too racy for Hickory Bough's kitchen, they cook in beige."

"Why do you think you'll be disappointed?"

"Oh, honey, Cincinnati has the best chili in the world, I'm spoiled!" Claire explained. "How do you think I put on a hundred pounds? I'd go eat a bowl of three-way twice a week, it's wonderful!"

"You gained a hundred pounds?" Hannah asked incredulously.

"Yes," Claire sighed, looking down at herself.

"I'm down some after my stroke, but at your age? Just a rail, and I could eat whatever I wanted. Your grandfather and I would go to this burger place that used to be downtown, where that Rio Bravo is now, and I'd have a burger, fries and shake, no problem.

"Tom teased me, said I should order double-burgers with cheese and bacon, 'so you'll get plump enough to cast a shadow.'"

The girls laughed.

"That sounds like something he'd say," Hannah said.

She called in their order and the pair continued their banter.

"I guess I chased off guys, Hannah," Claire added with a sigh. "Thin, and a head taller than any boy besides the basketball team, I had the body of Karlie Kloss or Elle Macpherson—nothing but leg. All the popular Randall High girls, I thought, had your build: chests, hips, curves.

"I spent a fortune on clothes to compensate. And, I guess I've always spent a lot on nice dresses, not that it did much good when I wore a robe on a lot of days."

"You sound beautiful!" Hannah replied sincerely. "I wish I had a figure like that, but that's not what my squatty grandmother looked like, and I got a double-dose of her genes."

Claire smiled.

"That's my point, we never see ourselves as we should, our strengths, we tend to dwell on our perceived weaknesses," she said thoughtfully. "Every month, I read *Vogue, Mademoiselle* and *Seventeen*—the new magazine then—cover to cover, but I looked at the clothes, not the models. If only I had clothes like that, then I would be beautiful!

"It hit me when I went to New York," she added. "Columbia University had this lady meet me at Penn Station when I got off the train.

"I remember the moment like it happened yesterday, down in a tunnel, this swirling mob of people, some had been on that train since Texas—two days! The porter handed me my suitcase, then I shuffled along, totally lost, bewildered, as we inched toward the stairs, and there she stood with a little sign: Miss Dearborn.

"We came out on Eighth Avenue and, oh, my goodness! Here came this gaggle of young, poised women taller and skinnier than me.

"It left me in awe, I'd never seen women like that! They all carried these big bags under their arms. What on earth?

"I asked my guide, 'What's this, who are these women? They grow them tall here!'

"'Fashion models, we're in the Garment District,'" she replied. "'They pose for all those fancy fashion magazines like *Vogue, Mademoiselle* and *Seventeen*.'

"Bang! I stood there, shocked, while she hailed a cab: They looked like *me*! Tall, thin women—sought after, successful, famous—because they looked like *me*!" Claire said, shaking her head disbelief.

"Why didn't I see that? I guess I had been an ugly duckling.

"To Tom's credit, he saw me as beautiful," she continued. "We sat out in that gazebo in my parents' backyard and talked a lot. Early on, I asked him once, 'Do you think I'm pretty?'

"I remember he snorted, which embarrassed me. He sat there for a minute with this smirk, then said, 'You are more than pretty, you are the most beautiful girl I have ever seen.'

"Oh, I wanted to believe him! Here, this guy I had chased for years, since third grade, actually saw me as beautiful. Imagine, lucky me!

"He told me several times while we dated how guys checked me out, but I never saw it.

"I never knew your grandmother, or course, but she proved inner beauty's important, the Bible talks about that," Claire continued. "To Tom's credit, he noticed, I guess he saw inner beauty in both of us.

"Tom's just a little biased," she added with a smile.

"And that's a bad thing? What's the difference in bias and love?" Hannah asked.

They both chuckled.

"The first couple years we dated I towered over your grandfather. He finally caught up with me, but whenever I wore heels I'd still be taller than him. I might still be taller if I weren't in a wheelchair."

"Ha! He's a mellow fellow," Hannah replied.

"Oh, I know that, and I guess that's why I loved him then and now. He's just go good-natured, gets along with everyone, doesn't let what he wants get in the way," Claire said.

"I have the opposite problem," Hannah said as she shook her head. "Every guy interested in me towers way up there, a foot-plus taller than I am," she said as she thumped the headliner.

"I need a short boyfriend!"

"I'll keep my eyes open, I sit down low," Claire replied with fake seriousness. "So, you're still having boy problems?"

Hannah sighed.

"If you only knew, maybe I should ask you for some advice?"

"Oh no, not me!" Claire said firmly.

"I am the last woman on earth you want to ask about men. I dumped the most wonderful man I have ever known, your dear grandfather, then took up with the worst man I have ever known, a total reprobate and miscreant murdered in prison. It's the grace of God I got Tom back.

"Honestly, Hannah, with all I've done, with all the places I've been, my happiest hours came in high school with Tom as we sat out there in the gazebo in our backyard. We just knew what our future would be, we would be together—forever.

"Dating him made a lonely school girl's wildest daydream come true."

Their food came and the girls munched as they talked.

"But give me a rundown, who's who in your life?"

"Let me start with Mark, he's Mr. Di Burlone's grandson, we met at your anniversary lunch, remember? Oh my, he's *fine*!" Hannah said as she chewed. "He's driven down to spend a couple weekends since your anniversary, and he came to see me in the hospital. We talk and do FaceTime on the phone a lot."

"He does seem nice. You know he's divorced?" Claire replied.

Hannah put down her burger.

"No, I didn't know that," she said, stunned. "He doesn't say much about his personal life, except the Navy, I guess you'd call them war stories. He talks all kinds of pilot stuff about 'the meatball' and 'the three wire.'

"Instead, it's all about me—what do you like to do, where do you want to go, what's important to you? We do things, golf, hike, movies. It's just fun to be with him.

"The thing I figured out: he's a lot older than me—hey, he may be thirty! He has to be to have done all of the stuff he talks about."

"He's in his early thirties, I know that from Tony," Claire replied. "I wouldn't let that stop you if he's the one."

"Claire, now Mark's the smooth talker you warned me about," Hannah said between French fries. "Boy, does he have some pickup lines! I've wondered, honestly, if he has something to hide. Do you know what happened, why they split?"

"No, I don't. I think his wife got tired of life alone while he pulled sea duty. It hurt him badly and that's why Mark resigned his commission. I think he did a lot of carousing back then. He cleaned things up to try to get her back."

"But it didn't work. Maybe she's married someone else by now, who's to say?"

"For what it's worth, young lady, you left Tony smitten, he thinks you are just the most wonderful thing. 'Maybe a butterfly net might work!' he said once when he got off on his let's-catch-Hannah-for-Mark project.

"Tom went along, we didn't know about Charley. I know that day turned awkward for you."

Hannah stared out the windshield.

"Mark's never said anything about a divorce, what else do I not know?"

"Sweetheart, look, we all have things in our past we don't like to talk about," Claire said as she chewed. "I told you some of mine, and even your dear, spiritual grandfather fell short sometimes—but I'll let him talk about that if he wants.

"What's important: Tell God we're sorry, then pick up, go on, do better. Think about the future, make life better! I think that's what Mark wants to do.

"Who's next?"

"Randy's the weird one, the boy who attacked me," Hannah said with a sigh as she took a drink.

"Really?" Claire asked. "You're interested in him?"

"No, I think the word for things between us might be 'toxic.' But oh my, we made the hot item back in high school! Sometimes I ask myself 'what if?' Maybe he deserves another chance. He has potential—if he'd let himself. If he'd truly settle down, I might be interested—even now.

"He called me from jail the other day and apologized, then asked me to come visit him. The last thing I wanted to do was see that reprobate after what he did. But Claire, honestly, I heard an audible voice in my bedroom say 'Go!' I did.

"I went over there with daddy, and the jerk said 'sorry' multiple times, said he's turned his life around, got right with the Lord, got all weepy, then declared his love for me, added I'm the girl of his dreams, he wants to make everything right."

"Well! That's unusual," Claire said. "I must say, as a retired judge, be suspicious."

"That's what we thought. But still, I sensed something different about him. There's a side to him I could, maybe, find attractive. But I don't, you understand?"

"Of course, he put you through terrible things."

"He's just done so much stupid stuff, and not just with me. He got kicked out of college for one of his stunts, he had other trouble with the law before he assaulted me."

"I understand your reticence," Claire said. "What about Charley? Remember, I warned you! Has he been sweet-talking you?"

"Ha, hardly! He barely speaks to me since our hike and he got sick, all that mess," Hannah explained. "And before? Well, Charley's polite and courteous, but he's certainly no smooth operator."

Claire finished her chili, then stuck the empty bowl in the litter bag and thought for a moment.

"I must say that does not sound like the Trottel I knew. Could I be wrong? I hope so for your sake," she added. "He seemed very pleasant that day we talked."

"He's a really nice guy, but introverted. You told me to be careful, then he broke things off between us in the hospital. He saved me when Randy attacked, you know."

"Yes, but he did what any normal person would do," Claire replied.

"We have had to see a lot of each other as we worked with the prosecutor, but it's all business, just-the-facts-ma'am, nothing personal. I met his mother, who chewed me out for what happened on the hike."

"Ah, now that sounds like the Trottel I knew!" Claire said. "When anything goes wrong, blame somebody else.

"So who else chases you?" she asked.

"Ugh! Aren't three enough?" Hannah said painfully.

"Okay, maybe I should ask, are you husband hunting?" Claire asked, looking at her young companion with a wise smile.

"Absolutely not!" Hannah said firmly.

"If it were me, I'd just as soon not have all this boy-thing going on in my life while I try to finish college. I never dated much, really, guess I'm a social butterfly, just flitting around with my girl buddies. The guys come to me!

"If I could choose, I'd start to look after I graduate and get a job, that'll be a year-plus from now. But I know when people come in, or go out, of our lives can't always be our decision."

"Oh, you sweet girl, I'm amazed at you," Claire said as she patted Hannah's leg. "You're so bright and upbeat—and pretty—I'm surprised there aren't a dozen more chasing you. At your age I had to conspire just to catch one guy: Tom. I chased him for six years before he spoke to me."

"I haven't felt very upbeat lately," the girl replied with a sigh.

"Well, all this will pass. Anyway, don't get in a hurry. Whoever, and whenever, it's your call. Don't get talked into things," Claire said, admonishing her young companion.

"But one bit of advice I can give: Whoever you keep, make sure your family stays in the loop. Don't lose them."

"Do I hear the voice of experience?" Hannah asked as she munched.

"You certainly do," Claire said as she finished her last tater tot. "It took years for me to heal the relationship with my family."

"Over this man, Mr. Trottel?"

"Oh no, over your grandfather!" came the reply. "My parents doted on Tom. They thought him the most wonderful young man ever, and when I dropped him to go to law school, they got very upset: 'Claire, what are you *doing*?'"

"The worst argument I ever had with my father occurred the night I left for New York.

"And you know what? They proved right. Listen to your parents, Hannah. They make mistakes, they're human, but they love you and want to do right by you. They've gone through things that you haven't, they have experience.

"I know now they thought they did the right thing when they demanded the two of us go to separate colleges, which led to our breakup. But they meant well, I see that now, it could have worked."

Hannah nodded.

"Anything else you'd like to do, or do you need to get back?" the girl asked.

"I don't think I can top this fun afternoon, it's been wonderful," Claire said thoughtfully. "But you know what I'd really like?" she added as she looked at Hannah wistfully.

"Sure, what?"

"Can you call me 'grandma?'"

Hannah looked at her, blank.

"I guess so."

"It's been 'Grandpa Tom and Claire' since we married, and I seriously want to be a real part of this family. It's not like I snuck around to replace your grandmother, I'm not a homewrecker. Your family has so much, it's wonderful, and I want, truly, to be a part of it. It means a lot," Claire said with intensity.

"Okay—*Grandma*!" Hannah replied.

"Trust me, we didn't mean anything by it. Grandpa's been in our lives forever and, well, you've been here less than two years."

"Understood. We're working up a series on adoption for the radio program. You know, Joseph adopted Jesus, wasn't his son, but obviously Joseph loved him," Claire added.

"Adoption may be the purest form of love: You're not mine, but I'm going to treat you like you are. We could go off on all sorts of things from that, salvation, suffering, innocence, loneliness, authentic love. We'll keep it simple and straightforward, you can't get deep in four minutes.

"Can you adopt *me?*" Claire asked with a nervous smile, looking at Hannah.

Hannah sat, astounded.

"Of course we can, we have. Really, maybe we just haven't said it. We think of you as family, truly we do."

"Thank you," Claire said softly as she leaned over the console. The pair hugged.

The Bluetooth rang: Josefina, Tom's had one of his fainting spells, passed out in Tony's room. You need to head back.

"Here we come!" Hannah replied as she started the Jeep.

Chapter 21
Letters and Memories

Hannah parked in the driveway just as the postman pulled away from the family mailbox. She walked back to see what came, and there among the ads and a bill she found a letter with her name on the envelope, poorly written, scrawled with a dull pencil. She checked the return address, some numbers above a local post office box.

She leaned against the mailbox and opened it:

Deer Hannah,

I don't think you know how hard it was to talk to you when you came in hear to see me. I hope you're father didn't think I'm wired. Ha. Ha.

Hannah, I really mean I'm sorry. I changed. I want to make things write between us but I don't know what to do. My cellmate said I shood rite you this letter and apologize, and hear it is.

Please forgive me. Please. Please. Please. Please. You are the girl of my dreams and I want to do whatever it takes to make things OK. I'm sorry for all the dumb stuff I done. Please let me know what to do and I will do it. You mean everything to me.

All my love,
Randy

It left her shaky, what on earth?

"Trash it!" she thought, but caught herself as she started to wad the page up. Part of that sinister defense ploy? This might be evidence. She folded up the page and put it back in the envelope.

Judy just then pulled in the driveway and Hannah walked over to greet her mom.

"Hi, honey, what have you done today?" the mother said as she kissed her daughter on the forehead.

"Grandma Claire and I went for a drive around town, then stopped for lunch at the drive-in," the daughter explained.

"That sounds like fun!"

"Mom, she asked me, very seriously to call her grandma, she doesn't like 'grandpa and Claire,' says she doesn't feel like she's really a part of the family," Hannah said.

"Well," the mom answered. "I can see that, hadn't really thought about it. But if that's what she wants, then, sure, 'Grandma Claire.'"

"That's all sweetness and light, then I get this," Hannah said, handing Randy's letter to her mom.

Judy opened the letter and read it.

"First off, he needs to work on spelling," she said with a sigh.

"Seriously, what do you make of it?" her daughter asked.

"Like we discussed after you and your dad went to the jail, I think he's up to something," Judy replied. "If he's not, and he means it, well, then you have another problem."

The prosecutor looked at the letter, front and back.

"I know where they're headed with this," she said glumly: "Oh, hey look, judge, really, no big deal here. The defendant and Miss Bentley dated in high school, they just decided to get back together and make a little whoopee—light the ol' spark, you know. Then this bad guy, Miss Bentley's jilted lover, Mr. Trottel, walked in, caught them in the act, flew in a jealous rage, and put a chair in the defendant's head. Mr. Trottel should be the one on trial for assaulting poor, innocent Mr. Smith!"

"But that's not what happened," Hannah replied earnestly.

"You know that, I think I know that, but the judge doesn't know it," she replied firmly. "Mr. Smith and his defense attorney could have saved us a lot of trouble if they had waived a preliminary hearing, but they didn't. Watch for theatrics. We talked plea bargain but his attorney's not interested, apparently thinks they can get the whole thing thrown out.

"The judge will decide. I wish we could have gone to a grand jury, we have solid evidence besides your testimony, but the county doesn't have one empaneled now, and it's not worth calling one for this and a couple other comparatively minor cases.

"So what did you tell Mr. Smith when you went to visitation?"

"He asked me to forgive him, I said that's fine if that's what you want, but it doesn't change things with the law. I'll tell the truth about what happened," Hannah said.

"Good, did anyone go with you? Could they corroborate your testimony?" the attorney asked.

"Yes, my father sat there the whole time right behind me, he heard everything."

"That helps, we have him subpoenaed, of course, since he saw the crime scene and can speak to your state, physical and mental, after the attack. Your dad's been very helpful."

"So what do we do now?" Hannah asked.

"Wait. We have to see the fall docket. I think they'll want to get this out of the way early so we could go to trial this fall. I know you don't feel this way but we're talking a minor felony here," came the reply. "At its simplest, assault and battery."

"No, I don't," Hannah said with a sigh.

"So, I could miss out on another semester at Mizzou? I've already missed the summer term," she asked with pain in her voice.

"Sadly, yes. Even if the preliminary's first thing on the docket, that will be early September, then the trial would be sometime this fall, maybe November, or it could be early next year. I'm afraid you'll have to sit around a lot," the attorney said. "That might leave you with nothing but incompletes for the term."

Hannah shook her head.

"Okay, I guess I can look into classes online."

"I'm sorry, what about Mr. Trottel? Isn't he at Missouri too?"

"Yes, some scholarship program, I don't know what limits he has on what he takes and when."

"Good luck, and let me know if I can help."

The ladies shook and Hannah walked out into the ornate hallway.

What a pain. Assuring Randy gets due process means everyone else suffers, she thought.

Why does justice demand injustice?

She headed toward the courthouse entrance as Charley came around a corner. He appeared to not notice her. Hannah deliberately stepped in front of him.

"Stop!" she said firmly, raising her hand like a policewoman.

He did, looking down at her.

"Yes?"

"Charley, what's wrong? Why do you hate me? Please, let's talk," Hannah pleaded.

"I have a meeting," he said coolly.

"I figured that, but tell me what's wrong. The lawyers can wait five minutes. What have I done? This hurts," she replied with a frown.

Charley shook his head.

"You haven't done a thing, I don't hate you, can we sit down?" he added, pointing to an empty bench.

"Certainly!"

"Hannah, look, my mother at the hospital made me realize the truth: I see too much in you, you and me will never work," he said.

"Why do you think that?" she asked.

"We are too different. It would take a big bridge to cross the gap."

"What does that mean?"

"Think about it: Mother and I live hand to mouth, we don't have much. Her old Pontiac barely runs. There have been times I had to walk a couple miles to buy groceries because we didn't have gas money. I had the grades to earn a scholarship so I got in college. Otherwise, I'd be a clerk at a C-store or in the Marines now.

"Then I look at you: rich. You lack nothing, your family has more money than it knows what to do with. I'm not jealous, well, a little.

"And, you have this loving, close family. Me? I don't have anyone but an indifferent, hateful mother. I can't imagine being related to famous people like Tom and Claire. I'm just happy to listen to their show, one in ten-million strangers in front of a radio or a computer."

"And another thing, Hannah, you're... uh, elegant," Charley said. "I'm not handsome enough for you."

Hannah clapped her hands, which echoed down the hall.

"Me? Elegant?" she replied as she laughed loudly.

"Oh, Charley, you're funny! I'm just a chunky little ex-cheerleader who'd rather sleep in a tent with her boots on as wear a ball gown to a fancy gala," she replied. "I drive a Jeep with camo seat covers, not a stretch limo. If you think I'm elegant, thank you, but I don't see it."

"I do," Charley replied firmly.

That caught Hannah.

"So, how could a Sad Sack like me make you happy? You need someone else, let me get out of your way."

She listened, concerned.

"Don't make excuses! Charley, look: you will be a success someday. Who made those grades that got that scholarship? *You* did!

"You're smart, you have talent, you're a hard worker, you're honest, you're polite, you treat people well. Success will come to you."

Charley snickered and shook his head.

"Says who?"

"Says my father!" Hannah replied brightly.

"He told me how people at the warehouse talked about what a hard worker you are in a staff meeting. They want you! They said how they want to figure out some way to keep you, it's such a pleasure to work with you."

"Did they say that?"

"Yes, yes they did."

"Oh!" Charley said, brightening.

"You've had bad breaks, sure, but I look at you and I know you'll make something of yourself. You'll go places, let's stay friends at least," Hannah said, leaning toward him.

"We share a faith, and we share experiences—the hike and all its problems brought us close together. And then this thing at Grandpa Tom's old house," she added with a nod at the prosecutor's office.

"I don't know what your mother said to you, she said tacky things to me in the hospital."

"She's good at that."

"Charley, look: Let's make this between you and me—not her. Maybe we can build that bridge. We can at least be pals, and who knows, maybe something more someday," Hannah said. "Bridges take you someplace. We both have a lot going on, let's stay connected, let's see what happens.

"Please?"

Charley sat upright, his back against the wall, as he thought.

"If God brought us together, then it'll work. Let's trust each other. I need people I can trust in my life," Hannah said firmly.

"I don't know," he answered. "Maybe I'm still in shock after that tick got me. This summer has been weird. I came down here for a quick weekend in May, it's August, I'm still here. Some weekend."

They sat, looking at each other.

"Can we give it a try? Besides, I like pianos," she said to add a little levity to their serious moment.

Charley's frown turned to a smirk.

"Okay, it's been so long since I played I may have forgotten how," he said with a shrug.

"Hey, why don't you come over tonight and bang away on ours?" Hannah asked. "Let 'er rip, maestro! Tell daddy to bring you home from the warehouse. I'll let mom know you're coming, you can have a real meal for a change."

Charley scowled, deep in thought.

"Okay, do you mind?"

"Mind? I would be thrilled! Maybe we can jump in the hot tub!" she said with a wink. "We never got to do that."

Charley blushed.

"And speaking of that mean ol' tick, did you suffer anything permanent?" she asked.

He shrugged.

"No, doctors don't think so. I'm tired of the tests."

He stood up and turned to walk off as Hannah bid him a chirpy "Later!" Charley turned and smiled down at her—the first real smile she'd seen on his face since that sunny afternoon in the Ozarks.

Finally!

Maybe this mess with Charley could get cleaned up.

Meanwhile, what about Mark?

A cloud had moved across their sunny relationship. If what Claire said proved true, they needed to have a long talk. Maybe it would work, maybe not. She had to know more.

As "grandma" noted, we all have things we don't like to talk about.

Trust Charley? Yes.

Trust Mark? Maybe.

And Randy? Trust?

Oh, good grief! One letter wouldn't do it. It might be a second step on that marathon.

Hannah walked in the front door with a cheerful "Hi, Mom!" Judy looked out from the kitchen and replied with a "There you are, how did the meeting go?"

"Fine, the attorney's suspicious too."

"Hey, you got another letter today," her mom said, handing her an envelope. It had the address in ink but it came from Randy, no doubt.

"Oh no, I don't know if I want to read it."

"Guess you better," her mom replied as she walked back to the kitchen.

Hannah opened it:

Deer Hannah,

One of the guys gave me a book of stamps he had so I decided to write you every day until I run out. Again, I don't think you know how hard it was to talk to you when you came in to see me that day. Thanks for coming, it meaned a lot to me don't you know it did.

Please, Hannah, I really mean it, I'm sorry. Forgive me. With all my heart I want to make things write between you and I. But I don't know what to do, please tell me.

Please. Please. Please. Please. Please. Please. Please. Please. Please. Please. Please. Please. Please. Please. Please. Please. Please. Please. Please. Please.

Is that enough? If not, I'll write some more until you get the idea.

You mean everything to me, I want you to be a part of my new life whatever that will be thin the two us could be together forever and that would mean a lot to me. I'll be whatever you want me to be.

All my love,
Randy

Hannah leaned against the wall and cried.

Maybe the poor goof-up really meant it.

Then what?

She thought back to those few, amazing weeks in their junior year, her first boyfriend, so exciting—and not just any boy! They shared so many happy moments before he got fresh, it had been great.

He laughed, he cut up, he teased, and she loved it.

She teased back. Randy loved animated, fun-loving Hannah at her best.

They worked together, yes, they really did. Those few weeks glowed in her memory.

Tom Junior gave her keys to the family Jeep after she got her driver's license that fall. To celebrate, Randy gave her a gift, that funny spare tire cover: *Silly Boys, Jeeps Are For Girls.*

What a hoot!

You wouldn't call him a gentleman but he behaved himself. She heard the whispers, she knew the rumors, but she could tell something more lurked deep inside him, something down there that wanted respect. Maybe it couldn't get out.

Randy wanted to be more than a dumb jock.

To date Hannah Bentley—one of *the* Bentleys, Randall's first family—would bring it.

Randy made her feel special, and to be Randy Smith's girl! Wow! Every girl at Randall High envied her!

Football Fridays: Here they came down the hall together between class, other kids stepped aside. Big Randy wore his blue jersey over his jeans, she wore her white-and-blue cheerleader uniform and white knee socks, the big, gray *R* on her uniform's front, and *Hannah* in script across the flap collar. She had a big blue-and-white bow in her hair.

She loved that outfit, it still hung in her closet.

To make varsity cheer, chosen from dozens who tried out: amazing! Then to be the love interest of the team's star player too? Wow!

Proud.

Hannah rolled over in her mind that early season victory, an upset, at Marshfield when he jogged off the field at the end of the game, dropped his helmet, picked her up like a sack of potatoes, then plopped her on his big shoulder pads. The star of the game came to *her*!

Then, he danced around between the other cheerleaders, holding her up, as the band played the fight song. She could hear the tune in her head:

> *"Go Rams, win team,*
> *Fight for our blue and gray!*
> *When our Rams go marching,*
> *Hear our cheer so loud and clear:*
> *Fight! Fight! Fight!*
> *Win team for Randall,*
> *And make our banner wave!*

Take the ball and push on through that line,
Hey! Rams, lead the waaaay!"

She waved her pom-poms over her head as Randy did a jig beneath her.

What a thrill, one of life's magic moments.

Then it ended.

Maybe she had been too harsh when she slapped him.

Maybe they could make the spark glow again. Maybe they could....

No, wait.

He tackled her at that playoff game. Then came the threats, he stalked her. Then came that horrible night at Grandpa Tom's old house.

Love-struck crushes can overlook dark sides. Melancholy tears turned to disgust.

No, even if he meant every "I'm sorry!" he had a long, long way to go to win her back. Much as she might want Randy then, she did not want Randy now.

Trust?

Randy?

None.

Judy came out in the hall and stopped, shocked, when she saw her daughter, red in the face with tears streaming down her cheeks.

"Wow, what did the letter say?" she asked.

Hannah wadded up the page and stuffed it back in the envelope. "Same thing.

"Oh, Charley's coming over tonight."

Chapter 22
Patience

Tom Junior strolled into his office from a late Rio Bravo lunch, whistling. Business looked great for the holiday season, although after all these years he still didn't understand why stores that sell garden hoes, toilet plungers, pliers and such did well at Christmas. Who puts shovels under Christmas trees?

And what about lawn mowers? Mower sales ticked up every December, why? Here you go dad: merry Christmas, enjoy your gift next April!

Whatever, the big sales season loomed just ahead as in every other year, and he had to make sure merchandise at the company's hundred-odd locations sat on shelves when shoppers arrived. Or more and more, that it popped up on the website at a mouse click. And the catalog, yeah, some people still shopped by mail. The marketing and inventory honchos did the heavy lifting but he had to do the signoff.

Truman had it right: The buck stops here.

Pressure.

He had reports to read, people to call, decisions to make—after lots of research to make sure the company achieved fourth-quarter success.

How can sitting at a desk make one so tired? All this to tend to, then the difficult times at home. Poor Hannah, it's not her fault. He stopped to say a quick prayer for her.

The tedious afternoon passed slowly as sunlight rotated across his office floor once again.

Another long day at Bentley Hardware headquarters finally came to a close, everyone else had gone home except for Tom Junior. A typical day for a good CEO: First in, last out.

He grabbed his briefcase and hurried through the dark reception area, he could see through the front door that Charley patiently waited in the Lexus, as usual, in the otherwise empty parking lot.

The receptionist's phone rang as he passed and the company's chief executive instinctively picked it up.

"Bentley Hardware."

"Yes, I'm with the Randall Public Library," a woman said. "I need to verify employment."

Let's see, he knew about everyone in the building. "Sure, who've you got?"

"We have an application here for a library card from a Charles Trottel, says he's new in town, doesn't have a water or cable bill for verification. His driver's license has a Neosho address, can you confirm?"

Tom Junior, dog tired, shook his head, sighed, and looked out the door again—the poor kid.

"Ma'am, yes, he works here. Give that fine young man any book he wants."

Chapter 23
Playing A New Tune

A garlic aroma greeted Tom Junior and a sheepish Charley as they walked in the door.

"Hello!" Judy called cheerfully to Hannah's big friend, "C'mon in, we're about to eat."

Charley weaved around boxes stacked in the hall, which he gave a curious glance.

"What's this?" he asked.

"Aunt Brenda's moving into a loft apartment downtown, and she plans to open a, what does she call it?, 'alternative arts' store below her place, ordered a bunch of merchandise," Tom Junior explained. "I put money into the developer, she's the first tenant."

Hannah peeked around a corner and called out a chipper "Hi!" to Charley.

"Hi," he said quietly.

"So if she moves out, may I move back in your spare room? That office guest room gets old," he said.

"I don't think that would be appropriate," the father replied pleasantly, but firmly. "I will get you in an efficiency down the hall from Brenda; nice."

"When?" the boy replied.

"This week if you want, the office folks would like for you to move along, someone in the Dearborn clan's coming down from St. Louis, Claire's grand-nephew or something, to check out the new place."

Judy had outdone herself with a top-flight Italian dinner, Hannah had grated the parmesan.

"Homemade spaghetti sauce," she explained to the guest. "My Italian great-grandmother brought the recipe with her from Naples."

The boy stuffed himself on spaghetti and meatballs with multiple slices of heavily buttered garlic bread. The conversation around the table had been lively and chipper, even usually wet-blanket Aunt Brenda sounded upbeat and optimistic as she talked-up her exciting new business.

But no one said a word about the one thing everyone thought about: Randy and the hearing. Why ruin a happy night?

"This is just so awesome, Mrs. Bentley," Charley said as he finished and leaned back, filled.

"We have spumoni for dessert," the mom offered with a wink.

Charley shook his head.

"Later, I can hardly move."

"Now remember, you're sort of singing for your supper," Hannah said across the table. "The deal's for you to hit the piano and entertain us, Gershwin!"

"My belly's so big I might not reach the keys," he replied.

The whole crew cleared the table and helped load the dishwasher, then adjourned to the Bentley's spinet.

Charley played a few chords, then turned to his audience.

"What'll it be?"

"Surprise us, you can play anything," Judy suggested.

He thought for a moment, then launched into the hornpipe from Handel's *Water Music*. His little audience listened, enthralled. Finishing, he turned and asked, "How's that?"

They sat, speechless.

Then he solemnly asked, "know this one?" as he started *Oceans*. They sang along.

"How do you get all that out of our dinky little piano?" Judy asked as the family finished. "I can't do *Heart and Soul* with Chad."

Charley shrugged.

"Dunno."

"I thought you said you forgot how to play," Hannah said.

"Well, missed some notes, you notice?" he replied.

"I did!" Brenda replied.

"How this?" Charley said, smiling at Hannah, then turning to play the andante from Mozart's *Concerto No. 21*.

She sat, enthralled, as the slow, lilting music drifted through the room. Put a piano in front of this guy and he could melt her into a mushy, romantic puddle.

He could do that—yet he envied *her*. What did Grandma Claire say about seeing our weaknesses and not our strengths?

Charley finished, which brought spontaneous applause.

"How about some stuff with a beat?" Chad asked.

"Sure," the pianist responded, and he leaned into Leon Russell's *Delta Lady* as he sang. Tom Junior and Judy jumped up and danced, joined by Chad and his sister. Charley followed with *Wide Awake*.

"Okay, you've earned your dinner," Judy said, out of breath as he finished. "Seems I recall something about you and Hannah in the hot tub?"

Charley blushed.

"Uh, no suit," he replied.

"Not a problem," Chad said, "you can borrow my trunks, I'll give 'em to Hannah."

Brother and sister walked back to his room and he pulled the swimsuit out of a drawer.

"Yes, yes, mom washed 'em since Mark came," he said, laughing. "Maybe I'll get to wear them someday. Hannah-banana, I need to charge rent with all these guys who come to see you!"

"Put it on my bill, you're a good little brother!" Hannah answered, reaching up and patting Chad on the head.

"Listen Sis, the time's coming when I'll need *your* help," Chad said, smiling down at her.

"And when that time comes, you have it, bro! You can count on it, you know that," she said solemnly. They gave each other a high five and winks.

Charley and Hannah changed, grabbed towels out of the linen closet and headed out to the gurgling tub on the nearly dark patio.

"Never done this, what's the trick?" Charley asked.

"No trick, just get in, have a seat and it bubbles away your misery," Hannah answered with a smile.

"Need that," he answered.

Hannah climbed in and Charley followed her, plopping down next to her. He clumsily leaned over, wrapped his arms around her, and passionately kissed the girl.

It surprised her.

"Well!" she said, gasping, as they parted. "Wow!"

"I'm sorry, I just forgot how special you are," he whispered, an inch from her lips, his face turned for another kiss.

"Nothing to be sorry about, you're special too," Hannah whispered back.

They kissed again.

"I think I saw someone showing off in there?" she said smiling, rubbing her finger down his wet nose.

Charley hung his head.

"I guess."

"And you're so good, what a gift!"

He shrugged.

They silently leaned on each other, watching night slowly fall over the town below.

"This is just so awesome," he said quietly.

Hannah sighed, maybe Charley could be more than a friend.

They just sat there a while, arms around each other.

Tom Junior finally poked his head out the door.

"You two oughtta' look like prunes by now, want to get out?" he called.

"Sure, Daddy!" she called.

She looked at Charley, he turned and held her cheek, they kissed again.

"Treat me like this, I'll come by more often," he whispered.

"Bridge building, that's all!" Hannah said with a giggle.

"And Charley Trottel, remember this night next time you talk to your mom, okay?" she said firmly, shaking her finger at him.

"Yes, ma'am."

Chapter 24
Awkward Moments

Aunt Brenda and Charley huddled and planned their moves. Tom Junior rented a truck first-thing Saturday and the fam organized after breakfast to haul stuff to the respective new digs. Chad packed too and planned to head back to Rolla for fall when they finished.

Charley could move in the Jeep.

Aunt Brenda could fill a semi.

Hannah had carried a couple boxes out of the hall, then hoisted them to Chad in the truck when her phone rang: Mark.

"Hi there!" she answered, stepping to one side as Tom Junior came up with another load.

"Hey, I'm in town, tried to call you last night but didn't get an answer. You busy?" he answered.

Ohmigosh, she forgot!

"I am so sorry! Uh, yeah, uh, we had company last night," she replied sheepishly.

"Company, or acquaintance?" Mark asked.

"Either one," she said.

"Understood," he replied with a chuckle. "Did we have a mix-up, thought you knew I planned to drive down."

"Oh, Mark, again, I'm so sorry, I did, I apologize. This has been a crazy week, I've been at the prosecuting attorney's office, the preliminary hearing's coming up, and we're moving my Aunt Brenda today."

"So, could we do lunch at least?"

"Sure, of course, uh, absolutely, I'm in the middle of the move right now, why don't I meet you at the new pizza place, it's just down from your hotel?" she suggested.

"I can see it out my window. Remember, I have Italian in me. Can you be there around noon?"

"Great! Again, my apologies, I truly am sorry," Hannah answered, embarrassed.

Think fast: How to sneak out to see Mark?

She rode over to the storefront downtown with the first load, just down from Rio Bravo. The neighborhood already smelled of fajitas before ten o'clock. Lugging stuff upstairs proved a chore but the sharp-looking apartments in the renovated building impressed her. Aunt Brenda had a one-bedroom directly above her storefront below.

"I should put in one of those firehouse pole things so I could just slide down there every morning," she said, showing off her new place.

Aunt Brenda had no sense of humor: She meant it.

Charley dropped his things in the efficiency three doors down. Its single window had a view of the courthouse. He unpacked what they had picked up at the family office as Tom Junior, Chad and Hannah hopped in the truck cab to drive back to the house.

She had to figure out some way to break off. Oh well, just do it!

"Hey, I have to meet a friend at lunch, gotta' go," she explained as Tom Junior backed into the driveway and stopped. The father winked at his daughter as she walked to her Jeep, adding "have fun."

She drove through town, what to say? Tell me about your divorce? Where do things stand? This could be make-or-break with Mark—and she forgot his visit. Dummy!

Her phone rang and Bluetooth announced "unknown caller." She clicked the steering wheel's button and answered "Hello?"

"Hannah, this is Randy."

She groaned. Charley-Randy-Mark all in one hour.

Not now, Randy, please.

"Hello," she answered painfully.

"Have a minute?" the boy asked.

"Okay," Hannah replied. "What?"

"I wanted to make sure you got my letters."

"Yes."

Silence.

"So what do you say?"

"Say about what?"

"When can we get back together?

Hannah did not want to deal with this, especially as she drove.

"Just a sec'," she answered as she slowed and turned onto a side street and parked.

"Randy, look, I'm driving. We're talking pretty heavy stuff while I'm trying to make sure I don't rear-end some dumb truck."

"I'm sorry, but this is important to me."

The vision of Randy high-fiving a lawyer flashed through her head.

"I'm sorry, I guess I'm not convinced. Has your attorney thought up some slimy trick?" she asked sharply.

"Oh no, trust me!"

Perfect: Randy, you just left yourself wide open.

"That's the problem, Randy, I don't trust you, I can't trust you.

"Can you understand that?"

Silence.

"Yeah, I have a lot to prove, don't I?"

"Yes, you do," she said firmly. "A lot has happened since our junior year, and it has not been good."

"Well, I have more stamps, I'll write more letters. You'll see! I'm sincere, I mean it, I want you back."

Tears started down her cheeks. She grabbed the sleeve of the T-shirt and dabbed her face.

"Randy, do what you think you have to do. I'll do what I have to do.

"But for me, I'm not there yet," she said with a heavy sigh.

"Did I upset you?" he asked.

"Yes!" she answered sharply.

"A few letters and a couple phone calls do not make up for threats, stalking and physical attacks."

"Okay, but I told you I'm sorry, I want to make you happy, I guess I'll try some more," he replied painfully.

"Okay, let's leave it at that. Hey, I need to go," Hannah said, drumming her fingers on the steering wheel.

"Hannah, I... I... I love you," Randy said slowly.

She hit the button and Bluetooth responded with its "call ended."

She dug in the console for a Kleenex. Why? Why now?

Hannah mopped up her face, blew her nose and put the Jeep back in first. Hot, sweaty, tear-stained and in her moving-day grubbies, Mark probably would run for the door when she got there.

But he didn't.

The Cheshire Cat, dimpled chin and all, smiled as she walked in.

Mark had a table ready. He stood to greet her, the restaurant lit up as he grinned, and they embraced. Oh my, forget a suit or blazer, this guy looked great in a Rams T-shirt and jeans. He kissed her sweaty, tear-stained cheek.

"I ordered you a Dr Pepper, that okay?" he asked.

"Perfect, thanks, I'm hot and thirsty from Aunt Brenda's move," she explained. "I have a lot going on."

"Oh, now she's quite the character. What's she up to?" Mark asked.

Hannah explained Aunt Brenda's plans for an "alternative arts" store.

"I have Grandpa Tony, you have Aunt Brenda," Mark said. Lightning burst through the dining room as he smiled at the thought.

They both chuckled.

The waitress brought menus. Here's a good segue, time to talk about families, she thought to herself.

"I guess I don't know much about your family besides your grandfather," Hannah said. "Uh, I'd like a Canadian bacon, maybe some mushrooms too."

"Works for me," Mark said. "I don't know what to say."

"My parents live outside Randall, you know. They retired and bought this A-frame on an acreage down in the Ozarks, just across the line in Arkansas. You'd love it."

He talked more about his folks, a sister in Florida, and some cousins in Michigan he never sees.

This didn't go where Hannah wanted, did she have to press the issue?

"So, has there been someone before me?"

The iridescent smile instantly vaporized, a frown formed as Mark hung his head.

"Yes," he said into the table, "divorced."

"What happened?" she asked, as innocently as she could.

Mark shifted uncomfortably.

"I don't like to talk about all that."

Smiling, confident, extrovert Mark suddenly turned into a silent, withdrawn introvert.

"I guess I'd tell myself mind-you-own-business, Hannah, but I'm kind of involved in it now, I'd like to know," she replied. "It may not change a thing—or it might change everything. It depends."

He grimaced and sighed.

"Sure, right, okay, I need to tell you about it, the relationship seems to be moving along a lot faster than I expected. I like that, but it's very hard," Mark said, staring away from her.

He sat quietly for a moment, then drummed his knuckles on the table and sighed.

"She's from Kenefic, Oklahoma, down near the Red River. Beautiful girl, strawberry blonde with blue eyes, about your height," Mark said, propping his arm on the table and his cheek in his palm, still staring off. "Journalism major, she worked on the student newspaper, came over to the campus armory one afternoon to do a feature story on, you know, isn't it funny—Ha! Ha!—landlocked Oklahoma has Navy ROTC?

"I may have been one of five, a half-dozen, people she talked to, including the detachment commander.

"I don't know, we just hit it off," Mark continued wistfully. "She interviewed me last, I bet we sat there and jabbered an hour. Then the story comes out, it's all about me. There I am in a page-one photo in my midshipman's uniform, up against a big anchor we had in the armory, above this corny headline: 'Sooners Aweigh!'

"Oh, did I get razzed! Wade, you swank!

"I looked her up and said thanks, which led to sushi that night up on Campus Corner. We started dating, I went to her folks' place several weekends and Thanksgiving, we flew up to St. Louis to meet my folks, everything went great.

"We married our senior year at OU, she thought life as a wife of a naval officer and a pilot would be exotic, exciting. Faraway places, strange-sounding names, and she would be there for it all!

Mark sat silently for a moment, then swallowed hard.

"She beamed at my commissioning, her parents drove up to Norman, my parents and Grandpa Tony came down from St. Louis. She didn't think about the months I'd be at sea, and that Navy towns can be pretty dull.

"We moved to Norfolk, she didn't know anyone—nor did I. Okay, that's to be expected that she'd be lonely, but thousands of lonely wives lived around the base. She didn't seem to want to do anything about it, lots of programs for Navy spouses, she just sat at home.

"When I came home after six months at sea, everything turned into a fight, an argument, both of us got frustrated.

Mark sighed again.

"It got easier to go out drinking and partying with the guys, guys who'd been with me every day for weeks, than to spend time with her. I knew them better than I knew her.

"The marriage just did not work," he said, then Mark stopped and swallowed again. "And truth be told, we both got into things with other people that we shouldn't have. I'm ashamed of all that, I know she is too.

"We landed once, excited, I'd been promoted to lieutenant, let's go celebrate! She said, 'So what?' A big deal for me, and she didn't care.

"We separated, Janeen moved to Dallas, got a job with some financial services firm so she could be close to her parents.

"It hit me: Mark, you idiot, what have you done? If I didn't want to lose her, I better change things, even if that meant I had to give up a Navy career. So, I resigned my commission, getting my life straightened out meant more."

He sat quietly and swallowed hard, still staring away.

"I slapped her once."

The personality change shocked Hannah.

"I got the job in St. Louis, I couldn't find a management slot in Dallas.

"But it came too late, I lost her anyway. I cleaned up my life, how do you say it, got right with God? I don't know, but it all came too late."

Mark looked back at Hannah painfully.

"I really am a nice guy, I see my faults. I'm sorry, I guess you don't want to hear about my problems," he added as the waitress walked up with their pizza. "Anyway, that's my side of the story."

"That's alright, everyone has problems, I do too.

"But I need to know, how do I fit in?" Hannah asked sincerely, taking his hand. "Mark, look, we're getting kind of serious. Am I a replacement, someone new—or a temp, a placeholder—until you get her back?"

Mark put down a slice of pizza and leaned back in his chair, shaking his head. He did not smile.

"Hannah, honestly, I don't know, I really don't. I guess that's not fair to you," he said. "I could have made it work if I'd tried harder and sooner. I still hear her shouting that night: 'That's it, I'm through!'

"It left me down in the dumps, now I turned into the lonely one. Thankfully, we don't have kids, the divorce came easily. We text each other now and then, we communicate some, we're friends on Facebook. You know, we tried, it didn't work.

"Then Grandpa Tony, always upbeat, started talking you up.

"Yes, you can thank the grandfathers," Mark said as he doused his pizza with cheese.

"I came down here to visit my folks last Christmas and off he went: 'How's your love life?' I told him not so hot, I'd asked this nice lady at work out a couple times and she turned me down.

"'Markie, my man, she may be a stick o' dynamite, but sounds like she's gotta' wet fuse. Forget her! I gotta' little hottie lined up for you right here in Randall!'"

"I hear your grandfather thinks I'm wonderful," Hannah said as she ate.

"Oh! More than that, if you need someone to do PR, hire him," Mark answered. "I'm sure your grandfather did quite the sales job on your behalf.

"And you know what? Those old guys are right, you really are wonderful."

Mark looked at her but didn't smile.

They both sat quietly, munching.

"Thank you, you're pretty wonderful too. But where do we go from here?" Hannah asked.

"I don't know. My fondest wish? Get back with her, I will be honest about that, and no slight on you, please."

"Understood."

"But maybe we won't, been two years now. I did so much to hurt her, I changed too late. And, well, she hurt me as well. You know, your sins will find you out, that sort of thing."

"That's certainly true," Hannah said, thinking of Randy.

"Hannah, you are really a delightful young lady," Mark said, lighting the room finally. "I enjoy time with you, I think you know that. These trips down here come hard, lots of windshield time, but it's worth it to be with you. You're fun to be around, you're smart, you have a wonderful family.

"I know you've had a tough summer, I don't know everything that's happened, but you're still the optimist. Stay that way.

"But me? Maybe I haven't decided yet, maybe I'd like to see you some more, maybe I need to think about things some more," Mark said, suddenly quiet again. "If things don't work out with my ex, I could get really, really serious about the two of us."

Hannah sat, listening.

"I've changed."

Echo! Echo!

Oh, had she heard enough of that line.

"Okay, maybe," she said quietly. "Let see how things work out, what's best for both of us. I like you, I really do, maybe it would work.

"You know about my, how do you call him, 'acquaintance?' Maybe I need to make some decisions too," she said seriously. "But with the court case, I have a lot happening, I'm not ready to make a big, life-changing commitment with anyone right now. I want to finish college first. I want to wait on a serious deal until after I graduate."

"Understood," Mark said. "Could we, maybe, drive down so you could meet my parents next time I'm in town?"

Hannah looked at him. Mark looked at her, his eyebrows up with a "Please?" expression on his face.

"Okay, maybe it's time for that," she replied.

"I have to ask: Are there more guys? I'm surprised there are only two men interested in you. You are quite the attractive young woman, you'd be a catch for any guy," Mark said.

"Let's not get into numbers," Hannah said, turning back to her pizza.

Chapter 25
Eyes

Hannah's phone rang, the prosecutor.

"Nine o'clock, September fourth for the preliminary hearing, the docket's out," she heard her attorney say. "Do we need to go over anything again?"

"I don't think so."

"I'll call you last, after the police, Mrs. Dawson, your dad and Mr. Trottel. I'll enter the medical records for you and Mr. Smith. Things will be cut-and-dried on our side, but be ready for anything from the defense attorney, I've heard he's a loose cannon," the prosecutor added. "Just answer his questions, yes or no, don't ramble, don't speculate, remember everything I told you. All we have to do at this point is prove to the judge there's enough evidence for a trial. We don't need to convict him."

"Okay, thanks," and they hung up.

The Labor Day weekend turned into a blur. Aunt Brenda set the grand opening of her shop, A Different View, that Saturday and asked her niece to station herself at the front door to greet customers "warmly, say hello and stuff like that. People like you, they'll want to come in and buy things," her aunt explained.

Hannah got lost on that one, why would a friendly girl convince people to purchase a hookah, Thai fisherman's pants, or a book of Allen Ginsberg poetry?

Oh well, happy to help, family's family. Charley came down from upstairs and they chatted as they waited for customers to wander in.

Randall's coat-and-tie mayor came by promptly at nine o'clock, opening time, to present Aunt Brenda, wearing an "Adlai Stevenson for President" T-shirt, with a city council proclamation, announcing the City of Randall's official "A Different View Day," with all honors, festivities, recognitions, perquisites, and appurtenances thereto.

The *Randall Ledger* photographer snapped a photo of the mayor and Aunt Brenda as they shook hands in front of a beaded curtain. She stood so her pelican tattoo showed.

"Where'd your aunt get this stuff?" Charley asked, looking around at the eclectic merchandise. "Here's a Happy Buddha with Confucius, how many Buddhists live in Randall, Missouri?"

"I have no idea, ask her," Hannah said, breaking off the conversation to greet an elderly couple with a cheery "Good morning!"

Business proved slow until numerous diners finished lunch at Rio Bravo and wandered in, toothpicks at work, to walk off their enchiladas as they roamed the aisles to look things over.

Between Inca flute CDs blasting loudly from multiple speakers and enough incense to hide the whole town in a London fog, there could be no doubt that "Randall's never seen anything like this" as one woman put it, as she walked out with a Frank Zappa poster. A bunch of Indian saris vaporized—the day's sales hit—after Aunt Brenda posted a big SALE! sign on one end of the rack.

Charley thumbed through a file of used LP's until he found ZZ Top's *Eliminator* album.

"Finally, something I've heard," he said, smiling, showing the disk to Hannah. "Can I find a record player?"

"I think she has one marked down, over there next to the scented candles," Hannah said with a smirk.

Outdoorsy Hannah liked the Ansel Adams prints, maybe she'd get one for her apartment in Columbia—would she ever got back there? *Clearing Winter Storm*, oh my, the clouds over Yosemite, beautiful! She thought of the Girl Scout camp she did there. Better yet, maybe Aunt Brenda would give her one after working all day—for free.

One long-haired young man came in, asking if the store had copies of *Das Kapital* by Karl Marx for sale?

"Right over there, next to Hitler's *Mein Kampf*," Charley answered without blinking. Hannah ran between the shelves as she stifled laughter.

Six o'clock, closing time, customers still packed the aisles. Hannah made it a point to flip the OPEN sign around on the door but it did little to stem the flow of curious shoppers. Things slowed by seven, she finally locked the door and turned to help Aunt Brenda close.

Charley had hung around all day too, Hannah noticed.

"Want to come upstairs? Dinner's on me, peanut butter sandwich or ramen noodles," he said.

"Either would be fine, I have so much smoke up my nose I can't taste anything," she answered with a cough as she pounded her chest.

What does a girl wear to court?

The prosecutor recommended she dress nicely, "We want the judge to know you're respectable, not riff-raff," she explained. That stretched Hannah, not that she thought of herself as riff-raff, mind you, but she favored denim jeans or shorts below flowery tops.

She had camo in her closet.

The girl dug back on the rack and found that springy-pink dress she last wore to Grandpa Tom and Cla—uh, Grandma—Claire's wedding. She found the high heels she wore that day, she couldn't remember wearing heels since.

Okay, maybe to the church's Christmas Eve service, everyone dresses up for that.

Makeup?

Usually an afterthought, she of the what-you-see-is-what-you-get philosophy when it comes to beauty. But this morning, Hannah spent extra time working on foundation, eye liner and shadow, and lipstick. Oh, and an ever-so-slight touch of rouge. No false eyelashes, no sir, not on Hannah Bentley!

She stepped in front of her full-length mirror to check the results. She wanted to look good for the judge, and, well, for Charley.

Hand on her hip, turning this way and that: very feminine, a real looker, quite the attractive young woman! Her eyes smiled as she winked at herself.

Tom Junior, in a not-unusual-for-him suit, and Judy left early to be sure and get there when court began at nine. The attorney had told Hannah, "We won't get to you until at least eleven, no need to rush."

The first day of the fall court term meant the usually listless Limestone County Courthouse turned busy, nearby parking spaces filled up. Hannah had to park down past Bea's Hen House and walk a couple blocks. She couldn't help but think of standing on that sidewalk three months earlier when Randy snuck up behind her. She could still hear the scary "YOU'RE MINE, HANNAH!" in her head.

How much had happened since then?

Her feet hurt, she wobbled a bit in her heels, by the time she got to the hallway bench outside the big wooden, double doors beneath an official looking "Circuit Court" sign. She arrived just as a skinny bailiff came out and loudly called "THOMAS BENTLEY!" She mentally dubbed him "Barney Fife."

"Hey, Daddy!" she called as she walked up and he stood to go in. They gave each other a kiss and a bear hug as he disappeared through the courtroom door.

"Pray for me, Ladybug," her father said.

"They're running late, imagine that," Judy told her daughter, glumly, as they sat down. Just then Charley came down the hall in a gray-pinstripe suit.

It hit her: They sat right here when the two of them worked things out—maybe—a few days earlier.

"Don't you look nice!" she called as Charley walked up. "That the suit you bought at Goodwill?"

The big boy smiled down at her.

"No, brand new!" he answered.

"So I have to ask, do I look elegant today?" she said with a wink.

Charley leaned back and squinted at her, head to toe with a playful "Hmmm..."

"Yes, sophisticated, less cute-more elegant!"

"Thank you!"

Charley sat next to her on the bench and they hugged, like in the hot tub. Best buds: They'd get through this.

The big clock down the hall ticked as they quietly watched an odd assortment of humanity shuffle past them.

"This place beats a bus station for local color," Judy whispered to her daughter. "Where do these people live, in caves?"

Noon came and went, the courtroom behind them finally emptied as the judge called lunch recess. Tom Junior came out, rolling his eyes. "Buckle your seatbelt when you get on the stand, that defense attorney's a doozy."

He shared "highlights and lowlights," as he put it, while they ate sandwiches in the crowded courthouse snack bar in the basement, then headed back upstairs for the afternoon.

They'd sat for a few minutes when Barney Fife came out and with authority called "CHARLES TROTTEL!"

"Wish me luck," he said as he stood.

"I'll do better than that," Hannah said as she stood, wobbling slightly, and kissed his cheek; lipstick!

"Thanks," he replied, then walked toward the bailiff.

Hannah surfed her phone and nervously checked the big clock in the hall. Two o'clock came and went, still no Charley. Three o'clock passed, the boredom made her sleepy. She yawned.

The door swung open and out came Charley with a loud sigh.

"That must be what a colonoscopy's like," he said as he sat down on the bench with a tired thud. Just then, Barney Fife reappeared, loudly calling "HANNAH BENTLEY!"

"Here we go," she said quietly. Judy and Charley both took her hands and smiled at her.

She walked toward the bailiff who sharply advised "follow me!"

The courtroom held maybe fifty people, family and friends, along with the usual assortment of folks who make hearings a hobby. And there sat Grandpa Tom, a pleasant surprise.

Stares.

She felt every eye in the courtroom, including the gray-haired judge's, as she, the victim, walked up the aisle—except for Randy. He sat next to his public defender in an ill-fitting suit and didn't look up from the table in front of him. The bailiff swung the bar's gate open and she stopped even with the prosecutor.

"Step-forward-please," Barney demanded in a rapid staccato.

"Raise-your-right-hand-do-you-swear-that-the-testimony-you-are-about-to-give-is-the-truth-the-whole-truth-and-nothing-but-the-truth-so-help-you-God?"

"I do."

"State-your-full-name."

"Hannah Judith Bentley."

"Please-be-seated-on-the-witness-stand."

Barney smugly stepped over and stood by the empty jury box as Hannah nervously stepped up beside the judge's bench and sat down in a large, wooden chair.

The hundred eyes continued to drill holes in her, except Randy's. He rocked back and forth, like that day at visitation.

Tension.

The prosecutor stood, coughed, and picked up a legal pad.

"Thank you, Miss Bentley. I know this isn't easy."

"No, ma'am," Hannah said just above a whisper.

And off they went.

They had rehearsed the questions and answers multiple times and Hannah mentally ticked off each in her mind. Maybe this wouldn't be so bad after all.

All went well until the prosecutor came to the one about, "Did Mr. Smith accost you on the sidewalk outside a restaurant, as you waited to eat dinner, on the evening of June first?"

"Objection!" the defense attorney said, springing from his chair. "The prosecutor asks the witness to speculate, to state her opinion, on an incidental encounter between the two parties that has no relation to these charges."

"Overruled, remember, preliminary," the judge replied, looking back at the prosecutor. "Proceed."

It rattled Hannah, she took a deep breath.

"Yes."

Then the questions got to the scary part: the night Randy attacked. The painful seconds, the struggle, her ripped blouse, the blood, the horrific terror—everything flooded back in her mind.

"Had you invited Mr. Smith to come to the office?" the attorney asked.

Hannah's hands shook, she covered her mouth.

"I'm, I'm sorry, could you repeat the question?" she mumbled. She felt tears welling in the corners of her eyes.

"Had you invited Mr. Smith to come to the office?"

"N-No!" she stuttered.

"Young lady, there are tissues in front of you," the judge said.

She pulled one out of the box and dabbed at her eyes.

The questions continued.

"How did the defendant know you worked there?"

"I don't know."

"Had you communicated with him in any way since he accosted you on the sidewalk?"

"No."

"Can you say you avoided the defendant?"

"Yes, definitely."

Hannah managed to get a grip on herself. The prosecutor winked at her as she continued.

"Were you aware at the time of the assault that Mr. Trottel had come in the building?"

"No."

"Objection!" Randy's attorney said, bouncing up again. "I believe we will show Mr. Trottel had a major and provoking role in this incident."

"Counsel, you'll have your time, overruled," the judge said, nodding at the prosecutor. "Proceed."

If the defense attorney wanted to rattle Hannah, it worked. Her hands shook.

She took a deep breath. Oh my, what will it be like when *he* starts to ask questions?

On they went. All these questions, step by step, took a few minutes in the prosecuting attorney's office, now they stretched seemingly to hours. Hannah glanced at Randy, who still sat staring down at the table, rocking slowly. His attorney scribbled furiously on a legal pad after every answer.

She had never seen Randy in a suit. His poorly knotted tie hung crookedly, caught on a shirt button.

The prosecutor finally finished, looked at the judge and added "no further questions, your honor" and sat down.

"Counsel?" the judge said, turning to Randy's lawyer.

Oh no, here it comes.

Randy and his attorney began heated whispering to each other. Hannah made out Randy saying "not that!" His attorney became agitated, slicing the air with his hand as he whispered to Randy and he exclaimed something about, "doesn't work."

"Do you wish to cross-examine the witness?" the judge asked.

"Just a moment, your honor," the defense attorney responded.

The intense whispers continued. "Are you sure?" the lawyer asked loud enough to be heard.

"Counsel, we need to move along," the judge said, prodding.

Randy's lawyer leaned back and threw up his hands in surrender.

"Your honor, may we approach the bench?" he said with a loud sigh.

"Certainly, come forward, and will the prosecutor come forward?"

Randy, slouching and looking at the floor, shuffled in front of the judge, standing next to the two lawyers. It made Hannah queasy to sit just feet from him.

Barney Fife still stood by the jury box, thumbs in his belt. He didn't appear much bigger than her, a lot of help he would be if anything happened.

The defense attorney shook his head.

"Your honor," the lawyer said slowly, "my client wishes to plead guilty to all charges," in a "what's the use?" tone.

The judge sat back, surprised. Hannah's jaw dropped, a titter went through the small crowd. She looked back to see Grandpa Tom sitting upright, surprised, with his hands on his cane. She noted Barney Fife's shock.

"Young man, do you understand what you're doing?" the judge asked slowly.

"Yes sir, uh, your honor, sir," Randy replied, looking up for the first time.

"You understand that you would waive your right to a trial, and the opportunity to present any and all evidence in your defense?" the judge asked, puzzled.

"Yes sir, uh, your honor, sir," Randy repeated.

"You understand, Mr. Smith, that what you ask constitutes something highly unusual? We have due process to assure you have the right to a fair consideration of your side of the story—and if you do this you will not have that opportunity?"

"Yeah, uh, your honor, sir," Randy said with a nod.

"Counsel, have you explained the result of what he wishes to do?" the judge asked.

"As best I can, your honor. He's emphatic."

"Has the prosecutor offered you any sort of immunity or clemency for this plea?" the judge asked.

The question stumped Randy, who cocked his head, puzzled.

"No sir, your honor, sir. I haven't talked to nobody, if that's what you mean," he replied.

The judge sat for a moment, lost in thought.

"Mr. Smith, do you wish to have new counsel?" he asked.

The question puzzled Randy, who stood quietly shaking his head.

"Do you want another lawyer, another public defender?" the judge asked.

"Nah, he's cool, sir, your honor, sir."

Snickers went through the crowd as the judge scowled.

"Mr. Smith, I'll give you one, final opportunity to change your mind and we will proceed with this hearing. If not, I'll end things now and we'll move forward to sentencing, based on your guilty pleas. Are you very certain this is what you want to do?"

Hannah sat stunned, her mouth open.

What had the idiot cooked up? What rabbit would Randy's lawyer pull out of his hat?

She glanced at the prosecutor in front of her, who shrugged an "I don't know."

"No, uh, yes, I mean I do, your honor, that's, that's what I want."

The judge shook his head, picked up his gavel and banged it.

"Let the record show that the defendant pleads guilty to all charges, that he has been advised of his ability to continue his defense, by both the court and legal counsel, and he has waived that right.

"Bailiff, please return the defendant to custody."

The judge banged his gavel again and announced "court's adjourned."

Barney Fife shouted "all rise!" as he headed for Randy. "Come along," the bailiff demanded as he took the big defendant's arm.

The judge stood to leave and the little audience behind the rail stood.

It erupted in loud chatter as the judge went into his chambers and closed the door.

Randy lunged.

Hannah gasped and recoiled as she put her arm up. Randy hugged the rail around the witness stand, leaning toward her, inches from her face.

"*Now* do you believe me?" he shouted, pleading.

"I've changed, really, I did this for *you*! If you want it, then you can have it! I just want us to be together again, whatever you want, it's yours!"

Hannah sat looking at him, gasping, speechless.

The bailiff grabbed his shoulder.

"I love you!" Randy said, looking back as the bailiff pulled him away.

Absolute, total shock: Hannah felt like she'd grabbed a live wire.

"What just happened?" the prosecutor asked as she rushed toward the witness stand.

"A poor, mixed-up guy tried to do the right thing," Hannah said, shaking her head.

Chapter 26
Bejeebers

Hippo.

Hannah curled around her chubby little stuffed friend in a daze as she stared out her bedroom window at the patio and the woods.

No lawyer-induced trick: He meant it, Randy Smith, the doofus, the thug, the jerk, the criminal, he really meant it.

The big oaf threw away any chance he had to beat the rap or plea-bargain to cut his sentence, and he did it in a way to maximize the impact. He did it right in front of everybody, most of all—her.

There could be no doubt.

Randy, for certain, had changed. Maybe that parabolic Bible had done some good?

All the celebratory handshakes, embraces and greetings in the hallway after the hearing rang hollow. It felt odd to get hugged by a prosecutor. Tom Junior offered to take everyone to Rio Bravo for dinner. No thanks, daddy, I just want to go home.

Yes, Randy would go to prison for what he did, justice had been served. Good riddance.

But her Randy problem had not gone away, only changed.

Could she love Randy again?

Maybe.

Would she love Randy again?

No.

Okay, well, maybe if an angel appeared at the foot of her bed some night. Wait: she *had* seen an angel, or something, out there in the woods as she desperately struggled back to the Jeep with Charley. If he, she—whatever angels are—hadn't shown up that day, the K-9 unit or the horse patrol might have found her crying over Charley's cold body.

Thank you, Lord.

But Randy?

Well come to think of it, she did hear voices, angelic or whatever, right there in her bedroom.

"Okay girl, this is getting spooky-weird," she mumbled to herself.

"Randy? Charley? What about Mark?" she said out loud to her empty bedroom.

Nothing.

Hannah turned and looked at the stack of unopened letters her mother left on her dresser. They loomed at her, scary, very real, and the pile grew steadily. As promised, Randy wrote every day, so she always received two on Tuesdays—one for Sunday and one for Monday. Hannah could not bring herself to open any more.

The image of a contrite Randy, in her face in the courtroom, beaten, frantic, afraid, shouting *"Now* do you believe me?" replaced the horror of him walking, sneering, toward her that awful night in the office.

Both scared the bejeebers out of her.

Hippo got another hug. Why couldn't they just roll back time, before that hayride, and start over? Up to that moment, it had worked. Yeah, she liked Randy, she really did, her first teenage crush.

Randy and Hannah—Randall High's all-everything couple, until....

All her fault? Did she overreact that night?

So instead of slapping him, she could have just grabbed his hand and quietly said, "Randy, don't do that." Then maybe she could have remained some kind of positive force to set him straight, to help him change his skanky ways.

Then maybe he would've had a scholarship to, say, Alabama, he'd be all-SEC by now, NFL scouts would run his name through computers to plot draft strategies—and she'd be Mrs. Randy Smith, WAG of a famous football player.

Yeah, maybe.

But on the other hand, when Randy got slapped, he could have politely said, "I'm sorry, excuse me," and that would've been that. They would have gone on lying next to each other in the hay, looking up at the stars.

They both acted like the dumb kids they were. She grew up and Randy did too, eventually.

Would he have sucked her down while they dated for a year or two? Would goody two-shoes Hannah Bentley have become just another "slutty girl"—his term—hanging around super-stud Randy?

What if she started to do things she didn't want; persuasion?

Okay, just this once….

Maybe not.

After all, why her?

Chunky little tomboy Hannah Bentley?

What did he see in her?

Randall High had prettier. Dozens of swooning girls would be more than willing to go along with stuff she would never, ever let herself do.

Some girls keep score: "Guess who I did last night?"

Why did Randy still chase her?

"You're different," he told her.

You got that right, Randy.

Five years had gone by, Hannah had become an adult. She could not, she would not, go back.

"Face it: You have three guys after you, not two," she mumbled to herself. "What are you going to do about it?"

Chapter 27
Parents

Hannah finished a paper for an online class, dull, but it felt great to get back into the college swing, even if it meant sitting at a computer in her bedroom. Her phone rang as "Mark" appeared on its screen: FaceTime!

"Hi, there!" she answered warmly and Mark's smile appeared on her screen.

"I hear congratulations are in order."

"I guess, what's new with you?"

"I'd like to come down this weekend, thought maybe you'd enjoy a drive out in the Ozarks, you know, meet the parents. See them?" he asked, pointing the phone at a portrait of a pleasant-looking, sixtyish couple.

Meet the parents? Already?

"Sure, uh, we can do that," Hannah replied. "What's the plan?"

"How about same as usual?"

"By the way, my aunt's moved into her apartment so the Bentley Hilton has space available if you'd rather stay here."

"Let me think about that," Mark said with a chuckle. "Gee, I won't get points but I'll get more of your mom's coffee. Let's see, mom wins!"

"Okay, see you Friday night!"

Charley?

Oh boy, this continued to get more and more complexer. Is that a word? Well, she'd look him up sometime.

The Grand Cherokee pulled in Friday night, Judy held dinner for Mark. Everyone had a great conversation as they ate. He, too, found the flowers on the guest room wall "different."

Saturday morning, they headed out with a stop at Hickory Bough, "no telling what my grandfather's got himself into now," Mark said. The smile lit up again.

Tony rolled backwards through the dayroom as they came in.

"About time you got here!" he called. "Let's go over and straighten out Tom."

"What's my grandfather done now?" Hannah asked.

"Oh, thinks he's a big shot! Some movie agent called, they're workin' a script. I wanna' make sure they get Jack Nicholson to play me."

The trio headed down C Hall to find Grandpa Tom and Grandma Claire talking as he scribbled on a legal pad.

"Figuring out how many bucks you'll make on the boffo box office?" Tony asked as they rolled in C 8.

"Oh, hi," Claire responded. "No, new topics for the show. Couple of writers plan to drive down from St. Louis next week and we'll record a new run, we do a month at a time, about two-dozen."

"So where do you record them?" Mark asked.

"Family Fellowship out on the bypass, where my kids go to church," Grandpa Tom explained. "They have a great A/V set-up, best in the area, they make a little money off us for studio time. We tape our parts, they upload 'em on Dropbox to St. Louis, and the crew there mixes them down. Then, weekly packages get bounced off satellites to all the stations and networks. Ain't technology grand?"

"The technology changes but the foundation stays the same: faith, family, friends, fellowship, future," Claire added firmly.

"Hey, good stuff!" Tony replied. "You guys could become famous talkin' like that."

They chatted for a while and Mark finally mentioned "we need to go, we plan to run out to my folks' house."

"Oh, good!" Tony replied brightly as he sat up in his wheelchair. "My daughter can help pick out the dress!"

Hannah covered her face.

A beautiful drive: Now she understood why Charley acted nervously on that Friday afternoon four, long months ago: What to expect? Will they like me?

It turned into a glorious day.

Mark's parents proved sweet, older than her folks. Mark's father knew Bentley Hardware well from his years with a St. Louis plumber. She impressed the old couple with her outdoor prowess—without details, you know, about last June's fiasco.

A large portrait of a younger Mark in his Navy ensign's uniform hung on the living room wall to one side of the fireplace. Hannah couldn't help but notice a light, bare rectangle of the same size on the wall, with a nail hole inside it, next to Mark's picture. A photo of someone, and she could figure who, had once hung there. A model of a Navy plane sat on the fireplace mantel.

On the opposite side of the fireplace hung two more photos, one of Mark's sister—with that same big smile—holding a toddler, and another of their handsome son-in-law. Can smiles be hereditary? Mrs. Wade energetically described a recent trip to Florida "to see that wonderful grandbaby!"

Lunch on the patio—with a gorgeous view of the mountains and Bull Shoals Lake—proved delightful, and the couple bragged on their son incessantly. Lieutenant Junior Grade Mark Wade personally had pulled Saddam out of that hole, according to their version of the war.

They chatted all afternoon as Mark's dad absentmindedly watched the Arkansas Razorbacks plaster somebody on TV. Grandpa Tony and his antics provided lots of laughs.

"Just imagine having him for a father!" Mark's mother said with a laugh.

Hannah found the Wades' big A-frame delightful with its knotty pine walls and floor-to-ceiling windows. Sandwiches for dinner, some polite hugs, and time came to drive back to Randall as the sun set.

What sweet people, what a lovely home! The Wades made her think of her own family.

Everyone waved as Mark backed out and drove down the gravel driveway through the trees.

"Well, did I pass?" Hannah asked quietly as they headed out.

"With flying colors!" Mark answered. "I bumped into dad in the kitchen as he topped off his iced tea during a commercial. He winked at me and gave me a thumbs-up. You're in!"

Back home well after dark, Hannah came out of her bathroom in her nightshirt, ready for bed, ready to curl around hippo. She noticed a MISSED CALL note on her phone: Grandpa Tom. He might not be up still but she called anyway.

"You rang?" she asked as he answered.

"Yes, sweetheart," he replied. "What on earth happened out there today? I've never seen Tony so excited. I thought he would jump out of that wheelchair and run down the hall—a miracle healing!"

"So they liked me?"

"Darling, like I said, Tony nearly did cartwheels."

She drove downtown late Sunday afternoon, after Mark left, to see Charley. She parked in front of A Different View and trudged upstairs. Aunt Brenda had some odd CD of wind chimes turned up loud. She knocked on Charley's door and the boy sleepily opened to her.

"Oh, hi," he said, "been reading, come in?"

"Sure," she replied.

"Spartan" came to mind as she looked around the little efficiency. He had a small table, two chairs, a love seat, a bed and a chest of drawers. Everything shined, spiffy and new, but no pictures hung on the wall, a dirty plate and glass sat in the sink—a single guy's apartment.

"What's new?" Charley asked as they sat at the table.

"Bunch of stuff, I'm thinking we need to get you a phone," she replied. "It's awkward to have to drive over here just to talk."

"Sure," Charley replied. "I've got a little money saved, can we do that now?"

"Let's go!" she replied.

They headed out to locate a phone store, any phone store, open late Sunday.

He found something, then they stopped for burgers.

"Hey," Charley said as they ate, "we need to go to Neosho, you can meet mom."

Hannah sighed.

"I've *met* your mom," she replied grimly.

"Oh, yeah, right," Charley said, squirting more ketchup on his fries. "Well, we can try to start off on a new foot."

More parents?

Next up: Randy will want to… no, please, Lord, not that. She visualized graying, doper Deadheads.

"Okay, I guess we can go next weekend. Tell you what, let's teach you to drive a stick, the trip to Neosho will let you practice— and I won't have to do all the driving!"

"Sure, but where?"

"How about the Bentley Hardware parking lot? It should be empty on a Sunday, except for a certain Lexus I can think of, and it sat in our carport when I left the house."

They turned in the lot's gate, stopped and swapped seats.

Charley climbed in the driver's side, scooted the seat back, then frowned as he adjusted the rearview mirror.

"How can you see, the mirror's down there?"

"Because *I'm* down there, silly!" she laughed. "I'm not six-foot-whatever!

"Okay, push the clutch in, the gears are in an H-pattern, first—up and to the left. Give it a little gas as you let out on the pedal," Hannah explained.

Charley tried with just a mild jerk-jerk-jerk, then shifted into second.

"Hey, it's like an organ!" he said with enthusiasm. "No big deal!"

"Only a musician," she thought.

Charley quickly caught the hang of it, they cruised Randall until well after dark, Charley shifted as smooth as silk at every stop sign and light. They drove along the bypass when the Jeep went "DING!" and the low-fuel light came on.

"Let me buy you some gas."

"Well, if you want."

"I want!" he replied. "This makes me feel like such a guy! I'll blow off college and drive a truck!"

Hannah burst out laughing. She had rarely seen Charley so talkative, so chipper.

"Not if you want me around, I want you home every night!"

"Oh, I could get one of those sleeper cab things, you'll be right there behind me. We can spend the night together at every truck stop in the country!"

"Those things may be bigger than your apartment!" she chuckled.

"Probably," he said brightly as he pulled in a station.

Charley got serious, the banter ended.

"That's crucial, will you be around?"

They stared at each other.

"Only if you want me," she said softly, surprised at his change.

"I do."

He leaned over the console and kissed her.

Hannah kissed back like she meant it, and she did.

She had kissed Mark like she meant it, and she did.

She remembered the time she kissed Randy like she meant it, and she did—then.

She sat back with a blank look on her face, which puzzled Charley.

He looked at her for a moment, forced a weak grin, then mumbled "be right back" as he stepped out to pump the gas.

She leaned on the door's armrest and thought as she listened to the gas whir into the tank. "Girl, your cup runneth over," she whispered.

Hannah buzzed by Charley's apartment first thing Saturday morning with a sack—still warm—from Donut Heaven and a Thermos of Mother Bentley's coffee—light cream, no sugar, what Charley liked. She beeped and Charley came down the stairs two at a time with an overnight bag.

"Hi, you want to drive?"

"Sure" Charley replied, as she jumped out and skipped around to the passenger side.

Off they went.

They polished off the donuts and coffee amid lively talk and satellite radio.

"I know you'll be disappointed when you see where she lives," he explained grimly as he edged into the stream of traffic headed for Oklahoma and beyond on Interstate 44. "You said a while back I'll be a success someday. I don't know, but remember: This is where I'm *from*, not where I'm *going*."

"Okay."

The tree-shaded mobile home park sat at the edge of town, off Interstate 49. It sported a collection of trailers that ranged from gleaming, showpiece-new, with immaculate flower beds surrounded by golf-green lawns, to ramshackle, with empty beer cans by their doors and dead cars on blocks, partially hidden by weeds.

Charley slowed and turned at one that leaned toward the ramshackle. A dirty, older Pontiac sat in front of the Jeep as he parked. It had an Illinois tag.

"Here we are," he said flatly. They grabbed their bags and Hannah followed him in. She felt a tingle of adventure, she'd never been in a mobile home.

"Hi, Mom," he announced as he opened the door and they came in. There sat Kristi Trottel behind a computer, cigarette in hand, bored.

"You'll have to sleep on the couch," the mother said, waving her cigarette, her only greeting to Hannah. The room reeked of stale smoke, a half-empty whiskey bottle and empty beer cans sat on the kitchen counter, dirty dishes overflowed the sink. Piles of papers and old magazines covered much of the sofa. A filled trash bag sat by the door on a dirty, orange shag carpet.

Hannah caught a faint whiff of that burning-rope odor she smelled in the dorm her freshman year. Do people this woman's age smoke pot?

"How, how do you do?" Hannah said politely, nodding.

"Are you ever gonna' go back to school?" Kristi said sharply to her son, ignoring Hannah.

"I'm taking classes online, we didn't get the hearing over until a couple weeks ago."

Charley stepped over to his mother and hugged her. She didn't move.

"Working?" Charley asked.

"Nah, just catchin' up paperwork. I passed my quota this week and I want to make damn sure I have everything to prove it to those SOBs. I could use a bonus. Those tightwads ship more and more work off to those buck-a-day coolies in India, that way they can get away with paying me less."

He nodded, then turned to Hannah.

"Want to see my room and the keyboard?" he asked.

"Sure."

They went down the narrow hall in the dark, thanks to a burned-out bulb, and Charley opened the door to the mobile home's middle bedroom. Spare and plain, but everything sat in perfect order, immaculate, in contrast to the disarray elsewhere.

The tidy room, Charley's tidy room, spoke volumes. A big Thompson Chain Reference Bible sat on the nightstand.

"Hard to believe, six months since I've been in here," he said with a shrug.

Hannah nodded.

"It's been a long summer," she said blankly

"And there, ta-da, my keyboard!" he said proudly with a wave. Usually dour Charley seemed excited.

"We can have a little concert later, have to keep it low. Mom doesn't care for it."

Hmmm, mom doesn't care for much of anything, Hannah thought to herself.

This woman bothered her.

She yelled at a sick Hannah in the hospital.

Her son hasn't been home in half a year, he brings a girl with him—and first off she barks, "You'll have to sleep on the couch."

And the clutter, and the dirt! Ugh!

Neat freak Judy Bentley, nor her daughter, would stand for this. Dirt at a campsite's one thing, but in a living room? No! Hannah wanted to find a mop and a vacuum and go to work, but that might not be well received by the resident.

How on earth could this depressed, and depressing, woman produce such a wonderful son? Hannah feared this would seem a very long visit—even if they left at lunch.

The pair went back in the living room, just as Charley's mom took the butt of the cigarette she'd been smoking and used it to light another. She took a deep drag and puffed a blue cloud.

"I guess I scared the crap outta' ya' at the hospital," she said, turning to Hannah. "Everything left me kinda' upset. Looks like you two get along okay."

"Yes, ma'am," Hannah said with a grimace. "We all got upset."

Kristi hacked with a loud cough.

"Mom, again, it just happened," Charley said, clearing the sofa so he and Hannah could sit. "No one's to blame, Hannah's quite the outdoorswoman."

Kristi brightened, then took another drag on her cigarette.

"Is that a fact? You mean you hike and stuff?" she asked, exhaling the smoke through her nose. She hacked again.

"Yes, ma'am, not as much since college. Biggest hike I've done went through the Swiss Alps."

"They have that nice trail in Rock Creek Park, along the Potomac, I used to walk that," the mother said.

No!

"Potomac," as in the Washington, D.C., Potomac?

Grandma Claire's warning came back.

Maybe she should make a run for it, forget this whole thing, throw herself at Mark: Take me!

She could hide in a dumpster and call her dad to come get her.

She took a deep breath.

"So, uh, you lived in Washington?" Hannah asked innocently.

"Yeah," came the answer as Charley's mom flicked ash off her cigarette on the filthy carpet.

"I got your hospital bill," Kristi said, changing the subject. "Lucky for us I have insurance with this gig I'm doin' now, otherwise I'd be in the poor house."

"I'm glad it worked out for you," Hannah said quietly.

"He's expensive, and that hospital bill didn't help," the mom answered as she pointed at her son.

How to make conversation? Be pleasant, think!

"Uh, Charley tells me the two of you have moved several times," Hannah said. "I guess you've lived in some interesting places."

"Yeah," came the reply.

Silence.

"Do you like Neosho? Seems like a nice town."

"Yeah."

Silence.

"Do you travel with your work?"

"Nah."

Keep trying, Hannah.

"So, uh, do you own this mobile home?"

"Rent."

"Uh, you have any hobbies?"

"Nope."

So much for conversation. Apparently Charley and his mom had one thing in common: they didn't talk much.

Hannah glowered at Charley with a "Help me!" look.

He caught it.

"Hannah wants to hear me play this afternoon, do you mind?"

"Nah, get me somethin' to eat first," Kristi answered.

"Sure, that pizza place still over by the college?"

"How should I know?"

"Let me see if I can find it on my phone."

"When did you get a phone?" his mother snapped, sitting up. "Am I gonna' have to pay for it?"

"Last Sunday, no. I made a little money this summer, I work for Hannah's dad."

"Okay, guess you can keep it."

"Here!" Charley said, showing mom the screen. "I'll text an order, be back in a bit."

He got up and Hannah followed.

They got in the Jeep as Hannah noted grimly, "This is not going well."

"Actually, it's going very well," Charley answered brightly. "She likes you!"

Hannah shook her head, "How can you tell?"

"She has not yelled at you once!"

Chapter 28
Randall Babylon

Another week's worth of study and online classes, so good to be back in the college groove! Mark had called, they'd talked for an hour Wednesday night. He wanted to come down again.

Sure.

He pulled in the driveway Friday night, right on time. "Punctual" defined the guy. Judy cooked a big breakfast Saturday, and they decided to head out to Hickory Bough to see Tom, Claire, and—of course—Tony.

"I noticed your Jeep's not here," Mark commented as he backed out.

"Yeah, loaned it to a friend," Hannah replied quietly.

"A friend, or an acquaintance?" Mark asked with a wink.

She pursed her lips.

"Both."

Mark sat quietly as the gate opened.

"Perhaps you'll need to make some decisions soon?" he asked.

Hannah sighed.

"Guess that works both ways," she said, turning to Mark with a weak smile.

He grinned at her but didn't flash the toothy smile.

"Yes, you're right."

Grandpa Tom and Grandma Claire sat glumly with large, softcover books in their laps stamped "DRAFT 1" in red as Mark and Hannah strolled in.

"Good morning!" Mark greeted them as the smile glowed.

"Ah, the happy couple! Hired the preacher yet?" Tony chirped as he wheeled up behind Mark and Hannah, huffing and puffing.

"Saw you in the dayroom, not as fast as you youngsters!"

Tony, Mark and Hannah chatted briefly until they noticed Tom and Claire sat quietly—too quietly. Grandpa Tom hadn't stood with his usual "Look who's here!"

"What's wrong?" Hannah asked.

"We finished reading the movie script, the biopic, this morning," Tom said glumly, his arms crossed.

"We don't like it," Grandma Claire added firmly, drumming her fingers on the book.

"Not what you expected?" Mark asked.

"It would get rated R, a hard-R," Grandpa Tom explained. "They have us out in the gazebo in Claire's backyard, clothes off, making whoopee: high school kids! The Malt Shop, that old burger joint where Rio Bravo is now, the teen hangout, nothing went on in there. The owner knew all the kids—act up and he called your folks. You did not want that! But the script has an orgy scene in there!"

"We didn't do things like that back then!" Claire snapped. "We grew up in the Forties, we had good girls and bad girls in our day—I *defined* good girl!"

"I told my kids the war story about when I turned down the sergeant who tried to set me up with a Korean prostitute," Tom added. "That happened. In the script, I pimp for her."

"And what about that scene where you get in the argument with your father, before you get on the train to New York?" Tom asked, turning to Claire.

"Same thing," his wife answered angrily. "True, we argued, bitterly, in the car that night. But the dialogue has me spewing curse words I've never used in my life, my father's shoving me around the waiting room, calling me names, using the B-word, like a barroom brawl.

"My father, my darling father, never, ever, laid a hand on me. That's unthinkable! I may have heard him curse five times in my life, he simply did not talk that way."

Even Tony stared.

"Remember that awful book about the movie business that came out years ago, *Hollywood Babylon*?" Grandma Claire continued. "I guess they want to film a 'Randall Babylon.' This town was and is pretty dull."

"Anything you did like?" Hannah asked.

"Catchy title: *Two Lives And A Love*," Grandpa Tom answered. "After that, well, things go down."

"But you still have Jack Nicholson lined up to do me, right?" Tony asked.

"Not hardly," Grandpa Tom replied. "I sent our agent a note yesterday, said no way, we hadn't even finished it yet. Thankfully, we have a veto."

"Tom will fly out there next week to talk to people," Claire said. "I'd like to go but, hey, you know," she said, patting her wheelchair.

"This may not work," Grandpa Tom added, "like our concerts or whatever you want to call them."

"Sorry, I didn't know you two did concerts," Mark asked, puzzled.

"I don't know what you'd call them," Tom answered. "Claire's nephew, Bob Dearborn, the one who works with us on all this stuff, proposed a series of events—I called them concerts—in big-city auditoriums: 'An Evening With Tom & Claire,' there's a poster in the closet."

"We did a test run in Cincinnati last January," Claire explained. "Bobby figured if we couldn't draw a crowd there, where I lived for twenty-five years, we couldn't draw a crowd anywhere. From there, he had a dozen more shows lined up, St. Louis, Dallas, Phoenix—I don't remember them all.

"We booked Springer Auditorium. My oh my, I had attended so many Cincinnati Symphony concerts there, and for me to be up on that stage. What a thrill!"

"So did anybody come?" Mark asked.

"Oh, sold out in two hours!" Tom answered in amazement. "Standing room only, the place absolutely packed out. Hannah, grab that DVD we have and play it for your friend."

Hannah stooped down in front of the cabinet, found the disc and turned on the TV. The picture began with a dozen young violinists sawing through a spirited rendition of *Foggy Mountain Breakdown*.

"That's the warmup, a youth strings group," Tom explained. "Fast forward to where we come on."

Hannah zoomed forward and then Claire's nephew strolled on stage and announced in his distinctive baritone, "Ladies and gentlemen, please join me and let's welcome Tom and Claire."

The crowd stood with thunderous applause and cheers as Tom pushed Claire's wheelchair to the marked spot on the stage, then he sat down in a chair beside her. The applause died down and just as the hall turned quiet Tom quipped, "Claire told me, 'I know a lot of these people, so wear a clean shirt.'"

The audience roared.

"Bobby plays Mr. Interlocutor, the host, to keep things moving," Claire explained. "Hannah, go to the end."

She zipped to the end of video, just as Tom concluded, "...So don't give up, keep going in life. God's working on you, so let Him! Great things will happen to you: Claire and I prove that, and I hope you enjoyed our little observations about life.

"Good night, everyone!"

Applause fills the hall as the crowd stands. Tom pushes the wheelchair backstage, then the couple comes out for a curtain call—twice.

"Looks like a hit to me," Mark said. "No wonder Hollywood wants you!"

"Oh, it hit," Tom added glumly. "Darling, tell them about the hit," he said to Grandma Claire.

She sighed.

"We go back stage, everyone's shaking our hands, congratulating us, someone hands me this big bouquet, then PLOP!, Tom hit the floor. He had one of his fainting spells," she explained. "We took him to emergency, out for hours before he came around.

"We loved Cincinnati, we had a great time, I had the chance to see lots of old friends, but we figured out these shows would not work. What if he'd passed out five minutes sooner, on stage? And, travel for me nowadays? Never easy."

"Bob cancelled the rest," Tom said with a heavy sigh. "So between a book, this movie script and the radio show, we have plenty to keep two old coots busy."

"Tommy, I told you long ago you have a face for radio!" Tony added.

The Gulfstream swooped around the pattern at Randall's little airport, the early morning sun gleamed off its shiny fuselage. The wheels dropped, it screeched on the runway with a puff of smoke, the plane roared to a stop, then taxied back to the base operator.

Grandpa Tom and Hannah waited in the bland pilot's lounge with his luggage, listening to the radio chatter.

"A G-Five? Wow, that's about the biggest thing to ever come in here," the lady at the counter said, impressed, as her mouse-eared line tech waved his wands at the pilot. "Looks like we may sell some Jet A this morning."

Claire's nephew and several movie studio reps came down the air stairs and sauntered inside to greet Tom as the pilots took a latrine break and filled a Thermos with coffee.

"Wish I could go with you," Hannah said as she hugged her grandfather. "I hope you can work things out, but stand your ground."

"Wish you could too, sweetheart, I will," he said, kissing her forehead.

"We better roll," Bob said. "The pilots have to light-load to get out of here so we'll have to do a refueling stop, Garden City, Kansas, I think, headwinds all the way."

Everyone headed for the plane, Tom tapping slowly across the tarmac with his cane. The co-pilot buttoned-up the hatch and the engines screamed to life. The biz jet taxied back out to the runway, turned around, the engines spooled up, and off they roared into the cloudless sky.

It made Hannah feel particularly lonely.

Grandpa Tom, what an amazing man. What had he seen, and done, in eighty-plus years? And hardly done yet, she thought.

She wanted a man in her life someday like him, or like her sweet daddy.

Could there be another one?

Chapter 29
Mr. Bentley?

The Jeep's phone rang and its disembodied voice announced "Daddy" as Hannah waited to turn onto the bypass to head home from the airport. She clicked the steering wheel button and gave her father a cheery "Hi!"

"Five years," Tom Junior replied calmly.

"Do what?"

"Randy got five years in the Boonville pen," he said.

"At least he won't be over at Fordland, the farther away the better," Hannah replied with relief. "Can they send him to Alaska?"

"You still get letters?"

"Oh yes, have you seen that stack in my bedroom?" Hannah said.

"Sweetheart, you need to write him, tell him good luck or something. I know it's hard but he has expectations and, well, you need to set him straight."

"Okay, let me think about what to say, love you!"

She got her college work out of the way, made a sandwich and decided to write the note, father knows best.

Hannah picked up Randy's topmost letter and opened it:

Deer Hannah,

I so want to here from you! You know how I told you in the other letters how I feel and I know we can have a happy life together when everything in my life works out like its supposed to be done or something like that in the future.

My love, I spend an hour on my knees at my bunk every night, praying for you and that God will bring us together again. I'm so stupid, why have I missed up my life so bad? I'm so sorry for all I done, I hope you know that.

Please say we can be together forever and ever. You mean everything to me and since I changed I want you to be a part of my new life. The chaplain here says I should think about the minister and I may do that. I red my Bible again, not much else to do here. But whatever, I'll be whatever you want me to be.

Please say yes.
All my love,
Randy

She cried again.

How do you answer that?

The one person in the world she hated, she despised, the person she could barely look at, spends an hour on his knees nightly to pray blessings on her. He sends letters daily confessing his devout and long-lasting love.

"Jesus, help me! Jesus, help me help him!" she whispered as she put the letter back on the stack.

Her reply had to be handwritten and she hadn't done anything in longhand in ages—not that her penmanship ever looked that great. She opened her computer and drafted a note, with multiple changes, then put pen to paper:

Dear Randy,

I learned this morning you will be going to prison in Boonville. I know this must be hard but I trust God will use your time there to bless you. May you enjoy good things that you cannot understand now, and I pray that you will have a long and productive life. Maybe your experiences will help others.

As I told you when we visited at the jail, I forgive you for what you did. We all do wrong sometimes. I pray that with your change of heart that what the evil one meant for harm, God can use for good.

But please understand, I cannot agree to a romantic relationship. Instead, think of me as a friend, maybe a sister. I want the best for you, truly, but I believe some other girl waits for you in the future, and you will love her and care for her. And, she will love you in return deeply in a way that I cannot.

If the time comes when you finish your sentence, I will provide a reference, and tell anyone the positive change I have seen in your life. Keep going, I believe good things lie ahead for you.

May God bless you,
Hannah

She read and re-read the letter, that about covered it.

She addressed the envelope, then had to rummage around her father's office to find a stamp. She couldn't remember the last time she'd mailed a letter. She walked out on the driveway just as the postman pulled up to the family's mailbox.

"Afternoon," the cheerful mailman said, handing her the usual junk mail and another letter from Randy. He took her letter, nodded and drove on to the neighbor's mailbox.

Maybe this would end it.

Tom Junior strode in his office after yet another huddle with his vice presidents. "Good grief, we have meetings to plan meetings," he mumbled to himself. Corporate bureaucracy threatened Bentley Hardware despite his best efforts.

"Your father's on line two," his secretary told him as he walked past her desk.

"Really? Thanks."

Odd, Pop would call Claire. He bent over his desk and picked up the phone.

"Hey, ol' Dad!" the son said.

"I'm here. We landed at Burbank a few minutes ago, everything's fine, we're headed down to the studio in a nice limo," Grandpa Tom replied.

"You gave me a start, I figured you'd call your wife," Tom Junior said.

"I did, didn't get an answer. I figure she let the phone battery go dead, you know how old people are," his father said.

What a card, Tom Junior chuckled.

"Okay, I'll check with her, thanks for letting me know."

"'Bye," Grandpa Tom said.

Now: back to work. The CEO sat down at his desk and pulled out some accounting report he had to read. His phone rang again, his secretary answered.

"Tom," she called through his open door. "A Randy Smith on line one."

Randy?

Oh, no, what could he want?

He took a deep breath and picked up his phone.

"Tom Bentley."

"Mr. Bentley? This is Randy."

"Yes, how may I help you?"

"The judge sent me to Boonville."

"Yes, I heard that, son, good luck."

"Well, uh, sir, not sure when they'll transfer me. But before I go, uh, I want your permission to ask your daughter to marry me. We could do it here at the jail, I checked with the chaplain, he's done that."

Facepalm.

Oh, help!

An image flashed in the doting father's mind: His precious Ladybug in a wedding gown, standing in front of a preacher, next to Randy in his orange jump suit—in a cell.

No!

Tom Junior sat quietly, thinking.

"Mr. Bentley, are you still there?"

His gut instinct wanted to burst out laughing. No, can't do that, Randy had come a long way. He should be rewarded for his progress.

"Uh, look," Tom Junior said with a cough. "I'm not sure I know what to say. I'm impressed with how you have turned your life around, Randy, that is a very good thing. Good for you! But marriage amounts to a lot more than being a responsible citizen."

"Yes, sir."

"Randy, I'm sorry, Judy and I adore Hannah, we want only her best."

"I do too, sir. It's a joy to be with her."

"I'm sure you do. But as a loving father, I'm concerned about her welfare, and I don't think marrying a man headed to a penitentiary would be the ideal way for her to start married life."

"I guess not."

Think, Tom, think!

"Uh, look, uh, I'm sorry, Randy, but I can't. Too much has happened, I know you have apologized, and that took a lot of courage, good for you. But I still see my daughter, lying on that sofa with blood all over her, screaming. That's a picture that's very hard for a loving daddy to get out of his mind."

"Yes, sir, I'm sorry."

"Randy, uh, I wish you well, I might see what I can do to help you when you get out, the state does work release and maybe we could do something for you here at the warehouse. But that's a long ways off.

"I'm sorry, otherwise, you ask too much. I simply cannot agree."

Silence.

"Okay, thank you. Good-bye," and Randy hung up.

His secretary came to the door, concerned. "Tom, you know I don't eavesdrop, but was that the big football star? What's that all about?"

"Uh-huh." What else could he say?

Poor Hannah, what she must be going through. He sat and stared at the family photo he had on his desk, all four of them on a beach in Belize, what a vacation! His sweet daughter, dear Ladybug, twelve and growing then, Chad only nine. That wondrous night around a big fire, shrimp and fish for dinner, just one good time out of dozens the four of them shared. Their guide pointed out the Southern Cross, low in the sky, as a million stars twinkled in the night and the surf slowly rolled in.

His family, what a treasure.

Hannah and Chad would leave soon but he wanted to assure, whoever they left with, would fit into his blessed little, close-knit clan. That did not include a convicted felon, no matter how good his intentions.

Pop's "my kids" echoed in his mind. Good ol' Pop would love to have more kids.

He took a deep breath: Back to work, what about that report? Oh, answer the secretary's question!

"Yeah, that's the one, too much to talk about," he said with a shrug and an ironic smile.

She nodded and walked back to her desk. The phone rang again. The secretary talked to someone for a while as Tom shuffled papers, then called out "Tom, a Mark Wade on line one."

Now what? He picked up the phone.

"It's Tom."

"Mr. Bentley? Mark Wade here, up in St. Louis. How are you?"

"I'm fine, Mark, what's new? You plan to be down this way soon?"

"Yes sir, and that's why I called, if you have a moment. As I'm sure you're aware, Hannah and I have spent a lot of time together recently and I can honestly say I love your daughter very much."

"Yes."

"Mr. Bentley, I want to ask Hannah to marry me, and I would like to ask your permission."

Now what? Had someone set up a joke?

Tom paused for a moment, he liked Mark. Now, here would be a real catch for his daughter.

"Well, Judy and I think a lot of you, Mark, we've enjoyed your visits. I can't speak for Hannah, of course, her decision. But if she says yes, then, we welcome you to the family. I think you would be a great fit.

"There will be some logistics to let her finish college but I suspect the two of you can work that out. We will support you."

"Thanks, that means a lot. Hannah is a treasure, it's a joy to be with her. I'll do everything I can to make her happy."

"I'm sure you will. So, do you plan to pop the question soon? I'll keep my mouth shut."

"I plan to come down Saturday after next, maybe we'll go out for dinner; you know."

"That would be nice, please keep me posted. And Mark, thanks for doing things right," Tom added. "We've enjoyed getting to know you."

"Likewise, see you soon, Mr. Bentley. Good-bye."

Okay, wait: something's going on, Tom thought, but he had to get some work done, back to the desk. He managed to digest the confusing report. Ugh! Thomas J. Bentley Jr. earned an MBA, then made CPA, and he still found these things hard to follow.

Accountants are not writers.

Oh, better check the email, anything there? He turned to his computer.

"Excuse me Mr. Bentley, may I see you for a minute?" Charley asked nervously, standing at the office door.

"Sure, c'mon in, Charley," Tom Junior replied absentmindedly, his back to the door, as he squinted at Outlook.

"Okay, what's up? Have a seat, how go things on the floor?" the CEO said as he swung around to face his visitor.

"Fine, thanks," Charley answered, sitting down in front of Tom Junior's big desk. "Uh, I want to talk about something, uh, kind of personal."

"You bet, sure."

"Mr. Bentley, uh, I, uh, well…. I would like your permission to propose to Hannah."

Tom leaned on his desk and held his head in both hands.

A full moon tonight?

"Sorry, uh, something wrong?" Charley asked, embarrassed.

Tom leaned back in his chair, sighed, looked at the ceiling, then got up and closed his office door.

"Charley, if you only knew," the father said, plopping in his chair.

"Knew what?"

"Never mind, so you want to marry my daughter?" Tom said with a here-we-go-again sigh.

"Yes, yes sir," Charley said, wringing his hands.

"Uh, so when do you plan to ask her?"

"Don't know, sir, uh, need to think about stuff, no money. We're still in school, guess I need to find a part-time job when we get back to Mizzou. I want to do the best I can for her."

"Charley, I appreciate that," Tom said as he propped his elbows on the chair's armrests. "I'm pleased, you've earned an excellent reputation around here, people want me to keep you on. I'm sure you'll do well anywhere you work.

"Otherwise, my Hannah's a trooper, she'll pitch in too. She'll flip burgers or whatever it takes to make things go, and smile and laugh while she does it."

"Yes, sir."

"Of course when Hannah moves out on her own, she'll gain a separate interest in the family investments, so that may not be necessary."

"Uh, not sure what that means," Charley said, puzzled.

"The Dearborn Interests: I'm not up on what would it be worth, very complex, you can take some now, save for later. But back of the envelope, I expect her disbursement could be as much as eight-thousand and change," Tom explained. "That, as you put it once, will buy a lot of ramen noodles."

Charley brightened.

"Well, that would pay for a wedding."

"No, no, you don't understand," Tom Junior added patiently, "eight-thousand-plus a *month*, somewhere around a hundred-thousand a year, gross."

Charley grabbed his chair and sat up—shocked.

"*What?*" he said, stunned.

"When Hannah, and Chad too, move out after they graduate and set up separate domiciles, they gain personal interests in the families' investments, the Dearborns and the Bentleys, separate from what Judy and me receive," the father said.

"I guess, frankly, I have to ask, does that make a difference? I know your family has had some tough times.

"To be blunt, Charley: Do you want to marry my daughter for her, or for her money?"

Charley sat, mouth open, slowly shaking his head. Getting the girl of his dreams would be wonderful—but he could get the girl *and* hit the lotto?

Unbelievable.

"Oh, gee, no idea, Mr. Bentley! That's been my big worry: how can I support us? I know we'll both get jobs when we graduate, but until then...."

Tom Junior scratched his chin.

"Look, I think you would make a fine son-in-law. You're a hard worker, you're going places, you're smart and talented, and I believe you could make some young woman a fine husband. And from the bottom of my heart, I will forever be grateful for what you did to help Hannah that night.

"But whether that woman will be her or someone else, remains to be seen."

Charley's face fell, he stared down at the front of Tom Junior's desk.

"So your answer's no?"

"Not at all," Tom Junior replied. "But it's a maybe. I want you to be honest with me, son."

Charley gulped, this hadn't gone the way he expected.

"No, truly, I would love Hannah if she were as broke as me. It's a joy to be with her."

Tom Junior coughed and squirmed.

"I've heard other people say that. That's what I want, and if it's the truth, you have my permission," he said firmly.

Charley brightened.

"Thanks, this is just so awesome!"

"Keep me posted, her decision."

The boy stared past Tom Junior's head, looking out a window at the Bentley Hardware complex. There rested a dozen shipping containers, next to a string of semitrailers. A couple boxcars sat on a siding. He had been down there, pushing around cartloads of stuff just minutes before, alongside a half-dozen other hourly employees.

In front of him sat the company CEO, the man who ran it all.

"If you don't mind me asking, sir, how did you make so much money?" Charley asked.

Tom Junior chuckled and smiled.

"There are two ways to become rich, son:

"One, be a crook. Our families would not do that.

"Two, live below your means, keep the outgo less than the income, however much you make. My father—Pop—had a goal, to live on three-quarters of his income, save the rest. Then, when opportunity comes....

"Our families have done that for generations. Keep your head down, work hard, be honest, it pays off. I know that's tough for someone like you, just starting out, but it works.

"What's the old saying? A rich man plans for retirement, a poor man plans for Saturday night."

Charley leaned forward, listening intently.

"To be frank, most of the family office money came from the Dearborn side. Claire's father, Campbell, Wow! Now, that guy had an amazing gift. He worked hard, but he had the vision thing, he could see how business deals would pan out. The Dearborns had made money since the Civil War as bankers, then he doubled-tripled-quadrupled their fortune. He hit it big in oil, among other things."

"We Bentleys have been blessed too. I learned from Pop to be a good steward, to share the wealth. I enjoy golf, but I don't play thousand-dollar-a-hole games.

"We support worthwhile charities and our church. We give money to this missionary foundation that drills water wells for African villages, for example. I went over to help a couple years ago, slept in huts out in the bush. I'd lie there in the heat, listening to elephants trumpet in the night. It made me appreciate that house we have all the more.

"Share the wealth: We'd rather do that than have a big boat or a vacation home down at Shangri-La we only get to once a year.

"To be frank, Charley, I want a man like Pop to marry Hannah."

Charley nodded.

"How come your family's so, like, normal?" he asked.

Tom Junior laughed and leaned back his big chair.

"God's grace," he told the boy.

"Define 'family.' Hey, we Bentleys have problems. You met my sister, Brenda, we hadn't seen her in decades, then she shows up minutes before the wedding last year. I'm pleased Pop and Claire talked her into moving back here and—for once—she took advice. Bless them, they made my strange sister a special project. Who knows what scrapes she got in over the years? Brenda opened that store, or whatever. She's here, but she still does her own thing.

"Is she family? Well, on paper, but we are not close.

"Pop had a blowout with his brothers, Brenda and me just kids then, they didn't like the way he and my grandfather ran the company. They sold out and moved to Kansas City, I have cousins up there I never hear from—except when money comes up.

"So what *is* family?

"For me, family's my wonderful Judy, Hannah and Chad, Pop and Claire," Tom Junior said, rubbing his face thoughtfully. "Someday, I hope we can add a husband for Hannah and a wife for Chad."

Charley slowly shook his head.

"That is just so awesome.

"Sir, believe me, I love all of you," the boy said. "I want to be a part of it."

Charley stood and smiled weakly. Tom Junior stood and the two shook hands across his desk.

"Let's see what works out," the father said.

Charley opened the office door, nodded, and walked out as the phone rang again.

"Who's next?" he muttered. "She's running out of guys."

"Tom, Claire's on line two," the secretary called.

"Whew! Thanks."

"Hey, Grandma!" he said as he answered the phone.

"Hello, just wanted to check if you've heard from Tom?" she answered.

"Oh, Pop called a while ago, everything's fine. Sorry, been busy. He said he called and you didn't answer."

"Oh, okay, sorry to bother you, I guess I had my phone off. What are you up to this afternoon?" she asked.

"Not much, just writing a Hollywood script."

Chapter 30
Proposals

Groceries: the library had Judy tied up with an elementary school book fair and mom asked the daughter to go to the supermarket, here's the list. Off to Price Cutter!

Sure, and Hannah could buy herself a honey bun, mom didn't need to know! She loved the things but her vitamins-and-veggies mom gave her a lecture when Hannah got caught with one.

The Jeep's phone rang as Bluetooth announced "unknown caller" on the way to the supermarket. She answered.

"Hello?"

"Hannah? This is Randy."

Oh no, not again.

Why did he only call when she drove? Maybe his cell had a window and he could see the Jeep go by. Silly, get serious!

She pulled in the high school parking lot and stopped.

"Yes."

"Can I, uh, talk to you for a minute?"

"You are, what?" she snapped.

"You know, I received my sentence."

"Yes, I heard. Did you get my letter?"

"Yes. But Hannah, please, I want us to be so much more than friends."

She banged her forehead on the steering wheel and sighed.

"Randy, I'm sorry. Like I said in the letter, I wish you well, I'm happy that you've changed your life."

"Ha… Ha… Hannah, will you marry me?" Randy stuttered.

Help, beyond awkward.

She flopped her head back against the headrest and looked at the headliner.

"Randy, oh please, no. I cannot have a romantic relationship with you. I'm sorry, it cannot happen."

"But…" he started.

"Hear me: No! There is no *but*," she added firmly. "I'm sorry, it's a long ways between forgiveness and marriage. Can you understand that?"

"But I want us to be like back when, when we dated in high school," he pleaded.

"Me too," Hannah replied, "but that cannot happen.

"Think about the future, Randy, not the past. We cannot go back, but we can go forward, okay? I can be a friend, I'll help you as I can, but no more.

"I cannot be your wife, I'm sorry."

She could hear Randy sniff.

What to say?

"Like I said in the letter, maybe God has someone better for you than me," Hannah added nervously.

"You think so?" he replied, suddenly cheerful.

"Yes."

"Okay, but please know I'll always love you," he said slowly. "Good-bye."

"Call ended."

She grabbed the phone out of her purse and angrily hit BLOCK NUMBER, enough of this.

Then she shut off the engine, cupped her face in her hands, and bawled.

Grandpa Tom called after dinner from Los Angeles and Tom Junior put Pop on the speaker so Judy and Hannah could hear. Negotiations did not go well, they might drop the whole movie deal.

"I made some demands on what we want, but they're trying to do stuff like cut our royalties if we make them rework the script," he explained.

"What does Claire say?" the son asked.

"She's with me all the way, she talked to her nephew, Bobby, he might have some pull. Maybe we should just forget this," Grandpa Tom added. "The book's in the works too. Maybe I won't get a star on Hollywood Boulevard after all."

"Stick to your guns, Grandpa," Hannah said, "don't trash-up the franchise."

"Oh, I won't. We'll meet again tomorrow, then I'll fly home. Can you pick me up at the airport, Hannah?"

"Of course, just call. Anything I can do for Grandma Claire?" she asked.

"I don't think so. Hey, better go, we're going to this great Chinese place for dinner. They wanted to do Korean but you know I how feel about kimchi, GAG!

"Pop, Korea's changed since your war days," Tom Junior said with a laugh.

"I guess, love you all!"

The trio said "'Bye" and hung up. Hannah did some homework and went to bed early. She just dozed off when her phone rang: Mark.

"Good evening," she purred.

"And good evening to you, Miss Bentley! What's the word in rowdy Randall today?" Mark asked.

Hannah sighed.

"Not too much, what are you doing?"

"Well, I'd like to come down this weekend if the Bentley Hilton has a room available."

"I believe it does, Friday night again?"

"No, let's do something different, think I'll leave Saturday morning, get there in the afternoon, then we can go someplace nice for dinner. How about steaks in Springfield? I hear there's a really great steakhouse there, let's dress up and hit the town."

Hmmm, did he have something planned?

"That sounds nice, let's do it!"

"Okay, see you then," Mark replied. She could see the smile. "And Hannah, I really miss you."

"I miss you too."

Saturday afternoon: She finished dressing as she heard the doorbell ring and her mom called "Mark's here!" down the hall. Mark stood in the front room in a perfect blue blazer, white shirt with a red-gold-and-blue regimental tie and khakis, chatting with Tom Junior.

Oh gosh, girls really do crazy 'bout a sharp-dressed man!

They hugged.

"You look mah-velous!" Mark said, holding her back as he admired her maroon pantsuit.

"And you look pretty good yourself, where to?" she asked.

"Jaime's, some friends tell me they have the best steaks in Missouri."

Chit-chat on the drive over, she could tell Mark had something on his mind—and she figured she knew what.

The restaurant had dark wood paneling, red leather chairs, red table cloths, and those drippy candles in old wine bottles. The tuxedoed maître d' seated them across from each other and handed over huge, heavy menus and a wine list the size of a phone book.

Hannah noted the huge, heavy prices.

What a pleasant evening, whatever might happen.

Then she heard it, straight behind Mark: Her eyes refocused across the way on some young man as he quietly played *As Time Goes By* on a grand piano. A half-full tip jar sat above the keyboard.

No, this would not work!

Whatever Mark had on his mind, a pleasant dinner or more, she could not sit with him as she thought of you-know-who.

Mark might be the one she spends the rest of her life with: focus!

"Uh, do you mind if I move to one side?" she asked. "I'm, uh, have some trouble hearing."

Mark looked surprised and mumbled "sure" as she moved to his left.

The filets proved delectable, accented by a superb Chilean Carménère, with twice-baked potatoes and asparagus. And here's an advantage to a date with an older guy: The waiter didn't card her.

They shared one insanely rich caramel nut fudge sundae for dessert—two spoons, please.

The conversation had been pleasant and at times funny, his Navy stories, her happy days at Mizzou, their travels. Maybe he'd get the plane again and they could have another hundred-dollar hamburger at Vinita. Sure! He ordered an espresso and the waiter refilled her water glass.

Mark took her hand.

"I want you to know just how special you have become to me," he said, barely above a whisper. "I covet these weekends we've had, and I would love nothing more than the opportunity to spend every day with you the rest of my life. I have come to love you, Hannah, truly."

Here it comes.

He reached in his coat pocket and brought out a ring box, sat it on the table and opened it.

Hannah gasped.

A big emerald, surrounded by tiny, sparkling diamonds.

"Oh, Mark!" she whispered, her hand on her chest, looking at the ring in awe. "It's, it's beautiful!"

"You know the question: Yes or no?" The smile lit up the room.

"Will you marry me?"

Echo! Echo!

Time stretched from seconds to hours. She sat there, slack jawed, her eyes locked on the thing.

What to say, what *could* she say?

Hannah sat in awe, what a gorgeous ring. Wow, to have that on her finger, and to have the terrific guy who goes with it! Wow!

"How about a destination wedding in Tahiti, or Pago Pago?" he added.

She sat back and fanned her face.

"Oh, Mark, with all my heart I want to say yes, I think you know that," she said, tears welled in her eyes. "You are wonderful, and I love you too. I know we could be very happy together."

Hannah sat, panting.

Oh my, she expected this, but when it happens....

"I truly want to say yes, I could spend the rest of my life with you, yes, and love every minute of it." Then she swallowed, "But I need to know, where do things stand with your ex?"

She looked at him longingly.

"Please, please, please say it's over!" she thought to herself.

"If I know she's history, I absolutely, positively say yes. I would be very happy as your wife, let's set a date," Hannah said, breathless. "But I have to know, I need your word."

Mark frowned.

"I guess I never fully answered your question, did I?" he said. "Maybe I rushed things a little, but I want to catch you before your acquaintance does."

Hannah grimaced.

"No, no you didn't answer. We could both be asking for trouble," she said, squeezing his hand. "Trust me, you're well ahead of the acquaintance.

"Look, Mark, I want with all my heart to love you and make you my guy. I'm romantic, but I'm practical.

"I've spent enough time in the out of doors to know a forest can be beautiful—but dangerous. Same for marriage, it can be beautiful, but you need to be aware of the dangers when you walk into it.

"I've seen girlfriends in our situation. They met someone who's been married before, he's very nice, everything's sweetness and light—happy, happy, happy! Then three years, seven years, trouble starts.

"You get up in the morning, the laundry's not done, the baby's crying, he needs a shave, she's put on weight, ugh! Then, the previous relationship, the ex, suddenly looks better, or he starts looking elsewhere. If he switched once, he can do it again—the grass in the other yard gets greener.

"I'm only going to do this once, Mark, so I'm very picky. I want permanence."

He nodded.

"So what do you want me to do?" he said.

"Can I tell you 'maybe?' I truly want to say yes, believe me, I do. But I need to know: Can you say she's history, or not?"

Mark took the ring, closed the lid, and slid it back in his pocket.

"That's one thing I love about you: You have a head on your shoulders," he said. "You're pretty, you're fun, you're smart."

"Thank you, I don't want to go into a permanent deal that, well, isn't permanent. Marriage must be about two people, not two people and an asterisk," Hannah said.

"So now?" he asked.

Hannah sat back, put her hand to her mouth and thought. Tears trickled down her cheeks.

"Call her and ask: Are we done? Are we really through? If she says yes, then let's set the date," she said. Hannah wiped her eyes. "I'm in, the answer's yes!"

Mark grimaced.

"Fair enough, and what about your acquaintance?"

"Yes, this works both ways, I know that," Hannah said with a frown. "I need to talk to him, I'll break things off. But we have not been married. We've had ups and downs, and I'm logical enough that I can see problems, major problems, if I were to get serious about him."

They sat, looking into each other's eyes. Mark flashed his smile.

"Let's see what happens," he said.

"Fair enough," Hannah replied. "You do your part, I'll do mine. Then we can get back together and make the call.

"And, don't do anything with that ring just yet," she said with a wink. "I love emeralds!"

Mark leaned forward and they kissed.

The drive back proved quiet, hands held. Sirius played dreamy New Age music, the stars shone through the moonroof.

They chatted with her folks until late, then headed down the hall.

"Tonight's been special," Mark said, taking her in his arms. "May I say I love you?"

"Yes, you may, and I love you too," she whispered.

"But: I love you enough that I want us to be honest with each other," she said as she reached up to place her finger on his lips. "Maybe it will work, maybe it won't. Let's both trust God here, okay? I want both of us to be happy—forever. And that might involve two other people who do not happen to be standing here in the hall with us."

They both glanced down the way, no one watching. They embraced and passionately kissed.

More teasing from gal pals at church Sunday morning: Isn't it time for another boyfriend?

Giggles.

"Could be, or something more," Hannah said at her cheerful best.

Lunch on the patio, a kiss at the Jeep's window, and another marvelous Mark weekend came to a close.

She stood, rolling thoughts, serious thoughts, over in her mind as he backed out and drove off:

Hannah Wade.

Mrs. Mark Wade.

She liked the sound.

Chapter 31
Something More

Charley?

Okay, she agreed to do her part, talk to him, where do things stand? She had to be ready to break it off, awkward as it might be. Talk about a sweet guy, she did not want to do anything to hurt him, but....

And if Mark and his ex got back together, well, Charley remained a factor.

Or, go back to your plan, Hannah girl: If he were interested, Charley could just check back in a year or two.

Fine.

"'Maybe' can get complex," she mumbled to herself. Doesn't Facebook have an "it's complicated" option for its "relationship" line?

Was she a two-timer? She did not want to be!

Surely Charley knew something, suspected something, when she disappeared.

But what to say? Had he lost interest? He had a phone now, he had her number. But not once had he called at an inopportune time, unlike Randy. Charley might be klutzy, but he had great timing.

They had to talk. Sleep on it, then decide.

Monday became Tuesday, Tuesday became Wednesday. She heard not a thing from him and she did not have the nerve to call.

Wednesday night her phone rang, "Charley" appeared on the screen.

"Hey!" she answered as brightly as she could.

"I haven't heard from you lately," Charley replied.

"That works both ways, Mr. Trottel, what's up?"

"Homework, didn't realize how hard online classes could be," he replied.

"Would you like to come over? It's cool enough outside we could turn on the hot tub's 'hot' tonight," she suggested.

"Sure."

"Good, be there in five minutes," she chirped.

Charley waited at the curb.

The Jeep stopped, he climbed in—and immediately leaned over the console, took her cheeks in his palms and passionately kissed her. She wrapped her arms around him. They held the kiss.

"Missed you," he said quietly, pulling back and smiling.

"Same here."

Hannah did a U-turn and headed back up Poplar. Chad's baggy trunks got more use as they climbed into the bubbling, warm water.

"Hey, nice!" he said as he slid next to her and put his arm around her shoulders.

They sat quietly, looking up at the stars.

"You're unusually quiet," he finally said.

"Guess so, have a lot to think about right now," she said matter-of-factly. Well, might as well bring it up, here goes:

"Charley, where are we going?" she asked quietly, looking at him.

"Where do we go from here? Our quick little summer weekend as June began didn't turn out to be little or quick. It's October, and we're both still stuck in Randall."

Charley sighed.

He scratched his chin and thought.

"Stay together," he added slowly.

"Okay," she said, nodding.

The tub bubbled away.

She sat up in the water.

"Look," she said, "even after all these months, I'm not certain if you came down here to see Grandpa Tom and Grandma Claire, or if you came to see me.

"Am I a friend who knows someone, or am I something more?"

Charley looked at her, puzzled.

"Both? I'm smart enough to know if I keep you, they're part of the deal."

"Well, that's true."

Hannah sighed.

"Charley, look, I'm sorry, I've, uh, I've had someone else come into my life," she said nervously.

"I know," he said calmly.

"You do?" Hannah replied, surprised.

"It's a small town, and I'm not as dumb as you think. I may be clumsy, but I'm not dense," the boy said firmly. "I know about both of them. Obviously, Randy didn't pick you out by chance at the office that night, I caught the way you looked at him in the park that afternoon. Then, I've seen you with the other guy."

Her jaw dropped.

"Did, did my father say anything?" she asked, concerned.

"Not a peep—ever. But I hear talk at work, you're the big boss's daughter."

"And you're still here, you put up with me?" Hannah replied.

"Yes."

"Why?" she asked.

Charley suddenly sloshed around and sat up, facing her.

"Because I want to *win*, Hannah!" he said. She drew back, shocked, she'd never heard that tone in Charley's voice—frustration, anger.

"Yes, I *am* jealous, I want you! I don't deserve you—but I want you, is that okay?

"You personify everything I want and do not have: a beautiful woman to love; family, faith, future. I want more out of life than I've had, and I could have it with you. That's what I want.

"I'm me!"

Now, that got Hannah's attention: He did not say "I've changed."

Charley is Charley—take it or leave it.

She liked that. Great that Randy and Mark started over, but not Charley.

They sat, staring at each other.

"You make your call, Hannah, and I hope and I pray, with all my heart, it's *me*!" he said firmly.

Hannah leaned back, her eyes smiled again, she crossed her arms.

"Thanks, that's all I need to know."

Saturday morning, the house smelled like coffee, breakfast out of the way. Chad came home Friday night with the usual college student's ton of dirty clothes, the washer and dryer spun in the laundry room.

Tom Junior suggested the family foursome go to the club for golf. They hadn't done that in months, what a hoot! No one kept score, plenty of double bogeys, how many balls went in the creek? Who cares? Burgers or tacos always followed at the 19th Hole, served up with lots of laughs.

Hannah went to her bedroom to get dressed when her phone rang: Mark.

Oh, wow! This could be it!

"Hello there," she answered brightly.

"Got a minute?"

"For you, always."

"Uh, bear with me, I need to follow up on last Saturday night. I thought I'd let you know I'm in Dallas. I parked on the courthouse square on my way out of Randall Sunday and called Janeen, first time we talked in a year. *Awkward* doesn't tell the half of it, we started yelling at each other.

"I told her I wanted to see her, I asked if I could come down, she finally said okay. I drove straight down here, didn't get to her apartment until well after midnight. I ended up driving around Love Field, missed my turn. I emailed my boss to take a week's vacation," Mark said.

"And?"

Mark sighed.

"And, well, Hannah, we want to get back together," Mark said without emotion. "There have been a lot of tears and apologies this week—and a couple great candlelight-and-wine dinners. You know, this town has some pretty good restaurants."

"I've heard that," Hannah said calmly.

"We had some great advice from a counselor last night at her church, we're looking to re-marry.

"Hannah, the spark's back."

"Congratulations," she said as affectionately as she could. "I'm happy for you."

She heard Mark sigh.

"Hannah, thank you," he said. "This would not have happened if you'd said yes last Saturday, and believe me, I wanted you to say yes. Really, I did. We have you to thank—you made me think, and I guess I made her think."

"You're welcome," she replied. "And I did want to say yes, truly, but…."

"I understand," Mark said.

"I've started a job hunt, I want to move down here, we'll make it work this time."

"Mark, honestly, I said I love you and that's still true," she said as her eyes got damp. She sat down on her bed and grabbed hippo. "Maybe I can love you as a very dear friend, if not as a husband?"

"Of course," he answered. "Same here, I will always think the world of you. If I can't love you as a wife, then I'll love you as one of my closest friends—platonic, a best bud. Thanks for a wonderful summer. I hope you meet Janeen someday, you're a lot alike, I think you'd be close."

The line went silent for a few moments.

"Are you disappointed?" Mark asked.

Hannah thought for a moment.

"Yes and no," she said. "You're a keeper, Mark Wade! I hope she knows how lucky she is. Maybe the word's 'melancholy,' what could have been? I think this will be for the best."

"I understand, I feel the same way," he said.

"Good luck to both you," she replied.

"I have to ask, what about you and your acquaintance?" Mark asked. She could see that smile flash.

"We talked, just like I promised, nothing definite," Hannah replied. "Hey, go ahead and give her that beautiful ring, I'll never tell."

"Oh no, I still have the ring I gave her back when, that warm night on the South Oval at OU," Mark said. "The last big argument we had in Norfolk, she took both rings off and threw them at me. I'm a dunce sometimes, but smart enough to grab them and stick them in a drawer. I'll have a jeweler polish them up.

"Thanks for everything," he replied. "I'll break the news gently to Grandpa Tony."

They both laughed.

"And Mark, when you come to visit him next time, text me," she replied. "I'll just so happen to come out to Hickory Bough about then by strange coincidence. I'd like to meet Mrs. Wade.

"She's one lucky girl."

So, no deal.

No Mark, certainly no Randy, what about Charley?

She hadn't asked for this weird, guy-centric "weekend" that suddenly popped up out of nowhere as June began and lingered now, even as November loomed. It certainly didn't fit her design. Her plan hurled the whole guy question off into some sort of vague, gauzy future.

Instead, for months she'd wrestled—sometimes literally—with a question she did not want to face until "someday."

After all, she had a fourth option: Pass on Charley too—back to the plan, stay organized.

But she had to make a decision.

Could she?

Would she?

Charley?

"Think like the accountant you are," Hannah mumbled to herself: T-account, assets and liabilities. Add them up, on paper Hannah and Charley did not balance. But she didn't draft a 10-K here, this involved people, not Wall Street and banks. She knew that, think subjective, not objective.

Charley.

The poor guy, stuck in Randall all summer—just like her.

His college plans messed up—just like her.

A hospital stay for a fun afternoon gone terribly wrong—just like her.

Not as exciting as Mark, Charley had never been in an airplane, far as she knew. Mark flew them, a macho, top-gun jet jockey vs. a, well admit it, wuss.

Columbia, Missouri? The biggest town Charley could remember. Mark had exciting stories of London, Singapore, Sydney, Tokyo, and more.

But oh, what Charley could do with a piano, she loved to hear him play! And, he could dance very well—music—despite his otherwise klutziness. She loved to dance.

Hannah thought back to that first slow dance they ever did at the Sisters of Spring social. They just fit together, up close, her head went right under his chin.

"Soft kisses on a summer's day, laughing all our cares away..."

He lived as a perfect gentleman, helpful, polite, thoughtful, courteous—honest. He made a girl, her, feel important and respected. And once in a while, the spark flared, it ignited exciting and romantic things—that dance at church, that horrible night in the thunderstorm, that evening in the hot tub. Just a nudge, and the desire popped up.

Charles Trottel had his strong points.

She sensed that this guy—clumsy, shy, unsteady, but very talented—would stay in a relationship for the long haul; permanence. Twentysomething Charley already had been through a lot and wanted a better life.

Somehow, Charley fit with her, and not just physically. He fit with her family—despite Grandma Claire's misgivings.

And he wanted her, oh gosh, he really wanted her. She could tell that.

She had never, ever, had to woo him. Not that Hannah Bentley ever had to woo any guy. Mark's "do you have any numbers left?" popped in her mind. You ditzy chick, how many guys chased you and you didn't even notice?

Dummy!

Again, she did not owe Charley anything—back to the plan! She'd finish college next year, then find a job, then find a guy. "And hey Susie Sorority, you *are* a Bentley. You're expected to marry some richy-rich, up-and-comer headed for the head shed," she whispered, "sort of like Mark." Cross Mark off that list, but there are plenty others like him—but without that smile.

Nah, wait.

Would Charley still be around in another year? Could they get serious then?

Maybe not.

"Jesus, help me do the right thing," she mumbled, staring at the floor. "I don't want to hurt him."

What did mom tell her when this crazy "weekend" began? "When opportunity knocks...."

Could he be more than a pal?

Yes.

Could she love Charley?

Yes.

They had to talk, again.

Chapter 32
The Rock Remains

Early Sunday morning, Hannah shambled in the kitchen, poured a cup of coffee, then shuffled back to her bedroom and closed the door. She picked up her phone and punched Charley's number.

"Yo!" he answered sleepily.

"Hey there, want to go to church?" Hannah asked.

Charley yawned.

"Sure, let me shave and get dressed."

The service turned fabulous, more terrific music, the worship team really cranked. Musician Charley loved it, standing and clapping, then swaying with hands in the air to the ethereal *Let It Echo:*

"*Ohhhh, let Heaven fall...*"

Hannah turned around to her girlfriends during the handshakes and one asked, "Another guy?"

She snickered and shook her head. "No, going backwards!" she whispered.

Charley and the Bentleys headed out with the crowd after the benediction.

"So what are you doing for lunch?" Charley asked. "Chad's headed back to Rolla?"

"Better yet, what are *we* doing for lunch?" Hannah answered, looking up at him.

"Flexible," he answered.

"Let's get a bucket o' bird and do a picnic at Hoot Owl," she suggested.

"Sure."

The Jeep pulled up at a picnic table above the big rock and below the big oaks in their autumn turn. Charley unloaded the sack and drinks as Quartz Creek quietly murmured.

"Don't tell my germophobe mom I ate lunch on a bare picnic table," she said with a nervous giggle as she spread an extra napkin out.

Charley grinned.

He grabbed a drumstick and started to munch. They sat, eating silently.

"Uh, what's up? You're quiet again," he asked, taking a drink and wiping his chicken-greased fingers on his jeans.

Hannah put down a fork of potato salad and looked at him, thoughtfully.

Tears started down her cheeks.

That startled him.

"You okay?" he asked.

She shook her head.

"Charley, I don't know what to say, honestly, except you *won*," she said.

He sat back, shocked, with a blank stare and put down the drumstick. "You mean...."

"Yes, but no details—ever," she said between sniffs. "You said you wanted to win, you have, and I'm glad. Of course, do you still want to win?"

He sat, staring at Hannah.

"Now what?" Charley asked, shocked.

"I think that's up to you," she said, dabbing her eyes with a napkin. "It's your decision, what do *you* want to do?"

"But, what do *you* want to do?" he answered.

Hannah furrowed her eyebrows in thought.

"For me, I'd just as soon wait to get serious. No offense, please, it's just that we both have been through a lot this summer," she said.

"But why?" Charley asked. "If we both want a permanent deal, let's do it now."

Hannah sat quietly.

"Okay, but my life has been so wild. Is it still summer? October? Whatever! All I know, it began with you, and after all the dumb stuff, you're still here. Somewhere in between, I saved your life, and you saved my life. Maybe we need each other, maybe we should stay close, forever."

Charley stared off into space.

"Uh, do I get down on a knee?"

"I don't know!" Hannah answered, crying and laughing at the same time.

He turned around and looked at the big rock, sighed, then looked back at her.

"Hannah, will you marry me?"

Echo! Echo!

She smiled, and her smiling eyes cried.

"Oh, Charley, with all my heart: *Yes!*"

He sat, stunned.

"Uh, okay."

Silence.

Hannah sniffed, the creek burbled on.

"What happened?" Charley asked.

"Our lives changed," Hannah whispered. "Are you happy?"

He nodded.

"Why me? I'm blessed and highly favored, why? Not all of God's blessings will come on the other side, you're one I'll have here."

He reached across the table to take the girl's hands.

"Somehow, this isn't what I pictured," he added, "no ring or anything."

"It never happens the way you think it will," Hannah replied. "Where's the moonlight? Where are the roses? Where's the violin? And no champagne!

"The two of us? We have fried chicken and baked beans on a Hoot Owl picnic. Maybe that says something about you and me. But it does happen, and for us it just did."

Charley propped his jaw on his hand and thought as he drummed his fingers on the table.

"This is just so awesome," he mumbled.

Hannah wiped her eyes and sniffed.

"And you, look at you! You big, goofy guy, I love you!" she replied, wiping her eyes as she laughed.

They sat, smiling at each other.

"Me too," he replied softly. "Never said this to anyone: I love you."

The romantic stares lingered.

"When did you decide to love me?" Charley finally asked.

Hannah leaned back, clapped, and let go a belly laugh.

"You silly thing, when I saw you standing in the hall in your underwear that night Aunt Brenda showed up," she said.

"Oh, still embarrassed," he said, dropping his head.

"Don't be," she replied. "It was just so good-old-Charley. You weren't trying to be sexy, just concerned-about-others-first Charley. You were so cute!

"And, when did you decide to love me?"

Charley smiled.

"First thing: That night when we met-met in the study circle," he replied. "You were too good to be true. I admire Tom and Claire so much— and then to learn they have an elegant and available granddaughter."

"You nut!" Hannah answered.

A puff of wind rustled the trees above, a handful of yellow leaves showered around them.

"Uh, I want you, more than you know. But I don't know much about husbands, never saw one up close," he said, rubbing his face. "I'll make mistakes."

"Charley, look, we both will, talk to Grandpa Tom," Hannah said. "He has a vested interest in his favorite granddaughter's husband."

"Sure."

Charley leaned back and crossed his arms.

"And Hannah, I have another question," he said solemnly.

"Yes?"

"Can I change my name?"

Hannah's jaw dropped.

"Do what?"

"No, really, I want to be a Bentley. I want you, I want your family," he said. "I want to be part of it."

"What family do I have? Nothing! I have one bitter, spiteful mother who says things like, 'I don't know why I kept you!' Then I look at all of you: Happy, affectionate, caring. Anything happens and you're all there. Claire joined your family, I want to join it.

"If we marry, I want to change my name first."

Stray bullet!

Hannah sat back, stunned.

Had Charley gone weird, some kind of joke?

No, apparently not. Rather awkward, but hey, that's typical for this guy—her guy.

"Well, you can do what you want. I'll marry you, whatever you call yourself," she said, awestruck.

Charley got up, walked around the table and sat down next to her. They kissed, then smiled at each other.

"You really sure you want to do this?" Hannah asked. "Walk away now if you have doubts, I'll understand."

"Oh please, please hear me, my darling, my dream, my lover, my life prize, I can do or say nothing but tell you, my precious Hannah, my sweet love, you wonderful, adorable, beautiful, vivacious girl, that I positively worship you, and I truly want you to be a part of my life forever and ever—more than you can possibly know or understand," he whispered as he caressed her cheek.

"That is the longest thing I have ever heard him say," she thought to herself.

"Oh, Charley!" Hannah said, resting her head on his chest as he put his arms around her.

The Jeep pulled in the driveway at dusk, Hannah walked in the front door. She could hear a football game blasting away in the media room.

"Hannah?" Tom Junior called down the hall as he hit mute.

"I'm here," she answered.

Hannah walked in to find her parents looking up from their recliners.

"Quite a long picnic, young lady," Judy said, smiling, as her daughter walked in and plopped on a sofa.

"So what's up?" her father asked. "The Cowboys continue to pound the Rams, give me some good news. A vendor offered me tickets, thought about driving up to St. Louis today, glad I didn't."

Hannah crossed her arms, played with her keys, and looked thoughtfully at her parents.

"I'm getting married," she said quietly.

Tom Junior and Judy didn't flinch.

"We know, but to whom?" her father answered.

Hannah sat up.

"You do?"

Both parents laughed loudly.

"Three guys asked my permission to propose to you, I told two of them yes. I think you can figure out who's who," Tom Junior said.

"And as spooky as you've been lately? You think we don't know something's rolling around in your head?" her mom added.

"Drum roll! And the winner is…" Tom Junior added.

Hannah slapped her cheeks, leaned back and laughed.

"Charley!"

"Oh, honey!" Judy said as she got up and trotted over to her daughter.

"Have you set a date?" the father asked.

"No way," his daughter replied. "That's way off, next year sometime, after we graduate. And here's the catch: Charley wants to change his last name before the wedding. He wants to become a Bentley."

"Do what?" Tom Junior replied, sitting up in his recliner. "Why?"

Judy kissed her daughter and Hannah hugged her back.

"He said he loves all of us, wants to be a part of us, like Grandma Claire," Hannah said, her eyes getting wet.

The parents sat, stunned.

"So, let me get this straight: When you marry, you would stay Hannah Bentley, but he becomes Charles Bentley?" Judy asked. "Correct?"

"Yes," Hannah answered.

"What do you think about that?" the father asked.

"Odd, but I like it," Hannah said as she stared into space. "I know Grandma Claire will be happy. She thinks he's related to some skanky old boyfriend she had years ago, a real bad apple."

"Well!" Tom Junior replied, "I suspect I know what you told Randy, but what about Mark?"

"He popped the question when we had dinner last weekend. I almost—almost—told him yes. But I said 'maybe,' he's divorced," Hannah explained.

"He'd mentioned that," Tom Junior replied.

"I could get around it from what he told me, but I asked if his ex is history, or not? Long story short: She's not, turns out they're getting remarried."

"So how do you see Charley? The booby prize, uh, Mister Congeniality?" Tom Junior asked.

"Oh, not at all!" Hannah answered brightly. "I think he's wonderful. Thank the Lord, it worked out perfectly, even for Randy."

Daughter and parents chatted for a long time, then a very tired Hannah grabbed a bite, showered and got ready for bed. She slipped into her pink nightshirt and went to the kitchen to get her usual nighttime glass of water before she turned out her light. Her parents had their bedroom door closed as she padded up the dark hall.

She could make out the murmur of conversation, she overheard her mom ask her dad, "Do you think he'll make her happy?" as she passed.

Huh?

She stopped to listen. Not to eavesdrop, but she had to hear this.

"Oh, I think so," her father replied, yawning. She could make out her dad punching his pillow to fluff it up, like he did every night before he slid between the sheets. "Charley dotes on her, you can tell that.

"I think he's in over his head, like a kid dropped in the deep end of the pool, who gets told 'Swim!' But in his own bumbling way, he'll figure it out. He wants to figure it out, he has to figure it out. He's a good guy, everyone at work thinks he's terrific. And you know what? He's gonna' pop off and do something great, he has talent."

"Do you really know him?" the wife asked.

"Hey, think about it: I've spent more time with Charley than Ladybug since this whole mess began with Pop and Claire's anniversary," Tom Junior continued. "I take him to and from work every day and I see him around the office. We talk.

"He's a bit of an odd duck but he's alright, I like him.

"And, we have Charley to thank that we still have a daughter. I get sick to my stomach when I think what could have happened."

"You think he's after her money?" Judy asked, concerned. "And that name-change deal, now that's goofy."

"Yeah, well, oh, nah," Tom Junior replied. "But I'll say this, I had my money on Mark, I really thought she'd go with him. I like the guy."

"Me too," his wife said. Hannah could hear the faucet come on in her folks' bathroom, she could make out her mom brushing her teeth.

"But bless her heart, the girl knew what could happen when there's an ex involved, might be a precedent, there could be problems," her father added. "She knew to ask, she confronted the issue, good for her. Hannah's sharp.

"Thankfully, she takes after her mother!"

Pa-tooey! Judy spit and chuckled.

"Well, her daddy's no dunce! Years of that strong, male voice: 'Turn off the TV and do your homework!' paid off."

"Thank 'ya, thank 'ya verra' much!" Tom Junior replied as both parents snickered.

Tom Junior yawned again.

"Well, whatever she wants, it's okay. I can eat with Charley if she can sleep with him," he said.

Hannah grimaced.

"Tom," her mother hissed, "don't be tacky!"

"Ultimately, it's her decision. We're like the queen of England—we can advise and we can consent," Tom Junior added.

Judy chuckled.

The bedroom went silent. Hannah could hear her mom slipping on her house shoes.

"The name change, well, don't know what to make of that. I guess it's a compliment," the father added. "He's had a rough life, he wants out. I can't blame him."

"Exactly, and that's why she looks so good to him. Hannah's a godsend. He'll fawn over her, I'm not worried," Judy said. "If things get tough, who does he have to run back to? No one! Charley doesn't have an ex, there's no family—he'll work to make it work. He wants something permanent.

"They'll share a nursing home room someday."

The parents laughed.

Hannah stood in the dark, all ears, holding her glass, afraid to breathe.

"But you know what, Judy-Judy? You and I have been blessed with a couple of really great kids, I trust both of them to do the right thing," her father said with a sigh. "They're sharp, they think. Not every parent can say that."

Hannah heard Tom Junior click off the lamp on his nightstand and the light under the door went away.

"I'm so proud of the way she handled that mess with Randy back in high school. I just about said something—the dreaded father lecture. She had no business with that thug. But smart kid, she broke things off herself. I can't imagine what she's been through with him, all over again, years later. I'm tired, let's go to bed."

"Yeah, trust, we have it," Judy said. "We've got a pair of the best, don't we? I'm going to the kitchen to get a drink, be right back, love you."

"You too, hon, 'night."

Move!

The girl quickly tip-toed toward her room as the parents' door opened.

Hannah smiled. It can be awkward to hear what people really think, even when they're on your side.

She climbed in her bed. What a blessing to have folks like that, and Charley could see it. Charley could see it in Grandpa Tom and Grandma Claire—and he could see it in her: Trust.

They wanted to do the right thing by him, like that pastor in Kentucky or wherever. Charley knew it.

She curled around hippo and sighed. She wouldn't need hippo soon.

Well, it happened. What a day, what a wonderful, wonderful day. No champagne, rather fried chicken in the park—outdoors, where she loved to be. No Superman, just a very loveable guy with potential. She could glimpse, somehow, what he might do—and he's crazy about her. She knew that, and her parents did too.

Her life plan had blown away long since, but it finally happened, more or less like she wanted all along.

Charley: A friend who's a boy, who becomes a boyfriend, who becomes a fiancé, just like she always wanted, always expected, but with some idealized guy-in-theory in that big plan.

Monday morning, the Lexus pulled up and stopped once again in front of A Different View at ten minutes before eight. Charley, as usual, waited for Tom Junior at the curb.

"Good morning, Mr. Bentley!" Tom Junior said cheerfully as Charley opened the door and slid in.

Charley looked blank.

"You know?" he asked.

"Of course I do, congratulations," Tom Junior said. "You'll learn we Bentleys don't keep secrets very long."

The two men shook hands, then Tom Junior slapped Charley on the shoulder as he smiled. "Welcome to the family!"

Chapter 33
Convincing Claire

FaceTime: Judy held Hannah's phone, focused up close on her daughter's new engagement ring.

"Sis, it's beautiful," Chad said. "Congratulations again, you still there, Charley?"

"Yes," he said.

"I know what I'll get you for a wedding gift: A swimsuit!"

The parents laughed with their kids.

"It wouldn't have happened without yours," Judy said.

"Thanks for the call, and congratulations to both of you," Chad said. "'Bye!"

"So, when do you break the news to Pop and Grandma Claire?" Tom Junior asked.

"Soon," Hannah said, "I've put it off. Grandma Claire has her doubts about this guy," she said, elbowing Charley.

Charley coughed.

"I'll vouch for him, if that helps," Tom Junior said. "And she needs to remember Charley's well-placed chair. Weddings beat funerals."

"I better hurry up and get it over with," Hannah said as she dialed Grandpa Tom's number.

Hickory Bough got quiet early, oldsters don't stay up late. Hannah led the way to C 8 and walked in to an affectionate "There you are!" from Grandpa Tom as he stood, braced on his cane.

Claire smiled.

Charley walked in behind Hannah.

Claire frowned.

"Have a seat," Grandpa Tom offered, "haven't seen much of you lately."

"I know, we wanted to come out and catch you up on things," Hannah said. She held up her hand to show off the ring.

"Well!" Grandpa Tom said, surprised. "Congratulations, young man, you've made quite the catch."

"I'm sure of that," Charley replied.

Claire continued to frown.

"I'm happy for you, I suppose," Grandma Claire finally said. "But be very sure you want to do this."

"Yes," Hannah said. "And that's what we want to talk to you about."

"Okay," Claire replied. "Have you asked him about what I told you?"

"No, I would like for you to tell him, Grandma," Hannah replied.

Claire slowly shook her head, then began the story of the evil man named Trottel she once knew.

Charley sat, mouth agape, astounded.

"Do you think you're related?" Claire finally asked.

"If I am, you just told me more about my family than I have ever known," Charley said, dazed. "I could be. I know my mom had me in Washington, well, Maryland, and she grew up there. My grandmother lives in Cleveland.

"It fits, but where's the connection? Maybe that's why my mother has been hiding, moving suddenly, to stay away from the mob. That's speculation, no details."

"Grandma Claire, please, if they're related I assure you Charley's not like the man you knew. And I think he has a way to prove it. Charley, tell them what you want to do."

Charley bent forward, sighed and wrung his hands.

"I want to change my name," he said. "I want to become a Bentley."

Tom and Claire both sat back, surprised.

"Why?" Tom asked.

"Simply, your family represents everything I've ever wanted and never had," Charley said. "I love this girl, I love all of you, the way you treat each other. Trottel means nothing to me.

"That includes you, Mrs. Bentley," he said, turning to Grandma Claire.

"What do you think, my dear?" Tom asked, turning to his wife.

"I don't have any say in the matter," she replied, looking away.

Tom, Hannah and Charley chatted for a while. Grandpa Tom gave both of the young couple big hugs. Claire hugged Hannah as the girl bent down to her, then offered Charley a weak handshake.

"That didn't go well," Charley said as they walked out to the Jeep.

"Let daddy work on her. You have a reputation, a good reputation, let it speak for you.

"And you know what?" Hannah said as they walked across the dark parking lot, "We're like Tom and Claire, we complement each other. We're different, but we work well together.

"Maybe Grandma Claire will see that."

Morning: Hannah stood in her bathroom, blow drying her hair, when she heard her mother shout "Hannah!" over the whirr.

"Yes?"

Judy rushed in, frantic.

"Grandma Claire's had another stroke!" she yelled. "They're taking her to the hospital."

"Your fault!" flashed through Hannah's mind.

"Let me finish up and we can go, I'll call Charley."

She punched his number and he answered on the first ring.

"Hi, I know," her fiancé answered, "your dad just told me. Do you want me to go too?"

"No, I don't think so, pray for her. Right now, it might be best for you to stay out of sight."

"Okay, love you."

"Love you, 'bye."

Grandpa Tom met mother and daughter outside ICU, rubbing his chin. Both hugged the old man.

"They have her on a tPA drip, we got her over here quickly. It hit just as she got up this morning" he said. "Classic symptoms: Face drooping, couldn't speak, her bad arm locked up again. I pushed the alarm, Clémence came at a dead run."

Tom Junior walked up.

"Hey, Pop, how goes it?"

"Son, it's never good, but we got her here in a hurry, that helps," he said.

Hannah shook her head.

"I have to ask, did we—Charley and me—cause this?" she asked.

"Honey, who knows?" Grandpa Tom answered, hugging his granddaughter again.

"She's certainly upset, she cried bitterly after the two of you left last night. Claire loves you and she's worried you are about to do the worst-possible thing she can think of."

Who should roll in but Gaylene.

"I came as fast as I could!" she said, looking worried for once. "Let me see my dear friend Claire!"

"I'm sure the doctor will let some of us back there soon," Grandpa Tom said. "Meanwhile, what do you always do in hospitals? Sit and wait."

They did.

Grandpa Tom and Gaylene went back for a few minutes, then came out to report to the others.

"She can't speak," he said.

"I trust the Lord for a full recovery!" Gaylene declared. "Gotta' go!"

More waiting.

Finally, Hannah and her parents went in to see Grandma Claire. Pale, wrinkled, her face contorted, her ever-present bun undone, Claire showed every one of her eighty-two years.

She had gone down.

"We're here, lots of prayers for you!" Judy said as she bent over to kiss her forehead.

Tom Junior took her good hand.

"Don't worry about a thing, please. We're all right here, we're going to get you everything you need, okay?"

Claire nodded weakly, then reached for Hannah with a grunt.

Hannah stepped forward, slid her arm under Claire's head and lightly hugged her.

"Please, don't worry about me, Grandma," the girl whispered. "I'll be okay, and you will be too."

Claire smiled a crooked smile.

Tom Junior took Hannah back to Bentley Hardware, lunch time.

"Here's the key fob, Ladybug, why don't you two grab burgers or something?"

"Thanks, Daddy!"

She tracked down Charley between the warehouse shelves, where he pushed a cartload of faucets.

"So, you're the lucky young lady!" a voice called.

"Oh, hi," she said, turning around and scrambling to remember the middle-aged man's name from when she worked past summers.

"We want to keep your guy," the man said with a wave as he walked out on a loading dock. "You gotta' good 'un!"

She smiled and nodded as he walked off.

"Not everyone feels that way," Charley said as he walked up.

"True," Hannah said as Charley bent over to kiss her. "Maybe we can ask him to go by the hospital."

The had fast-food tacos for lunch.

"I've had another thing come up," Hannah said as she crunched lunch. "My roomie graduates in December, forgot about that. I need to decide what to do with the apartment, I've been paying my share all summer. Do I want to keep it? I need to make a decision."

"Well, that would be convenient if we get married before the spring semester," Charley answered.

Hannah gasped.

"Wow! I've been thinking next June—maybe the old folks' second anniversary? Could we do it sooner?"

"Why not Christmas Day?" Charley said. "Give everyone time to open gifts, maybe set it for, like, noon?"

"Are you kidding me? That's less than two months!" Hannah answered.

"Well, Tom and Claire did a wedding in less time."

She stared vacantly at her plate.

"Deal!" Hannah said firmly as she slapped the table. "I like it! I want to get a ring on you before you change your mind."

"No chance," Charley said as he poured salsa on another taco.

Grandma Claire came back to Hickory Bough a week later, rolling in the front door to a welcoming party led by the manager.

"We've missed you," Mr. Pérez said.

Claire grunted.

No one greeted her more warmly, or affectionately, than her husband.

"I missed you terribly," Grandpa Tom added.

"Mmm, too!" she mumbled.

Just then Aunt Brenda hurried in carrying a large envelope.

"Father, I came as fast as I could!" she said, panting. "Here!"

Grandpa Tom looked blank.

"And this?"

"We took up a collection for Claire's medical expenses at the store," Brenda explained. "Everyone's worried about her."

Grandpa Tom opened the envelope and a wad of bills and change fell out.

"That's $137.81, everything the customers gave. I threw in a five!" she added proudly.

Tom and Claire considered the situation; dear Brenda.

"Well, we appreciate it," he said.

"I know these homeopathic doctors are expensive, I hope she's not stuffing herself with a lot of high-priced, synthetic medicines," Brenda said firmly.

"Uh, we're getting the best stuff available," Grandpa Tom answered.

"Good! And when they give you the list of herbs and supplements, you let me know. I can get a discount, just let me know," Brenda said, rushing out the door.

"Well, everyone wants to help," her father said with a sigh.

Claire's nephew, Bob, came down from St. Louis that afternoon to arrange for a speech therapist to drive over from Springfield. They absolutely, positively had to get her talking again for *Actionable Anecdotes*. A couple weeks' worth of programs sat on the electronic shelf, then a couple weeks of reruns—one month. The lively, give-and-take banter between the old couple sparked the show.

If Grandma Claire couldn't come back, then what?

Bob suggested Hannah as a temp, given her cheerful personality and infectious laugh. A grandfather-granddaughter tag team might work briefly—as though Hannah had nothing else to do.

But everyone knew the truth: No Claire, no show.

The therapist began her work with excellent results. "She wants to do it, that helps," she told Grandpa Tom.

Tom Junior came over to Hickory Bough one evening, unannounced, tapping at C 8's door.

"May I join you?" he asked as the old couple looked up.

"Certainly, we'll try to make room for you someplace," his father said, waving across the empty suite with his iPad.

"So, what are you doing, Pop?" the son asked.

"Facebook, people posted about Claire's stroke and now I'm deluged with messages, emails, that sort of thing," Grandpa Tom answered.

Tom Junior bent over and kissed Grandma Claire.

"I'd like to talk to you for a few minutes," he said as he sat down, taking her good hand.

She nodded weakly.

"I want to ask you to accept Charley," he said softly. "We know how you feel about him. But trust me, I've seen this boy close-up at the warehouse for more than four months and I believe he's a keeper. We seldom have temporary employees who work as hard as he does. He's dependable, he's smart, he has a good attitude, regular employees like him."

Claire listened with a blank stare.

"And let's not forget what he did to save Hannah," Tom Junior added. "He helped her when she needed it most. We might not have her now if it hadn't been for him."

Claire closed her eyes and shook her head.

"Granted, he has an uncertain background. But he wants to get out of that, to change. That's commendable. And Claire, honestly, he loves Hannah with all his heart, and Ladybug's one of the most precious things in my life. You know that.

"He's not what I pictured as a son-in-law, but then I might not have been what Judy's parents pictured for her. But twenty-five years later, we have a great relationship with them, I've proved myself.

"Claire, he's a keeper. Please, give him a chance!"

"H-h-hard," she mumbled.

"Listen, you're a judge, you're an attorney, you know you cannot presume guilt, only innocence. Forget his family, what has he done wrong to Hannah?"

Claire sat silently.

"Pop, what do you think?" Tom Junior asked.

"Well, he seems like a good kid," the old man said, rubbing his moustache. "But I understand why Claire feels the way she does. He makes her think of a very bad time in her life, bad people. I understand how she feels."

"H-h-hard," Claire repeated.

"I suspect Charley's had some bad times too. Let's work together to give him some good times, he wants to be a part of our family," Tom Junior added.

"Can we do that? Please?"

Claire started to cry.

"'Kay," she managed.

What about Kristi?

Charley's mom needed to know.

"Can we make it a day trip?" Hannah asked as she listened to Charley absentmindedly practice Gershwin on the Bentley piano. This guy could do *Rhapsody in Blue* and not think of United Airlines.

"I guess," he replied as he stopped and turned to her. "I did the best I could for you last time, you got my bed, I took the couch."

"And I appreciate that," his fiancée replied. "Look, I have a vested interest here, she's my future mother-in-law. Maybe she'll be happier if I'm not around."

Charley tapped on the trailer's door and walked in with a smiling "Hi, Mom!" Kristi sat in the same pose as at their last arrival, in front of her computer, cigarette in hand. The half-empty whiskey bottle had been replaced with a half-empty gin bottle, more beer cans cluttered the counter.

"Make it quick, a client's had a blow-up on the web, I'm supposed to monitor stuff," Charley's mother replied grimly.

Charley gave her a perfunctory hug.

"So, you're getting married?" she asked without emotion.

"Yes ma'am," Hannah replied, moving the sofa's stack of papers so she could sit. "Charley bought me this beautiful ring." She held her hand up.

"And how're you gonna' pay for it?" his mother demanded, looking up at her son.

"Half down, half credit," he replied.

"You put my name on the account?"

"No."

Kristi took a long drag off her cigarette, then blew a perfect smoke ring.

"So, if you marry, I'm not responsible for you any more, right?" she asked.

"Guess not," Charley replied.

"Do it!" she ordered.

Charley sat next to Hannah, looking at the shag carpet, thinking.

"Guess I need to get my stuff," he said.

"Fine," Kristi replied between coughs.

Hannah and Charley cleaned out his room—a few clothes, some books and his Bible, the keyboard. Everything he owned fit easily in the Jeep.

They came back in the mobile home and sat down on the sofa. Charley took Hannah's hand.

"And Mom, I want to change my name."

"Fine," his mother replied absentmindedly, focused on the computer screen, tapping on the keyboard.

Charley and Hannah looked at each other, he shook his head.

"Mom, will you come to the ceremony?" the son asked.

"When?"

"Christmas Day."

"I guess, won't be busy, holiday. Maybe I can get that damn car runnin' by then. I'm almost out of beer and baloney, gotta' do somethin'."

"Can we go buy you some groceries or take you somewhere?" Hannah asked politely.

"No."

"What about grandmother, will she come?" Charley asked.

"I'll shoot her an email."

Charley grimaced and looked at Hannah.

"Uh, Mom, I need my birth certificate, the name change," he said.

Startled, Kristi sat up and put down her cigarette.

"Oh!"

She took a drag on her cigarette, crushed the butt in her ashtray, then stood up with an exasperated sigh.

She walked down the hall to her bedroom. They could hear a filing cabinet open and she noisily rummaged through papers. The drawer closed.

"Can we come visit, like, once a year—for lunch?" Hannah whispered.

"Okay," Charley said quietly.

Kristi came back, crying.

"Here," she said, thrusting the document at her son. Charley opened it and read it for the second time in his life.

The "Father" line showed that name of some man, somewhere, he did not know.

He wasn't sure his mother knew him either.

Chapter 34
The Checklist

With pleasure
Thomas Junior and Judith Bentley
and
Kristine Trottel
Request the honour of your presence
at the marriage of their children
Hannah Judith and Charles
Noon, Christmas Day
First Presbyterian Church
Randall, Missouri
Reception and lunch to follow
Randall Country Club
Répondez S'il Vous Plaît

So much to do, so little time, the old couple offered to help the young couple. A Christmas wedding sounded romantic but proved impractical. The Bentleys' big Family Fellowship planned no Christmas Day service and the office staff really didn't want to open up the hangar-sized building, sorry. Besides, its thousand-seat auditorium would be too big, it's hundred-seat chapel too small.

Claire could still hardly speak despite the therapy, so she had Grandpa Tom call First Presbyterian downtown, the church where the high school sweethearts worshipped together long ago, before Korea, before law school.

Grandpa Tom just had to say "Dearborn" and the church secretary said "yes." The church has a Christmas morning service, we'll be out by ten and it's yours. Don't worry about a fee.

Claire closed her eyes, sighed, and leaned back in her wheelchair as she put a wrinkled hand to her mouth, thinking. The moment shimmered in her mind's eye:

A different decision, a little more patience, and here *she* came up First Presbyterian's aisle, past the Corinthian columns, toward the big stained glass window behind the choir, to take the hand of strapping Capt. Thomas J. Bentley, handsome war hero just returned from Korea, standing at the altar in full Army mess dress, shiny medals on his chest.

The silly crush, the rapturous dream, of a little, pig-tailed third grader, fulfilled.

Everyone, turn and look: That tall, slender, beautiful young woman in gleaming white, with the ever-present blonde hair over her right cheek, hiding brilliant blue eyes above that funny smile. She held a bouquet as she half-stepped, pulling a long train. The organ played and the choir sang, the packed congregation watched in awe.

What should have been, the wedding of Campbell Dearborn's only daughter—Randall's wedding of the year.

No, Randall's wedding of the decade.

The old lady sighed and dropped her hand on her wheelchair's worn arm. It never happened.

It never happened because of her.

Instead, she went off to a spectacularly successful legal career, and lonely nights at home. Tom confessed his post-Army alcoholism to her before they married and blamed himself.

She knew better.

Judge Dearborn agreed to officiate very few nuptials in her thirty years on the bench. She'd stand there in her chambers, in her robe, in front of a smiling couple—and think of Tom.

Claire turned and looked at her husband, right beside her with his cane. She got him anyway, thank the Lord, even if it took six long decades. He smiled back at her quizzically and pushed his glasses back up his nose.

And who would officiate for Charley and Hannah? The Cross Members director in Columbia had family plans that day, ditto the ministerial staff at Family Fellowship.

Gaylene, who else?

"Great idea, she's neat!" Hannah replied to Grandpa Tom's suggestion.

"Fine," Charley answered with an indifferent shrug.

Gaylene gushed.

"I would be honored! Oh, so wonderful, such sweet children!"

"And Gaylene," Grandpa Tom added. "We cut you short, TV networks and all that. This time, let 'er rip!"

Claire continued to roll things over in her mind, as she did about everything. This Charley? No Tom Bentley.

Okay, maybe he is honest. The clumsy lug made Hannah happy, and that made her beloved Tom happy. They say he's talented, but she didn't see it. And that name, no, she harbored serious doubts.

Not thrilled, but she'd go along with it. Maybe the evil Bert Trottel didn't breed true, he didn't do anything else in truth.

Sweet, loveable, bouncy Hannah could have done better— Tony's jet-jockey grandson would have been a fabulous catch. Well, kids don't always do what their families want.

She didn't.

Judy and Hannah broke loose one day and roared through Springfield's bridal shops to buy a dress off the rack, a special mother/daughter ritual. They had no time to waste.

"No puffy sleeves, no full skirt," Hannah admonished her mom. "No bigger than I am, I'll look like a big, white beach ball!"

They stopped at the printer to pick up the invitations and brought them back before dinner.

Pizza! Then the parents and the couple started an assembly line of envelopes, invites, response cards, address labels and stamps.

"Just make sure you wash your hands first," mom cautioned. "Bad form to have a big orange thumbprint on an invitation!"

Levity, everyone laughed.

Charley took on the manager-of-postage job, pulling two-hundred stamps off the sheets he'd bought, then sticking one on each reply card and envelope.

"You kids don't know how good you have it," Tom Junior said, scowling, as he lifted more envelopes out of a box.

"Wait, here comes a dad joke!" Hannah said, grinning at her father.

"Why… back in our day… we had to *lick* the stamps!" Tom Junior told them in mock horror, eyebrows furrowed.

"Oh no, and you had wood-burning televisions!" Hannah gasped as the foursome laughed.

Charley sat, amazed. He never heard banter like this in his home—a reminder of why he wanted to be a Bentley.

The stamp chore out of the way, Charley did what he always did at the Bentleys when he had free time: the piano. His fiancée tagged along and sat down on the bench next to him. He plinked at this song and that, they sang a few lines together, before he launched into Robert Palmer's *Simply Irresistible* as the two of them ad-libbed the song's catchy "Bad-dada-BUM! Bad-dada-BUM!" beat. Hannah clapped and sang the words she remembered.

"Like that?" Charley asked.

"Of course, do you think you can play as well wearing a wedding ring?" Hannah asked with a twinkle in her eye.

"Better!" her fiancé answered.

They both laughed, her eyes smiled.

"It will be nice to have that guy around here," Judy mumbled to herself, listening to the merriment as she went in the kitchen to clean up. Her sweet daughter, Tom Junior's beloved Ladybug, returned to her happy, bubbly self.

Bless you, Charley.

Hey, maybe they'd all like something to drink? Great idea, she'd check.

The music had stopped as she came down the hall and turned the corner, and there sat Charley and Hannah on the piano bench, arms locked around each other in tight embrace, in the middle of a passionate kiss. Her daughter's engagement ring sparkled on her finger, over his hair.

Oops!

No, it will not be nice to have that guy around here.

It will be wonderful to have that guy around here.

Judy had picked up a stack of those bridal magazines at the mega bookstore in Springfield after mother and daughter set up a website registry.

"Who buys all this stuff?" Judy asked as she thumbed through one issue the next morning, coffee at the ready. "Look at this: clothes, appliances, cars, trips to the Caribbean, golly! We've got more scratch than most folks and we can't afford all this junk."

"I know, and I don't want it all," her daughter replied, as she shuffled up to her mom in her bathrobe.

Two taps on the front door and in walked Charley. The Bentley routine had changed. Most nights, the Wrangler sat in front of Aunt Brenda's store, Charley loved the Jeep. He bent over to kiss his fiancée as she sat up to meet him. A Saturday, maybe they could knock some wedding chores out?

"Oh hey, you kids look at these things, I'll make some pancakes. Heard anything out of your father?" Judy asked.

"What's up?" Charley asked, as he sat down where his soon-to-be mother-in-law had been.

"I just try to find meaningful things in here. Greenland? For a honeymoon?" Hannah asked, looking at an ad. "Not in December!"

"Nope," Charley said, "they have camo bridal gowns?"

"Oh, don't tempt me!" Hannah said, clapping her hands and laughing. "Mom would die!

"Now, here's something useful," Hannah said, looking back and turning a page, "a checklist. We need to go over this."

"Anything on the groom's name?" Charley asked.

"Hmmm, think they left that one out, how's your application?"

"Fine, the usual fill-out-a-form. Your dad got a lawyer, she filed the petition, should be no problem," he answered. "I have to go to the newspaper, buy an ad, legal notice."

"Wait!" Hannah said, scowling as she poked a finger at the list. "Attendants! We haven't chosen attendants! Ohmigosh!"

"Let's see," Charley added. "I could have a guy at Cross Members come down. How many do I need?"

Hannah shook her head sadly.

"Fifty."

Charley sat up.

"Do what?"

"I know so many girls in this town and at Mizzou—and my sorority sisters! I bet I could have fifty attendants," she said with a blank look. "And I wouldn't dare leave anyone out, hate to think of the drama trauma."

"But I don't..." Charley said.

"Look, I've already been a bridesmaid five times and a maid of honor once," Hannah added. "Also, a quinceañera, I don't know if that counts."

Her mom had walked up with plates to set the table.

"You don't have to have anyone, you know," Judy said.

"But that wouldn't be any fun!" her daughter replied.

"Tom and Claire?" Charley suggested. "They brought us together. If your name were Hannah Hornswoggle, I would have never stopped you."

"Charley, that's brilliant!" Judy replied. "No one will feel left out."

"I like it!" Hannah said.

Grandma Claire had her glasses on, reading scripts for future shows, as Hannah and Charley walked in C 8.

"Well hello! The lovebirds flew out early this morning," Grandpa Tom said, standing to give his granddaughter a peck on the cheek. "What brings you here?"

"Grandpa, we have a special favor to ask," Hannah replied as she and her fiancé sat down. "Charley...."

"Uh, well, Hannah and I talked, we'd like to ask you to be our best man and matron of honor," he said.

The old couple looked at each other.

Claire mumbled and shook her head.

"No."

"Grandma, I will marry a Bentley, not a Trottel," Hannah said firmly.

She sat back and sighed.

"S-s-strange, 'kay."

"Fine by me, but maybe I'll ask Gaylene to cut it short after all. It's embarrassing when the best man goes to sleep and falls over," Grandpa Tom said.

Who should roll in the door but Tony.

"Hellooo, baby! Good to see 'ya!" he called brightly to Hannah as he pushed his wheelchair up beside his buddy Tom.

"Hello, Mr. Di Burlone," Hannah answered.

"And you, young man," Tony said as he glowered at Charley, "I hereby proclaim a curse upon you: Fifty years of wedded bliss! May you be the envy of every man who ever lays eyes on your wife!"

Charley gave him a puzzled look.

The five of them chatted about wedding plans. Hannah would just as soon Tony did not talk about Mark—and thankfully he said no more.

"What about a honeymoon?" Grandpa Tom asked. "We spent ours here at Hickory Bough, I'm sure we could arrange that with José."

A wedding night for twentysomethings in a nursing home? All five laughed.

"Could we do something simple, outdoorsy—but December?" Charley explained, "We can't camp, I've never skied."

"You mentioned that house your parents built in Montana?" Hannah asked.

"No," Claire answered, "rent."

Speech still came hard for her.

"You see, the family office rents it out over the holidays at a premium. Whitefish has become a very popular ski area," Grandpa Tom explained. "It would be tough to break a reservation now, and we'd mess up someone's Christmas plans."

Claire nodded.

"Hmmm, 'simple?'" she said, thinking. "Paper," she said, motioning to Grandpa Tom.

He reached over to a table and grabbed a yellow legal pad and pen, then handed them to her.

Claire swallowed hard and twisted her mouth.

"Jus' thing," she said awkwardly. "Caddle ranch, Okah-homa, Grand River, priddy!

She swallowed again.

"Sunny day, stroll river. Code an' cloudy, someding else!"

Her speech began to clear.

"Map."

And she drew one, stiffly. Her perfect penmanship had become jerky: Drive down Interstate 44, get off Oklahoma's turnpike at Miami, go through town, take Main Street, that's Highway 125 south, like you want to go to Fairland.

"Turn left, grabel road here," she said, drawing an X. "Go cubble miles. Look, bare post, right side o' road, no mailbox, turn right, long driveway, big ranch house, there. Boody-full!" she explained as she wrote.

Grandpa Tom nodded.

"She told me about the place, old and quaint, rustic luxury! It's very nice, remote, quiet—it has lots of antiques and some Western paintings. They say Will Rogers stayed there back in his cowboy days, before the movies, before the Ziegfeld Follies. His father owned the big Dog Iron Ranch near there.

"The family office rents it out in the summer, doesn't get much use this time of year."

Claire smiled, her voice continued to come back.

"You be alone 'dere, barn, corral, no neighbors. F-f-family mine stayed years, horses, weekend rides, river. Marty call foreman, heat and water."

She coughed and swallowed, she hadn't talked this much since the stroke.

"Use back bedroom, most priddy, when sun comes up, boody-full river, big trees."

"You'll hear the cows moo," Grandpa Tom added.

"Uh, two keys, under flower pot on porch, front door and barn," Grandma Claire added.

She tore off the paper and handed it to Hannah. "Here!"

"Thank you!" the girl said brightly. "Uh, does it have a piano?"

They laughed.

"Yes, baby grand," Claire said.

Claire turned to Tom and smiled, then swallowed. The words still came slowly, she labored with a thick tongue.

"Darling, we almost went," she said.

"Oh?"

"Remember that Sunday, you proposed on porch, before Korea?" she asked.

"I remember, like it happened yesterday," Tom replied.

The old lady brightened suddenly, the words came easier.

"Oh! You sat there, uniform, new lieutenant, so handsome! Told you, 'If you ask me, you know I will say yes. I guess we could drive down to Miami, Oklahoma, and see justice of peace tonight. But you know, it's not what we want.'

"B-big mistake," Grandma Claire said, sighing. "I got on train afternoon, go back college and almost—almost—turned around, get off.

"You know me, thinker, planner. What if? Where spend wedding night? The ranch, no Highway 66 motel."

Tom shook his head.

"You, my dear, never cease to amaze me."

"What if had turned around? I step up in vestibule, said, 'Can't do it!' What if I turn to conductor, said, 'Please, help me down.' How lives different?

"A few seconds, one decision, and lives—everything—changed.

"But for whatever reason, God's plan, got second chance."

Her eyes watered as she looked at her husband.

"I'm so glad, I'm so glad."

Tom bent over the arm of her wheelchair and they hugged.

"Maybe God gives us more chances than we know," Tom replied.

"Yes," Charley said, turning to Hannah.

Grandma Claire smiled a crooked smile.

"I can speak! Happy thoughts, I can talk again, happy thoughts!"

"You're a tough ol' gal, I knew you'd pull through!" Tony said.

"And we would be married sixty-plus years by now," Tom added as he took Claire's hand. "As wonderful as that would be, these kids would not be here," he said, pointing at Hannah and Charley.

"Look at us!" Grandma Claire ordered the young couple.

"You'll be where we are before you know."

Chapter 35
Who'd Miss This?

Thanksgiving proved special, less than a month to go. Judy got Kristi Trottel's email address from Charley, no phone. She sent a note, introduced herself, then warmly invited her to join the Bentleys for the holiday.

"No," Kristi replied curtly.

Tom Junior checked Pop and Grandma Claire out of Hickory Bough. Tony came along, mumbling that his daughter and son-in-law "have other plans this year."

"Like, maybe, a trip to Dallas?" Hannah thought.

Grandpa Tom's best friend proved in rare form, bantering, teasing, kidding over the turkey and dressing.

"Charley, my pal: You got less than a month, there's still the priesthood," he said sternly to Hannah's fiancé.

"He better not, I'll take back the Jeep!" Hannah answered with a laugh.

The season's first snow ended November. "Oh my, please, no white Christmas this year," Hannah mumbled, as she sifted through details of the ceremony with Charley in the front room. The white stuff piled rapidly on the lawn.

No romance, paperwork mostly, it felt like paying bills, and maybe that's the way it should be. The spark didn't have to glow all the time, their spirits were the same—if the personalities were not.

They knew it, they just fit together.

Opposites do attract.

Hannah watched the postman slowly drive by in the snow but he didn't stop at the Bentley mailbox.

"It's over," she whispered, her hand to her mouth, as she stared blankly out the big windows.

"What's over?" Charley asked, puzzled.

"The weekend, our awful six-month weekend, it's over, and we're still together," Hannah replied as she turned and smiled weakly at him. "Maybe we can get on with life now."

"Yeah," her fiancé replied, catching her thought.

The Bentleys' usual, impressive holiday lights sprung to life as darkness fell, a big tree stood in the front windows. But this Christmas? Things felt different, odd.

Ah, next year will be normal, quiet, she assured herself. She and Charley would be there to open presents on Christmas Eve, the Bentley family tradition. They'd drive in from St. Louis or Tulsa or Little Rock—wherever the two of them landed after graduation next summer. Charley would play carols. Just the five of them—unless Chad has someone by then, so make that six.

Chad and a girl, who knows? Stranger things have happened in a year. Ha! If asked about a "Charley" at Christmas a year ago, Hannah would have frowned, put a finger to her cheek and asked, "Who?" She glanced at her ring again just to make sure she hadn't dreamed all this.

A judge rubber-stamped the name change and the *Randall Ledger* ran Charley's ad.

"Anyone notice it fell right below the 'Equipment-Used' section in the classifieds?" Tom Junior pointed out as he thumbed through that week's edition. "Not sure what to make of that."

One week until the big day, Randall's quiet downtown seemed to bustle a bit more than usual. The courthouse had its nativity on one side of the steps and menorah on the other. Charley parked the Jeep on the square and the couple walked in the courthouse from the cold, hand in hand as they passed the prosecuting attorney's office.

"It doesn't feel right unless we stop there," Hannah said as they headed down the hall to the county recorder.

"No problem," Charley said.

It took some explaining to the clerk, yes, we both have the same last name.

But your driver's license says....

Do you have last week's issue of the *Ledger*?

Yes.

See, right down here.

Oh.

Then came a day trip with Judy in the Beast to Columbia to help Hannah's roomie move out, then haul Charley's stuff over from his dorm's storage room. On a cold, blustery December day, the shuffling and box-lugging became a chore. Their cheeks glowed red. At least they didn't have to fight traffic around Lake of the Ozarks this time of year.

Winter: Who came up with the idea to get married at Christmas?

Okay, Charley did, it seemed romantic. No, they would do the right thing, special, despite the weather.

Hannah returned from Columbia to work a pile of mail—other than Randy's now trashed letters—Judy left on her dresser: Greeting cards, congratulatory letters and gift cards from relatives and friends. She found opening them fun, but she feared them, like watching for a snake in a pleasant garden. Would she find a note from Randy? His letters had stopped, she did not want another.

A sweet card with angels and flowers contained a $50 check from someone named Rice in Drumright, Oklahoma. Who's that? Where's that? Some pal of her dad's? Well, she'd send a thank-you note.

The letter opener split open an envelope with no return address, just a DALLAS SCF postmark. She opened it to find another greeting card with pleasant sentiments, signed *Our Best Wishes, Mark Wade, Janeen Wade.*

How sweet of him.

Wait!

Two signatures—written with two pens, one black ink and one blue ink.

What did she know?

What had Mark told her?

The rehearsal and rehearsal dinner on Christmas Eve done—tomorrow, it really would happen. They went over last-minute details at Charley's empty apartment.

"I want to talk to you," Charley nervously told Hannah as they wrapped things up.

"Yes?"

"On this husband thing, I, uh, well, had a heart-to-heart with Grandpa Tom the other night, like you suggested," Charley explained. "He helped."

Charley rambled a long monologue, very odd for him.

"He told me, 'Hannah has a lot of my first wife in her, always cheerful and upbeat. But Linda could be modest to a fault, brought up poor. You can take a girl out of poverty, it's hard to take the poverty out of the girl.'

"That hit me, hard. Maybe that's *my* problem.

"'Hannah's different. That's no reflection on Hannah, she just grew up in another world. But they both have that charming, agreeable personality. Linda blessed me, Hannah will bless you.

"'Linda's parents? Broke most of the time, kind of like your mom, on commodities. I think you can identify with Linda, maybe through Hannah or something. Maybe the two of you click the same way that Linda and me clicked; odd.

"'You'll have to bend and accommodate, but do it. Whatever you do, make her first in your life, you don't want to lose her. Lose everything else, keep Hannah,'" he said. "'Money isn't important—people are.'"

Charley stopped and thought for a moment. Hannah stared at him, puzzled.

"Maybe the most important thing he told me was, 'You've had a lot of hurt in your life, now God's giving you healing, He'll take care of you. We can pass on curses, Charley, or we can pass on blessings. It's up to you what you pass along to Hannah.'

"Look, uh, I've moved around a lot. Some find home in a place, others find it in a pair of arms. Maybe I want both, with you."

Hannah quietly nodded.

"I just wanted you to know," he said sheepishly.

Obviously, this husband thing meant a lot to him, and whatever Grandpa Tom said impressed this guy, who in a matter of hours would be her husband.

"Okay," she replied, unclear on what he meant. Then Claire's words came back:

'It wasn't what he said and did, but the way he said and did things.' That could work both ways.

Charley shrugged as he finished.

"I'll try."

"We both will," Hannah answered. Her eyes smiled.

The honeymoon, back to Columbia and the spring semester, then summer session, and finally graduation. Then what would they do?

Whatever, they'd be together. She wanted a permanent deal— and so did Charley.

"Guess I better go, see you tomorrow at the church, say, around noon?" she asked with a wink.

"Sure," Charley answered.

"Are you going to give me a good-night kiss?" Hannah asked as she stood to leave.

"Okay," Charley replied. "I have a better one in mind tomorrow night."

"I hope, I'm not taking hippo," she replied, smiling up at him and looping her finger around one of his shirt buttons. "Hippo can't cuddle back."

Their lips met just as BANG! BANG! BANG!, somebody pounded on Charley's door. They jumped, what on earth? Their noses bumped as they both jerked away, he opened the door.

"SURPRISE!" came a chorus from the hall—eight guys from Cross Members piled into the little apartment.

"You really think we would let you get hitched to the cutest girl on campus and we wouldn't come to see it?" one of his pals said as he slapped Charley on the back. "Who'd miss this? Besides, we get free food!"

"You goofball, we're afraid you'll drop your lines," said another with a laugh. "If you forget to say 'I do,' we're here to jump up and shout 'HE DOES!'"

More laughter, banter and teasing followed.

"How did you get here?" Hannah asked, as surprised as her fiancé.

"Simple, eight guys crammed in an old Toyota, the biggest car anyone has."

"Uh, happy to see you, don't have any place for you to sleep," Charley said, shocked.

"Nonsense, look at that perfectly good floor," came a reply.

More laughter.

"Why Christmas?" someone asked.

"So this big block o' rock will never forget our anniversary!" Hannah said as she hugged Charley. "If he does, he'll get a bundle of switches!"

"Excuse us, just about to kiss good night so Hannah can get home," Charley said.

"Fine, we want to see it!" someone yelled.

"Smack 'er, Charley!" added another.

"Why not?" she said, giggling.

Charley, awkward Charley, blushed.

Oh well, he bent down, took petite Hannah in his arms, bent her over backwards, then put a kiss for the ages on her to loud cheers.

Coming up for air, Hannah hugged Charley with all her might as she laughed.

"Be right back," he said, as he ushered his fiancée into the hall. They found Aunt Brenda peeking out her door with a "what on earth?" look.

"There goes the neighborhood," Hannah said with a shrug as they passed.

"You know about this?" Charley asked as they went down the steps.

"Not a clue," Hannah replied. "See? You have more friends and family than you know."

"Yeah," he replied.

Christmas Day, dreary, cold and cloudy, the sanctuary filled well before noon.

Hannah, served by Judy, some of the bride's besties, and mom's closest friends, had been in the ladies' lounge since ten o'clock prepping to look her absolute, radiant best. It all seemed a bit much, Hannah thought, but then the moms had been through this, she hadn't.

Listen and learn, Hannah!

All the fussing did take longer than she expected. The ladies had nearly finished and the bride sat, jittery, as they checked every detail—minutes to go. Her phone, on a table next to her, made an odd beep. What's that? She bent over to check.

NUMBER BLOCKED.

Randy!

Hannah shivered. No, give it up, please. She started to answer the call.

Don't do that!

No!

She shook herself: focus, girl!

The organ had played for a while when she finally stood up and looked at herself in a full-length mirror.

Wow, just look at that: Tomboy Hannah, in white, she could strut with any gal!

The circle of women oohed and aahed. Lace and chiffon, off the shoulders, she looked magnificent.

No, Charley's word: elegant.

Hannah enjoyed décolletage that made the dress work, she never looked more beautiful or more feminine. But she wore pumps, not heels, she didn't want to wobble walking in.

Gaylene rolled in the room in her vestments and proclaimed "You look splendid!" The priest laid hands on Hannah, as did the friends and moms, to proclaim a blessing. They adjourned as Hannah went out in the hall and found her bouquet. Tom Junior smiled at his beloved daughter and took her hand.

The time had come.

She could hear the congregation rise through the open door. She took a deep breath, anticipation. An usher nodded as the organ played again. Father and daughter came around the corner and into the aisle.

Eyes.

She thought of that painful afternoon in court when she came through the door and all eyes focused on her.

But today? Different!

Of course, she looked straight at Charley, standing at the altar in his almost-new pinstripe suit, a boutonnière on his lapel. His mouth dropped as he saw her. She would remember that look.

Grandpa Tom, standing, and Grandma Claire, sitting, waited with him. "Pained" might best describe the look on Claire's face. Hannah checked the packed sanctuary as they slowly passed the rows of friends, then family, as the organ played. The Bentleys and Dearborns could barely stuff themselves into three pews on her left. Kristi and her mother, the seventyish Sue Trottel, sat alone in one, otherwise empty pew on the right.

The video crew and photographer shot away.

Father and daughter stopped, just short of the old couple and Charley as a final chord played.

"Who gives this woman in holy matrimony?" Gaylene asked.

"Her mother and I," Tom Junior answered, who then kissed his daughter, shook hands with Charley, and extended her hand to his.

Gaylene seated the crowd and Chad stepped to the lectern.

"A reading from the prophet Jeremiah: *'For I know the plans I have for you, says the Lord, plans to prosper you and not to harm you, plans to give you a hope and a future.'"*

Then Gaylene—at her bouncy, talkative best—grabbed the ceremony.

Yes, the sermon went long, but Gaylene preached good stuff.

"Charles," she said as she finished, looking at the groom, "isn't your bride beautiful today?"

He nodded.

"Keep her that way. Remember, the countenance of a bride will reflect the security and love she enjoys from her husband. Treasure her, protect her, and she always will be beautiful.

"Hannah, look at the handsome man beside you."

She smiled up at Charley.

"Always treasure him, support him, and he will treasure and support you. Put each other first, and you will have a long, happy and successful marriage.

"Jesus in the Gospel of Matthew promises us that the Father wants to give all of us good gifts. You are gifts to each other, never forget that."

A soloist sang, they recited their vows and exchanged rings, then went on their knees for Communion.

Tom stood, leaning on his cane. He peered around Charley and Hannah to see his wife. Claire gamely smirked back.

He envied her, sitting there. Whatever the kids pay Gaylene for this, they'll get their money's worth, he thought with a smirk: Genesis to maps.

Finally, "And now, under the authority granted me by God and the State of Missouri, with great pleasure, I proclaim you husband and wife.

"Charles, you may kiss your bride."

He did, to wild cheers from the eight guys and polite applause by everyone else.

Chapter 36
The Harem

The Randall Country Club ballroom blazed in festive glory. Streamers, lights, balloons—a magic moment: Christmas Day and a wedding, rolled into one.

Perfect crystal-and-china place settings awaited guests atop linen table cloths, along with flowers and candles. Three forks, two knives, two wine glasses, a dessert spoon and fork: ready for a substantial feast. No wonder the guys drove down from Columbia, this beat ramen noodles. Waiters hustled around trays of champagne flutes.

The DJ played mingle music while the guests queued to greet the newlyweds.

Hannah glowed.

Charley beamed.

The line ended, everyone watched the day's special couple as they slowly walked to the family table.

A typical pose: animated Hannah looked up at her new husband to tell him something, hands gesturing, a big smile, a laugh. Charley, arm around her, quietly nodded sure-yeah-fine-okay.

They sat down with their families to polite applause. Gaylene gave an invocation and Tom Junior proclaimed "enjoy your lunch!"

Beef, chicken or fish?

Aunt Brenda loudly questioned the lack of a salad as a waitress waited for her order. Why did the club discriminate against vegetarians? That's against the law!

No ma'am we're not, yes ma'am, we have an entrée salad if you prefer.

Grandpa Tom and Grandma Claire, obviously unhappy, sat at the end of the family table, their name cards awkwardly placed across from the two Trottel ladies.

Oh well, go with it.

Months later, Grandma Claire told Hannah of the painful conversation that afternoon—some of it, anyway.

It began light and polite as Grandma Claire sipped a Moscato Tom Junior ordered for her from the bar. Grandpa Tom quietly played with his iced tea. Sue and Kristi worked their third or fourth highballs.

What a lovely bride.

Charley looks so handsome.

What a beautiful church.

Did you have a nice flight out from Cleveland?

The couple seems so happy.

The TV weather lady said we have a chance of snow. Ha, ha, yes, well, it's Christmas.

The salads arrived, the small talk continued.

Claire sprinkled her salad with pepper, looked at Charley's grandmother, and asked calmly, "So how did you meet Bert?"

Sue gasped.

Stunned, she turned pale and put down her fork.

"How… how did you know Bert?" Charley's grandmother asked, visibly shaken.

"I slept with him too," Claire replied calmly.

Tom laid his hand on his wife's arm, she didn't flinch. The thoughtful, intense—scheming—Claire sat by him now.

The ballroom's music and conversation murmur continued, but the far end of the family table turned deathly silent.

"Mom…" Kristi said.

"Uh…" the grandmother replied, "uh, umm, well, didn't know Bert ever lived in Missouri."

"He didn't," Claire said flatly. "I lived in Washington."

Sue Trottel sat shocked, her eyes large.

"Claire…" Tom whispered.

"What's your name again?" Sue asked, eyebrows furrowed.

"Claire, Claire Dearborn back then."

Sue perked up.

"You're Granny!" the woman replied, pointing at Claire.

"Do what?"

"Granny! Bert called you 'Granny.' What a small world!"

"There must be a mistake," Claire replied, as she sipped her wine. "He never called me that, you must think of someone else."

The uneaten salads waited.

"Maybe not to your face, but that's how I knew you."

Sue took a swig of her Jack and Seven, bit her lip and thought.

"Okay, look, let's talk about this," she added flatly. "It may help, we both still hurt."

"Fine," Claire replied bluntly.

Sue took a deep breath.

"I was Mrs. Bert Trottel," she said.

"I thought so, thanks for filing that divorce," Claire said.

"No, I'm the *other* wife—he had two."

Now Claire turned pale. "I didn't know that."

Sue sighed.

"I started work for Bert in Cleveland, receptionist, right out of high school, 1967," she explained. "We, how shall I say? We clicked. I quickly had more than just a job. In a few months he transferred me to his Washington office, I'd never been on an airplane before, nineteen years old. He put me up in this swanky apartment off Dupont Circle, oh boy!

"Officially, I handled the mail and answered the phone in his law office. My off-the-books job involved keeping up with his 'harem,' as he called it. He kept a little black book—showered those in it with dinners, trips, flowers, concert tickets, clothes.

"Why am I telling you, you know what he did!" Sue added, exasperated. "I sent you stuff for him, I could fake his signature!"

Claire shuddered.

"I kept his calendar. He'd tell me what to put down: Send Ricci some gift Monday, thanks for that file; take Joy to dinner Tuesday night; buy flowers for Terri, thanks for that great evening, wink-wink; remind me to call June, she free Thursday night?; Friday's Jennifer's birthday, send her something; take Granny to the ballgame Saturday.

He'd look it over, wave his hand, say 'fine' and I made the reservations, ordered the flowers, whatever. Our florist had a stack of 'Love, Bert' cards to attach to bouquets we ordered—I wrote them."

Claire sat, shocked.

"But why 'Granny?'" Claire asked.

"Because you were so much older than the rest," Sue replied, "forty."

"No, thirty-nine when we met!" Claire answered sharply.

"Anyway, the rest of his girls? Twentysomethings, not long out of college. He made it a point to butter-up young women at the White House, congressmen's offices, the agencies. He didn't have anyone over thirty in his book besides you.

"You know how Washington works: lots of young people, just out of college, they get prestigious staff jobs, thanks to their parents' political connections. They're young, they're ambitious, they like to party, and Bert knew how to hook them. They saw him as a bigshot—and they all wanted to be bigshots too.

"And for the young men who liked young men, he'd find them the right young men.

"The payback?

"They answered Bert's calls and, well, other things. He made it worth their while.

"They ignored lobbyists or staffers, they funneled him information from supposedly confidential files, they put him or his cronies on agendas for this or that agency or commission. He found it all very useful, in addition to other favors.

"We thought relationship—Bert thought quid pro quo."

Sue coughed.

"But I never gave him confidential information, at least not intentionally," Claire said thoughtfully. "I didn't squeal."

"Probably you did more than you know—unintentionally. You ranked high enough at Justice he could get a feel for what would come down the pike in a conversation over dinner, and he took you out to eat a lot," Sue replied. "Or baseball, you talk during baseball."

"Yes, yes he did," Claire replied. "We always had great conversations."

"He had only one contact at Justice—you—that I recall, you had extra value, well up the chain."

"Well, maybe you're right," Claire said, sitting back in her wheelchair.

Sue laughed, which stunned everyone.

"And you had another thing: He worshipped tall blondes. Bert would have gone nuts over Ann Coulter if she were around in his day.

"If you did nothing but check your watch and give him the time, he would have gone for you," she said. "I can just picture him sitting there, holding a martini, ogling you. He could undress a woman with his eyes."

Claire blushed.

"Yes, he could. But, I never saw myself as attractive."

"C'mon, it's not what you think, it's what the guy thinks! We both know that," Sue continued. "How does this guy feel about you?" she asked, pointing at Tom.

Tom, beyond embarrassed, looked at his lap.

"To be honest, I really think Bert did care a bit more for you. You were smart, you were experienced, you were poised, you could carry an intelligent conversation. You didn't giggle and, boy oh boy, did you have looks.

"But that's all relative, don't let it go to your head, don't get mushy. Bert could be brutal when a girl failed to deliver. Pillow talk better pay.

"And those he liked, those who delivered?

"Well, gifts got more extravagant. Claire, he took you to France that one year. He'd move others along, promotions, as he could. Bert always had his ear to the ground. Some senator's receptionist became a congressman's chief of staff, stuff like that.

"And Claire, here's your proof you made his shortlist: I remember when he heard about the judgeship in Ohio. 'Let's get that for Granny,' he told me.

"'Remember, we have that girl, that little spitfire—what's her name? Kim? Yeah, her, at the White House. Her dad's an Orange County Republican honcho, races horses. She can re-type a memo and slip it in a file, or some such.

"'I'll call her, then you send a big box of chocolates tomorrow, she can get creative with chocolate.' He gave me this evil wink.

"So, I became a federal judge for a box of chocolates?" Claire asked incredulously.

"Yeah, that's about it. And you know why, don't you?" Sue asked.

"I suppose if some mobster got in trouble?"

"Exactly!" came the reply. "He had lots of shady goings-on in the Midwest from Cleveland, he or his lowlife pals might need protection."

Claire sat speechless.

"Silly me, I thought myself his one-and-only, then I read about the divorce," she said sadly. "I became physically ill."

"Honey, they all did, *we* all did," Sue replied flatly.

"We all just knew we were the one, Bert could do that.

"I thought I was the one for a long time, believe it or not," Charley's grandmother continued. "Think about it: I set him up with all these young women—but of course I figured myself special, me, the list keeper! I'd have him to myself someday, he'd come home to me every night. Ha!

"You were not alone, Claire."

Sue's comment hit hard.

Claire sat, hand over her mouth, and thought. It dawned on her: She did not face enemies across the table, but fellow victims. And Kristi? Kristi could have been her daughter.

"I never got into his mob stuff," Sue continued. "He didn't trust me with that, but I knew about it. He'd take calls in front of me while I sat in his office: 'Yeah, we don't need him anymore.'

"That meant kill someone.

"I got scared when I heard this. He said, 'We don't need him anymore' on the phone in front of me once about this guy who'd been in the office, young attorney, nice guy. Sure enough, a few days later the *Washington Star* had a headline on the front page: 'Airport Police Find Lawyer's Body.'

"His corpse had washed up on the rip-rap in the Potomac, underneath one of the runways at National Airport. No marks, no wounds, no poison, no drugs, the Virginia coroner ruled it suicide, he must've jumped from a bridge.

"Yeah, sure he did.

"I kept my mouth shut. I made twenty-thousand a year in 1970, plus that apartment. Experienced attorneys made less than me, officially a file clerk. No way in heaven could I make the money Bert paid me to straight-up answer the phone or lick envelopes someplace else," the grandmother said.

"Money talks, and so does fear. I knew he could say 'we don't need her anymore' and something really bad would happen to lil' ol' me.

"They'd find my body in an alley sporting a bullet hole. Where's her purse? Obviously, a robbery!

Both women sobbed.

"I'm sorry for you," Sue replied, smiling weakly.

Claire wiped her eyes on her napkin.

"He hurt me more than anyone," Sue continued.

"He got me pregnant just as the divorce decree came out in Ohio," she added, patting Kristi's arm. "Here she is. The FBI already had been in the office with a subpoena, rifling our files. Bert knew warrants would come shortly.

"I told him, 'Marry me, you filthy rat, so at least this kid has a name, or I give the FBI even more dirt! Remember: I have lots of contacts, phone numbers, and notes. And they're all with a friend you don't know, so if I disappear....'

"Well, not really, but he believed it.

"So, he did! Two weeks before I gave birth, we went to see a judge over lunch. Wanna' swing by the deli and grab a sandwich on the way back to the office? How romantic! Ha!

"I went to labor and delivery alone, he filed for divorce a month later," Sue added sadly.

"Wedding to divorce, forty-six days, I never even got a ring."

The wait staff swapped the uneaten salads for entrees.

Sue stopped, sniffed and cried.

"I grew up a man hater," Kristi began. "Mom told me story after story of the evil things Bert had done, the lives he destroyed. I vowed I'd be different, no man in my life!

"Well, guess what? Yeah, stupid teenage girl, I fooled around, got lights-out drunk at parties a few times, who knows what happened, or with whom?

"And of all things, I had a *boy*," she said, pointing down the table at Charley.

"I hated men, every man I knew made me miserable. And now, there in a bassinet, I had one of my own. I cried for days.

"I didn't know what to do with him. And frankly, I still don't. But for whatever reason, I kept him, I could have had an abortion."

All three women cried loudly.

Sue and Kristi stood up, came around the table, and hugged Claire. Charley, Hannah and the rest of the family table stopped and looked: What's going on down there?

Grandpa Tom looked back with a painful shrug.

"So who killed him?" Claire asked as the tears slowed.

"I don't know who exactly," Sue answered flatly. "I could have done it, I hated Bert.

"He squealed on a drug-running racket at the Miami airport, ratted on air freight handlers paid to look the other way. The Colombian syndicate would trans-ship coke through Guyana, Venezuela, Ecuador. 'Oh, gee! We don't need to open this box. Next!' The K-9 unit somehow never walked down that line.

"In payback, the Bureau of Prisons put him in Seagoville outside Dallas—that Club Fed prison—instead of ADX, the hard-time super pen out in Colorado.

"Really? C'mon!

"The Miami operation floated like a small potato in the organized crime stew. Nothing! But some of his mobster buddies made a lot on that arrangement.

"The autopsy found poison in his system, strychnine. Well, some dopers take strych in small doses to get high—an OD!

"Never mind Bert didn't touch drugs ever, well, except booze. He drank like a fish. Hey, we'll hold an investigation! Forty years later, I haven't heard a thing."

"And the two of you?" Claire asked, wiping her eyes.

"We did some stuff, okay?" Kristi said.

"Organized crime has, well, employees. I worked supplying dope, mostly coke—premium merchandise! Also, pills, benzos, to wealthy people around Baltimore and Washington—embassies, law offices, trade groups. Dictators send their idiot kids overseas to get rid of 'em, make 'em a naval liaison or adviser. They love to snort, they have lots of money, thanks to the Third World peasants daddy fleeces back in Flyspeckistan, or wherever.

"Some would buy serious amounts of coke from me, then stick it in diplomatic pouches for some toady in the foreign office back home to sell. I made money, they made money, everyone came out happy.

"I'd go somewhere in a business suit, dress for success, all professional looking, I carried a big purse. The office door closed, I passed the packet, they handed me however many hundred-dollar bills it took. We'd shake hands, I'd say, 'Nice to do business with you' and walk out, always thanking the receptionist—big smile—as I left."

Kristi stopped, thought, and chuckled.

"I drove a Bentley, get it?" she said. "That's some kind of karma."

A moment of levity broke the women's dark mood.

"I got tired of looking over my shoulder: I quit. Most cops work straight, other runners might take me out. There could be a coup d'état someplace. Daddy dictator gets hanged and his kid gets arrested by the secret police—who tip off the FBI. And, I had to walk around with dope and thousands in cash.

"Nervous? You bet!

"But could I quit? Snuff jobs, I saw a couple: My oh my, the brakes went out on that lady's fancy car, fatality wreck tied up the Beltway. Too bad, hate to hear about that sort of thing.

"I had a baby now, and well, I guess that mother-type stuff kicked in. What if I didn't come back to daycare some afternoon? What would happen to him? Cute thing, okay he's a boy, I hate boys, but he's cute about it.

"You don't quit the mob—ever," Kristi added firmly. "That's why I kept moving, I'd stay hard to find, more trouble than I'm worth to eliminate," she explained. "Out of sight, I didn't talk, lived in out-of-the-way places, used assumed names. The big syndicate I worked for doesn't operate in Podunk, not enough money."

"And you?" Claire asked, looking up at Kristi's mom.

"Ask me no questions, I'll tell you no lies. I had to make a living when Bert went to the can," Sue replied.

"Please, please, never—ever—say anything to Charley," Kristi begged. "He's a good kid, in spite of his rotten mom. Think about his family, if you want to call us that: raised by a single mom in the mob, who was raised by a single mom in the mob.

"No wonder you straight-arrow, church-going Bentleys look good to him. That's him, that's his personality. Charley is Charley.

"Some parent I've been. He should have died from an overdose or in a shootout. He should be covered with gang tats, his teeth should be rotting out. Every post office wall should have his photo.

"But no, not Charley! He'd come home from school, I'd be drunk or stoned, passed out on the floor. He'd just step over me and go back to his room and do his homework, play his keyboard. More than once, he cleaned up my vomit while I nursed a hangover."

Kristi cried again.

"If he hadn't married that beautiful girl this afternoon he could be pope," added Sue.

"That little gal doesn't know what she's in for, he's going places," Kristi said. "She'll have to hang onto the rocket, zoom!"

"Hannah's quite the go-getter herself," Tom added, stepping into the conversation. "I treasure the little thing, lots of spunk."

Claire looked at the two women in a new way: friends. The three of them could drop a bitter past.

"I can keep secrets," she said quietly. "Let me count both of you as dear, and bless that boy," she added, motioning toward Charley. "Let's quietly enjoy the show, we knew them when."

"You ladies have helped me close a dark, bitter chapter in my life," Claire added. "Okay, misery loves company, but I can see I'm not alone."

"No, no you're not," Sue replied as she hugged Claire. "There are others who hurt, just like the three of us. All of us let ambition get in the way of doing the right thing. All of us could have said 'No!' But we didn't."

Grandma Claire turned to Grandpa Tom.

"Do you love me any less?" she asked.

"Let's talk grace," he answered.

Claire turned and looked down the table.

"Charley! Come here!" she commanded loudly.

Huh?

The shocked groom wiped his mouth, stood and nervously walked to her. Hannah sat on the edge of her seat, eyes wide, looking down the table, puzzled, anxious.

"Yes?" Charley asked.

"Come here," Claire repeated, reaching up for a hug.

"Son, I love you with all my heart," she said as she kissed him.

Chapter 37
Home on the Range

A great lunch, with entrée salads for any and all who preferred one, led to the cake cutting. Multiple toasts, led off by Grandpa Tom and his iced tea, then Gaylene proclaimed an energetic blessing of the couple from her *Book of Common Prayer*.

The dancing started. Tom Junior and Hannah opened with a tearful *I Loved Her First*. He had mascara on his shirt when they finished.

Charley and Hannah did a romantic solo waltz, then the dance floor opened. Coat-and-tie Grandpa Tom slow danced with daughter Brenda, who wore a T-shirt that proclaimed PARTY HEARTY. Chad wheeled Grandma Claire out to share the *Hokey Pokey*. She got into the fun, lifting her right foot up, then her right foot down, then Chad took her wheelchair and spun her all around.

The high point came when Hannah and her fifty friends, or quite a few of them, did a—what would you call it?—synchronized routine to *Higher Love*. The fashionably dressed young women, the star of the day still in her gown, formed a chorus line, arms flying and feet swinging. The DJ turned off the lights and the disco ball sparkled above: A sight to behold, it brought down the house. The Steadicam moved down the line, along the kicking feet, to save the lively moment for future anniversaries.

A sweaty, puffing Hannah stumbled back to Charley's arms as the music ended to cheers.

"Old cheerleader and pep club deal," the bride explained as she caught her breath, "afraid I'd spill out of this thing." She grabbed her wedding gown by her thumbs under each armpit and yanked it up.

"I'm speechless," he said.

"You're welcome to take my Lexus," Tom Junior offered his new son-in-law, arm around Charley's shoulders, as the dancing continued. "Only the best for the happy couple!"

His face showed the excited melancholy every father feels at the marriage of a dear daughter.

"Tempting," Charley answered, "but we have our stuff loaded in the Jeep. Don't want to get off on the wrong foot with my father-in-law when I run his car in a ditch."

Tom Junior laughed.

"Suit yourself, buddy."

Charley shook his head, incredulous: Him? Drive a Lexus LS? What a thrill to ride in it, going to and from work.

My gosh, he had the girl of his dreams, the family he wanted, what's next?

The guests began to trickle out past tables that groaned with gifts. No time for a shower, everything came at once.

They did the garter toss as gentleman Charley, down on his knees beside Hannah's shapely legs, looked the other way in good taste as she hoisted her skirt. But he seemed to take his time on her thigh, Hannah thought.

Touching: what to make of that? Well, she had a husband now, and to be honest with herself, she might get a little freer with her hands.

Sure enough, one of the Mizzou guys caught the flying blue band to cheers from his pals.

Then the bouquet toss over her shoulder to squeals from Hannah's gaggle of girlfriends.

Tom Junior and Judy called for everyone's attention, then unveiled a splendid, three-foot by five-foot portrait of Hannah with smiling eyes, seated in her white gown, a long-stem yellow rose across her lap beside her sparkling engagement ring. Everyone applauded.

"I'm going to burn incense in front of that thing," Charley whispered to Chad. Little brother exploded in laughter.

A joke! Quiet Charley told a joke!

Or did he?

The couple slipped out and changed.

Hand in hand, they came back and told Tom Junior and Judy, then Grandpa Tom and Grandma Claire, good-bye.

Hannah gushed her love with hugs and tears.

"Thanks," Charley said.

"Happy to help," Grandpa Tom replied with a wink. "Glad you got around to making it official faster than we did."

"Come down here and hug me too, you dear, sweet boy," Claire called to Charley, and she kissed him again.

The bird seed flew as they dashed out through the cold wind. A posed kiss for the photographer and a wave for the video, and off they went at dusk.

Flurries began to fall.

A bone-tired Tom Junior noticed Hannah's tire cover had disappeared as the Jeep went out of sight. Now, that's odd.

"What just happened?" Hannah asked as they rolled through the deserted downtown. Christmas lights overhead lit the falling snow.

"Not sure," her husband replied, "it's just so awesome."

They drove in silence, hands joined on the console.

It started to snow harder, big and fluffy flakes, as they turned on the bypass and headed for the Interstate.

"You want the radio on, honey?" Hannah asked.

He noticed, she'd never called him that before.

"No, I want to savor this," he replied. "What if we sing together?" He launched into *Home on the Range*.

Now, who sings that on a honeymoon? Goofy guy!

"Seems appropriate, stay at a ranch," he explained.

"Oh, Charley, it's perfect! You know me, if the weather were warmer I'd bring a tent," she said.

They laughed.

Yes, she would have.

And Charley would have followed right along—whatever Hannah wants. He'd remember the bug repellent and an EpiPen.

Charley wanted to be more like this wonderful girl that somehow, by miraculous intervention, he'd caught. He saw everything in her, what could she see in him?

Dreams do come true.

The storm picked up.

Down Interstate 44 they drove through the dark, barely going forty in a seventy zone, edging around semis with their emergency flashers on. Cars peeked out of ditches, rear bumpers in the air. The wipers whipped back and forth.

Here came the familiar turnoff through the flying snow and dark: It felt odd to stay in the left lane, I-44 West Tulsa, rather than right, I-49 South, Neosho Fort Smith Exit Only. When would they go to Neosho again, or would they?

Miami's streets proved slick as they turned off the toll road, no sand bombers out yet.

"Slow down and shift it into four-wheel," Hannah advised, pointing to the lever on the hump. The expected thump came as the transmission shifted and the Jeep suddenly felt more sure-footed.

"Glad we didn't take your dad's offer," he replied with a pat on the Wrangler's dashboard.

"True, we've given our guardian angels a workout lately, I'm sure they would appreciate a day off," Hannah said.

"Yeah," Charley answered as they inched along icy streets and over the thankfully sanded Grand River bridge.

Hannah pulled Claire's map out, turned on the reading light and checked it, surprisingly accurate, given that the old lady drew it from years-ago memories. Miami disappeared behind them, the blowing snow made it hard to see, they crept along, looking for the turn.

Alone, no one passed them on the little highway.

Finally, they could make out the gravel road and Charley turned left—and the Jeep went broadside, sliding across the highway, narrowly missing a telephone pole.

"Let go of the wheel! Let go of the wheel!" Hannah shouted.

"What's this about you, me and bad weather?" she added as the Wrangler straightened itself and stopped in a shallow ditch. Charley backed up, then headed down the snow-covered chat.

"Don't make me laugh, enough trouble," Charley answered glumly as the wipers flopped.

They crept on, call it a blizzard now. Snow blew past the windshield sideways. Claire's "couple miles" on her hand-drawn map seemed to take forever as they crept along.

The bare post with no mailbox appeared at last, snow stuck in a white line on its north side. The long, rutted driveway led off into the night. A weak porchlight glowed somewhere in the distance.

They turned, and the big ranch house loomed ever larger in black, silhouetted by a light over by the barn, as they neared. Big gables, a broad porch, a hitching post by the steps, they could tell its rustic beauty.

"Okay, keys under the flower pot," Charley said, peering into the night as he pulled to a stop in the yard, just short of the steps.

Except, count 'em: eight-nine-ten flower pots between the pillars. Which one?

She hopped out and scrunched through the snow up the steps—cold! "There's a reason why people get married in June," Hannah whispered with a chuckle. She pulled her coat tighter and put on her gloves.

A romantic old ranch house? It seemed like a good idea at the time.

Now, a honeymoon suite at a Springfield hotel might have been better—bet ol' Charley boy would like that!

Shivering Hannah started turning the pots over as he unloaded, setting their luggage and a big ice chest of food—and a bottle of champagne—on the porch.

"What a honeymoon, we might be stuck here for days," she complained over the wind.

"Let's hope," Charley replied.

"Silly!"

He winked down at her over his muffler.

She smiled up at him.

Hannah searched on in the porchlight's feeble glow.

"Here they are!"

She jumped up with the keys, unlocked the door, they stomped snow off their shoes, and hustled quickly inside with their stuff. The lock clicked.

The bitter, snow-laden wind whistled on around the old house through the black night, drifts started around the Jeep.

Whatever the storm did outside, they would stay cozy and warm inside, just the two of them, Mr. and Mrs. Charles Bentley, safe and dry.

Yes, they would spoon again. They knew everyone makes it through storms, for one night, a weekend, or a lifetime, the same way: stay close.

# # #

Acknowledgements

Thanks to all of you who told me how much you enjoyed my first visit with Tom and Claire in *Something Surprising*. Your compliments humble me. I must say I found their charming and vivacious granddaughter a joy, she proves that what we make of life is our call. Perhaps I'll have time to visit with the Bentleys and Dearborns again soon?

My thanks to Greg Derrick, Evelyn Gravitt, Suzi Harkey, Vicki Hart and Michelle Thompson for their help in telling another very special love story. And, a special thanks to Katy Michael for helping me wrap the whole thing up.

Paul Hart
April 2020

Made in the USA
Monee, IL
03 March 2021

61780985R10194